A Letter
to the
Last House
Before
the Sea

BOOKS BY LIZ EELES

HEAVEN'S COVE SERIES
Secrets at the Last House Before the Sea

THE COSY KETTLE SERIES
New Starts and Cherry Tarts at the Cosy Kettle
A Summer Escape and Strawberry Cake at the Cosy Kettle
A Christmas Wish and a Cranberry Kiss at the Cosy Kettle

THE SALT BAY SERIES
Annie's Holiday by the Sea
Annie's Christmas by the Sea
Annie's Summer by the Sea

LIZ EELES

A Letter
to the
Last House
Before
the Sea

bookouture

Published by Bookouture in 2021

An imprint of Storyfire Ltd.
Carmelite House
50 Victoria Embankment
London EC4Y 0DZ

www.bookouture.com

ISBN: 978-1-80019-392-5
eBook ISBN: 978-1-80019-391-8

*For my marvellous mum, Margaret, who's coped with
so much over the last few years but is still smiling.*

Prologue

Iris Starcross was finding it hard to breathe, but wasn't particularly surprised. It was time, she supposed. She'd had her three score years and ten, plus another twenty-nine years on top. That was greedy, really, when some people had so few.

Slowly, she moved her fingers and felt the pressure of another hand gently tighten around hers. Lettie had been sitting next to her bed for hours. Or maybe it was days. Iris was losing track of time as all the joys and sorrows of her life played out like a movie reel in her mind, and condensed to this moment.

She rather hoped that dying wouldn't hurt, and Cornelius would be waiting for her. The vicar had assured her that he would be. But Iris had given up on God after what happened all those years ago, so she couldn't be sure of it.

She drew in another shallow, rattling breath and felt the delicate gold key on a chain around her neck slide across her collarbone. Gradually, painfully, she moved her free arm until her fingers found the metal of the key, its smoothness and familiarity a comfort. If only she'd been able back then, in the midst of her grief, to uncover its secret. But it was far too late now for if onlys.

'Keep this safe,' she croaked, her voice little more than a whisper. 'And find out for me, darling girl.'

When she was gone, the key would go to Lettie – the only person in the family who was like her. Iris sent up a fervent prayer to the God who might or might not be there that her beloved great-niece would choose a life filled with lasting love and happiness.

Darkness was creeping at the edges of Iris's vision and she closed her eyes, worn out with it all. She was aware of Lettie's voice, gently calling to her, but her thoughts were focused on a handsome young man in army uniform. The life she could have had. Iris Starcross took her last breath and slipped away.

Chapter One

Five weeks later

Lettie

Lettie stepped out of the taxi and sucked in a deep breath of warm sea air. It was fresher than the mash of exhaust fumes and sweaty humanity she was used to, and the view before her was a world away from her tiny balcony in London. That overlooked an ugly brick warehouse and a cemetery filled with blackened gravestones. Whereas here…

Lettie gazed around, at the ocean stretching towards the horizon, a moving sheet of navy blue, and the clifftop sprinkled with yellow gorse. And there, in front of her, stood a whitewashed building whose front door was flanked by stone pots overflowing with flowers.

So this was Driftwood House. It was described online as being 'on top of the world', and Lettie could see why.

It was the only building perched on the steep cliff that towered about Heaven's Cove, the pretty village her taxi had just driven through – a village of quaint cottages and gift shops that was currently rammed with tourists. Several had prompted a stream of muttered swear words from her taxi driver by wandering obliviously across the road. And his mood hadn't improved when he'd seen the potholed track that led to the top of the cliff.

Lettie brushed auburn curls from her eyes and watched his taxi bump its way back towards the village. Then, she ran her finger across the rail ticket from Paddington still nestled in her jeans pocket, hardly able to believe she was here.

This trip had been a last-minute decision. She'd jumped on the train to Devon with hardly a second thought, even though she'd never been a spontaneous sort of person. Her approach to life was rather more low-key and cautious.

But perhaps losing someone you loved and then being fired from your job just five weeks later made you braver. It certainly made you… Lettie drew in another deep breath and tried to make sense of the jumbled thoughts racing through her mind. It made you unsettled, she decided; unsettled, scared, and sad. Very, very sad.

Tears filled her eyes as she touched the gold filigree key hanging around her neck. Here she was, where Iris grew up but without her beloved great-aunt by her side.

If Iris were here, she'd know just the right thing to say about being 'let go' from your job, thought Lettie, glancing at the seagulls screeching overhead. She'd know how to make Lettie laugh and ease the sadness that had washed over her in waves for weeks. How ironic that the only person whose cheerful chatter could ease her low mood was the very same person whose death had initially caused it.

A warm wind blew through Lettie's hair as she made an effort to pull herself together. Iris would want life to go on, and Lettie's family certainly seemed to be coping with the old lady's death far better than she was. They hadn't even seemed that upset at the funeral, though it had reduced her to a snivelling wreck.

Thoughts of her family prompted Lettie to check her phone that she'd switched to silent a few hours earlier. There were four missed calls and a barrage of texts from her sister, Daisy. The latest said, simply: *Where the hell are you? Stop being such a drama queen and call me back.*

For a trainee life coach, Daisy wasn't the most empathetic of people. Lettie pushed the phone back into her pocket, picked up her case and walked to the front door of Driftwood House. She knocked and waited, noticing that, although the whitewash on the walls was pristine, the wooden window frames and tiled roof were more weather-beaten. Up here, on top of the world, strong winds and storms must sweep in off a deep, dark sea and batter the building.

Lettie shuddered and had just raised her hand to knock again when the door was wrenched open.

'There you are! Welcome to Driftwood House! How was your journey from London? It can take a while, especially if there's a queue for the taxis at Exeter station. Do come in.'

Lettie blinked under the verbal onslaught but stepped over the threshold into a sunny hall with black and white floor tiles and a grand-father clock in the corner. She'd assumed that women who ran seaside guesthouses would be on the older side of middle-aged, but the woman delivering such an effusive greeting was around thirty, like her, with bright brown eyes and fair hair that flicked up where it hit her shoulders.

'Welcome to Driftwood House,' the woman repeated, then winced. 'Sorry, I think I've said that already. You must be Lettie. My name's Rosie. Can I give you a hand?' She picked up the suitcase and smiled. 'Wow, you travel light.'

'I didn't need to bring much with me,' answered Lettie, realising she'd forgotten loads of stuff, including her walking boots, socks and moisturiser.

She'd been in a rush to get away from London, which was silly really because – bereavement and unemployment aside – her life there was OK. She had family and friends who cared about her, and a tiny rented bedsit of her own.

But an increasing sense of loneliness was hard to shake these days. Her closest friends had either moved out of London or settled down and had babies, or both. And now Iris was gone too, and Lettie, in her more dramatic moments, felt as if she'd been cast adrift with no particular purpose in life.

She automatically felt again for the key hanging around her neck, as though it was a magical talisman with all the answers.

'Let me get you settled in,' said Rosie, breaking into Lettie's thoughts. 'Shall I give you a quick tour of the house and then I can take you to your room?'

'That would be great. Thank you. It's nice to meet you too, by the way.'

Rosie gave a wide, bright smile and, still carrying the suitcase, led Lettie into a sitting room that smelled of polish. Red roses were arranged in a vase on the stone mantelpiece and framed paintings of wild moorland lined the lemon-yellow walls.

'You're welcome to use this room whenever you like,' said Rosie, standing next to the window with its view across the cliff to the sea. 'There's only me in the house at the moment so please make yourself at home.'

'Is it just the two of us? I thought you'd be really busy during the summer months.'

'To be honest, I've only just opened as a guesthouse and you're my very first arrival. That's my excuse for being horribly over the top when you arrived.'

When she wrinkled her nose, Lettie grinned. 'You were only a tiny bit over the top, and you were *very* welcoming.'

'That's some comfort, at least. You weren't supposed to be my first guest. A couple from Birmingham were due to arrive yesterday but had to cancel at the last minute because of illness.'

'That's a shame.'

'It was very disappointing, so I was delighted when you rang last night and asked if we had any rooms. If you don't mind me asking, what made you choose Driftwood House?'

'I was looking up the house online and when I saw on your website that it had been turned into a guesthouse, it seemed like fate that I should stay here.'

'What made you search for Driftwood House in the first place?'

'History.' Lettie looked around the cosy room, imagining an echo of children's voices from long ago. 'Actually... I'm pretty sure my great-aunt Iris and her brother, my grandfather, were brought up here.'

'In this actual house?' Rosie sat down on the stone window ledge, her eyes open wide. 'Really? That's amazing. I grew up at Driftwood House too. When did your family live here?'

'It would have been years ago. Iris and her family moved away from Devon in the Second World War. My grandparents died before I was born, but Iris only died last month.'

Rosie's face clouded over. 'I'm sorry. I lost someone close to me, recently, and it's hard, isn't it? Is that why you're here in Heaven's Cove, to see where your great-aunt lived?'

'I guess so.' Lettie paused, not willing to share her real reasons. 'Iris never told me much about the place but I'm curious to see where she came from.'

'Well, I think it's wonderful that my first ever guest has a link to this fabulous old house,' declared Rosie, hopping off the window ledge. 'That sounds like fate, indeed! Let me show you the rest of the place. Some of it won't have changed much since your great-aunt lived here.'

First, she took Lettie into a conservatory at the back of the house that had sweeping views across the Devon countryside.

'This wouldn't have been here in the war but it's a great addition to the house. You can see almost all the way to Dartmoor,' said Rosie, shielding her eyes against the sun streaming in through the salt-streaked glass. 'The pictures on the sitting room walls are of Dartmoor too. They were painted by my mum.' She glanced at a photo on the bookcase, of a woman in sunglasses smiling into the camera.

'Was it your mum who…? You said you'd lost someone too.' Lettie hesitated, worried she was speaking out of turn.

But Rosie nodded. 'Yes, my mum died earlier this year.'

'I'm really sorry.'

'Thank you. She was an amazing woman.' Rosie gently brushed her fingers across the photo before pulling back her shoulders. 'Anyway. Next stop, the kitchen.'

Lettie followed her into the hall, imagining young Iris walking across the shiny tiles or running her hand along the polished bannister rail. The divide between past and present seemed wafer-thin in this windswept house.

'The kitchen's just been refurbished,' said Rosie, opening a door into a large, sunny space. 'But the butler sink is original, and the quarry tiles too.'

After a whistle-stop tour of the room, with its wooden worktops and cupboards painted dove-grey, she led Lettie up a wide staircase onto a sunny landing.

'My bedroom's along here, and there are four more bedrooms for guests, but I've put you on the next floor if that's OK.'

Lettie followed her up more stairs to a large room at the very top of the house, tucked under the eaves.

'This is such a lovely space.' Lettie placed her case on the bed and gazed out of the Velux window.

The view from up here was magnificent. The village lay far below, its cottages clustered around the church. And the sea that edged Heaven's Cove had already changed colour from navy near the horizon to bands of aqua and moss-green closer to shore.

Rosie beamed. 'I'm so glad you think so. The attic has only just been converted and I'm delighted with it. There are towels in the en-suite and a hairdryer in the drawer over there.' She started shifting from foot to foot. 'I used to work in a B&B in Spain, but I've never run my own place before, so please do say if anything isn't quite right. I won't mind.'

'Everything's perfect,' Lettie assured her, sitting on the bed and surveying the bright, uncluttered room. 'Thank you.'

'Good. Then I'll leave you to unpack and I'll be in the kitchen if you fancy a cup of tea later. There's a lot to see in the village and the beach is wonderful and very safe for swimming on a day like today.'

'I don't swim,' said Lettie quickly, batting away an image of dark water and trailing seaweed wrapping around her limbs.

'Maybe you can have a paddle instead. The cove is definitely worth a visit, and the old castle, and there's a lovely café in the High Street that does fantastic cream teas.'

'I'd quite like to visit Dartmoor, too. Iris, my great-aunt, had a photo of Dartmoor hanging on her wall so I think it was special to her.'

'It's a very special place.' Rosie smiled. 'There are buses that go out that way, and I can find you a timetable while you're settling in.'

After Rosie had gone downstairs, Lettie unpacked her clothes and the toiletries she'd remembered, and placed her half-read book – a weighty history of London – on the bedside table. Then, she opened the window and stuck her head outside.

Had this view greeted Iris every day when she was growing up: a vast, never-still ocean and a huge, arcing sky? It was certainly different from the view she'd had towards the end of her days. Her great-aunt's London flat was perfectly fine, but overlooking a gasworks was depressing. How she must have yearned for the countryside and the fresh sea breeze – though never enough to return.

Lettie had offered a few times to bring Iris to Devon, so she could retrace her footsteps and relive her younger days. But her great-aunt had always declined and rarely talked about her life here. The Dartmoor photo on her wall – of a magnificent, gushing waterfall – was the only clue that she'd ever lived in Devon at all. She always changed the subject if Lettie asked her about it. The same, too, if she was ever quizzed about the key around her neck.

Iris's past was a mystery while she was alive and was even more so now she was gone. And it was emotional to imagine her great-aunt here in this house, young and full of life, when her final days on this earth were so different.

Watching someone she loved die had left its mark on Lettie; now she knew that death wasn't always a gentle fade into darkness. Iris's final moments were peaceful but the days leading up to them were filled with pain and fear and a succession of medical professionals in her flat.

Lettie had moved in for a few weeks so Iris could spend her final days at home. And she was glad she had – even though the long hanging on, the slow slide towards the inevitable, had been almost too much for both of them to bear.

When Iris did finally slip away, people told Lettie it was for the best because the old woman's pain and suffering were over. Her great-aunt had gone, and she must feel relieved. But she hadn't so far. All she felt was deep sadness and flutterings of panic at the thought of never seeing Iris again. She missed her so much it hurt.

The key around her neck felt warm in her fingers as she raised it to her lips and let it rest there. She felt closer to Iris here, in this storm-battered house on top of the world. Lettie lay back on the soft duvet, the sun streaming through the window onto her face, and closed her eyes.

Chapter Two

Lettie woke with a start and blinked furiously. The sun had tracked down her body and was warming her thighs. For a moment, she thought she was at home, but the screeching of seagulls outside, rather than the rumble of the Underground, reminded her where she was. And a glance at her watch revealed she'd been asleep for over an hour.

'Damn,' she said out loud, starting to regret her impetuous flight from London. What did she think she was going to achieve by coming to Heaven's Cove? It certainly wouldn't bring her great-aunt back, and she should be job-hunting at home.

Sitting up, she swung her legs off the bed and smoothed down her long hair that had a mind of its own. Then she went into the en-suite, with its gleaming new shower, and did her teeth. The minty fizz of the toothpaste made her feel more awake though the face staring back at her from the mirror still looked dozy. She blinked her big hazel eyes, raked her fingers through her unruly red hair and yawned. Sea air certainly wasn't energising, she decided, wandering back into the bedroom and spotting more missed calls on her phone.

Lettie sighed and switched her mobile from silent. She supposed she'd better let her family know where she was because they'd be wondering what on earth she was doing.

But she winced when the phone suddenly started ringing and Daisy's name came up on the screen. This was going to be tricky. She took a deep breath and clicked on 'answer'.

'There you are, Lettie! What's going on? You practically do a runner from Mum and Dad's yesterday, then you send a text at stupid o'clock this morning saying you're going away on holiday when you're supposed to be babysitting tonight.'

Lettie closed her eyes and groaned softly. That was the trouble with being spontaneous. It caused all sorts of upset.

'Well?' demanded Daisy, before her voice softened. 'Say something! You're all right, aren't you?'

Lettie hesitated. How did one define 'all right'? She hadn't felt all right for ages.

'I'm fine,' answered Lettie, knowing that was what Daisy wanted to hear. 'I just needed a break.'

'Why? You haven't got kids driving you crazy. And what about work?'

'I had some time owing,' lied Lettie, desperate to avoid both the disappointment and unsolicited advice that telling the truth would unleash.

Starcrosses held down solid jobs for years before retiring, like her father, to watch endless repeats of *Midsomer Murders* and *Cash in the Attic*. They didn't hanker after new, unattainable careers, and they certainly weren't fired for 'inappropriate behaviour'.

'So where have you buggered off to, then?' demanded Daisy. 'Spain, Italy, Greece?'

'I'm in Devon.'

'Devon? Why, when you have no responsibilities and can jump on a plane to anywhere, have you gone to Devon?' spluttered Daisy, to the sound of children bickering in the background. 'What the...?

Hang on a minute. Elsa, please give the remote control to your brother and stop biting him. Honestly, you two are testing my patience today.' She waited until everything went quiet before continuing. 'So why are you in Devon? You didn't mention anything about it and you should be here. You know it's my weekly date night with Jason tonight and you always babysit.'

'Sorry, Daisy. I'm afraid I can't this time.'

'What about next week?'

'Possibly,' answered Lettie, feeling, as usual, more like Daisy's au pair than her sister.

'Possibly? What is going on? You never go on last-minute holidays. Were you spooked by Mum trying to set you up with that sales guy?'

'I could have done without it, to be honest.'

Nicholas, the son of one of her mum's work colleagues, had been roped in to have an evening meal with her family and, as blind dates go, he'd seemed fine. Polite, clean-cut and with a good job. Just Lettie's type, according to her family. He even looked a little like Christopher, her ex.

But all Nicholas talked about was his job selling kitchens, and he hadn't seemed terribly impressed with her job in customer care for a firm that made a range of different types of adhesive. He'd have been even less impressed if she'd told him the truth, that she'd just been 'terminated'.

'Mum's only trying to help,' said Daisy. 'We all are, and he was better looking than I expected, plus he's got a career, and an Audi. You need to stop being so picky. Nigel, or whatever his name was, could be the man of your dreams.'

'I doubt it, and I really don't need you all to sort out my love life.'

'You really do,' snorted Daisy.

Lettie sighed. 'Nicholas seemed very nice, but he was a bit boring.'

'Boring? What do you expect from life, Lettie? Passionate romance and adventure? Let's face facts here.'

Oh, dear. Lettie closed her eyes, ready for the sisterly onslaught.

'You're twenty-nine years old, you live in a crappy bedsit, you don't make the best of yourself, and you spend your days listening to people complaining that their glue doesn't stick. You're not exactly a romantic dream yourself, you know. The trouble is all those old books you read and the endless history exhibitions you go to. You've always got your head in the past, with no time for real life.'

Lettie slowly turned her history of London face-down on the bedside table. 'That's not true.'

'I know not everyone can have an amazing marriage, like me and Jason,' continued Daisy, now in full flow. 'But you're getting on a bit and need to be realistic. So settle down with a solid, decent man and stop worrying Mum and Dad. That's what normal people do.'

Lettie sincerely hoped that Daisy adopted a more positive tone with her new life coach clients. 'I don't mean to worry Mum and Dad.'

'Not consciously, maybe, but subconsciously you're trying to attract their attention all the time because you're the youngest child of three. It's classic behaviour.'

Daisy seemed to have her all figured out. Lettie drew in a deep breath. 'I'm very sorry I can't babysit tonight but Mum might step in if you ask her nicely. I'll be home…' She hesitated, suddenly feeling rebellious. '…in a week or two.'

'Two?' whined Daisy. 'Mum won't cover two date nights, and I was thinking you'd do an extra babysit next weekend 'cos it's Jo's fortieth birthday party. She'll be devastated if me and Jase can't go.'

'I'm sure you can work something else out.'

'Huh,' harrumphed Daisy down the phone. 'I'll let Mum know what's going on but you need to call her yourself to apologise.'

'What for? I'm allowed to go on holiday.'

'Apologise for just taking off like that. It's a bit thoughtless, Letts.'

'Just because I didn't get everyone's permission first doesn't mean I'm th… oh, whatever.'

Lettie knew this argument was pointless. The Starcrosses were close. Everyone said so. The very embodiment of a close and caring family. But sometimes close and caring could tip over into micro-managing and suffocating.

'Well.' Daisy sniffed. 'Let me know when you're coming back, and I'll be in touch.' She paused for a moment. 'Sorry. I don't mean to nag. Of course you're allowed to go on holiday, but just don't stay away too long, OK?'

Once Daisy had rung off, Lettie sat quietly for a moment. Tendrils of guilt had started wrapping themselves around her brain, as they always did when her family implied she was letting them down.

'I have a life of my own,' she said, grumpily, into the empty room. Even though it didn't always feel like it.

That was the trouble with being the third child – a surprise baby who'd arrived seven years after the birth of Daisy and nine years after brother Ed was born. Her siblings' head start made all the difference.

Daisy had married her second ever boyfriend, Jason, at the age of twenty-three and now had two children and her coaching course to keep her busy. Ed, a school teacher, was married to Fran, had three small children and lived in a new-build house just within the M25 corridor.

They were settled and successful, which made Lettie's lack of direction and hopeless love life all the more obvious. It also meant that she'd slipped into the role of helper.

Neither Ed nor Daisy had the time – nor the inclination, Lettie suspected – to help out when it came to their parents. They were happy to pile round to Mum's for a Sunday roast but disappeared sharpish when she started talking about a shopping trip to Lidl or needing someone to accompany her to a hospital appointment.

Lettie always stepped in to help, and Iris was the only member of the family who never seemed to expect anything from her.

'You're too obliging for your own good and your family take advantage,' she'd often chastise Lettie, when they sat together, drinking tea. The older woman would light up a cigarette and puff smoke out of the open window as she advised: 'You need to strike out and be your own woman. And remember when it comes to men, follow your heart and never settle for second best. It's far better to be on your own than with someone not good enough.'

Lettie smiled at the bitter-sweet memory. Iris had certainly stayed true to her word, never marrying and, in fact, never mentioning any romantic attachments at all.

There was the sound of footsteps on the stairs before a tap sounded on the door.

'Sorry to bother you,' said Rosie, poking her head around the door. 'But I've just made a pot of tea and wondered if you'd like a cup?'

'That's really kind of you but I fell asleep and think a quick walk to clear my head might be a good idea.'

'That should do the trick, and you're spoiled for choice around here. You could walk down into the village. It's such a beautiful day, though it'll be very busy with tourists. Or the walk across the cliffs, from here to Sorrell Head, will be more peaceful and the views are wonderful.'

Lettie set out across the cliffs five minutes later, her hair scraped back into a ponytail and her small handbag slung across her body.

Rosie hadn't been exaggerating. The view really was magnificent from up here. She was so high, it felt as though she was flying alongside the seagulls that swooped above her. People were tiny ants in the winding lanes of the village far below, and when she strode as close to the cliff edge as she dared, she spotted a curve of sand lapped by azure waves. Heaven's Cove was aptly named.

Lettie walked on and on, feeling the stresses of the day melt away, until she reached a headland that jutted out into the ocean. Was this Sorrell Head that Rosie had talked about?

A salty breeze smoothed her flushed cheeks as she imagined her great-aunt playing here as a child, and wondered what had made her leave this place and never return.

Lettie had asked her mother years ago why Iris always changed the subject whenever growing up in Devon was mentioned. Her mum, faintly disapproving of her husband's outspoken aunt, had pursed her lips and shrugged. But her reply: *There were whispers of some sort of trouble or scandal,* had only served to make Iris even more interesting in Lettie's eyes.

Sitting on the grass, Lettie pulled an envelope from her bag and stared at the writing on the front of it: *For the attention of Miss Iris Starcross, Driftwood House, Heaven's Cove.*

She held on to it tightly so it wouldn't be snatched away by the wind and pulled out the sheet of paper inside. The paper, yellowed with age, bore the same curling handwriting in black ink as the envelope, and the briefest of messages:

Sit where I sat, darling girl, with the key to my heart and all will become clear.

What would become clear? Lettie had re-read the words so many times, she knew them off by heart. The mysterious letter had been carefully stowed in the lining of Iris's handbag and Lettie had found it whilst clearing out her flat. This was the real reason she was here now, in a picturesque seaside village miles away from home.

She'd almost asked her family about the letter but it had seemed too personal to share, and they'd never been particularly interested in Iris's life anyway.

Lettie sighed and gazed across the water. Brightly painted fishing boats were bobbing on the waves that sparkled like diamonds under the sun. It was truly beautiful here and Lettie already felt calmer being away from the constant buzz of London.

She knew what she wanted. She would stay at Driftwood House for a week or two, benefit from the break, and take the chance to find out more about Iris's life in this tiny village.

Perhaps that would shed some light on the key around her neck and this mysterious letter. And maybe she could grant her great-aunt's dying wish, whispered as she had passed Lettie the delicate key: *Find out for me, darling girl.*

Chapter Three

Fifteen minutes after walking down the cliff path, Lettie turned into another narrow lane and realised that she was near the edge of the village already. Ahead of her stood the ruins of what looked like a castle, with tumbled stones and ivy growing on its stunted walls. Heaven's Cove was absolutely tiny. It would fit into one small corner of London and be swallowed up in the general hubbub.

She looked around at the cottages, some of them whitewashed and some made of attractive local stone. Several had thatched rooves and tiny front gardens filled with vibrant gerberas and sunflowers. London was the only home she'd ever known, but this must be a wonderful place for a child to grow up. There were lanes to explore and countryside all around – the view across the county from Driftwood House's conservatory was breath-taking – and then there was the sea.

Lettie had a complicated relationship with the ocean and its murky depths. She would never set foot in the sea again, but she had no problem with looking at it. Sunshine sparkling on white-crested waves was always cheering.

She decided to find the local beach. The castle ruins were fascinating but they could wait for another day.

She was weaving her way through tourists browsing gift shops when a sturdy woman suddenly blocked her way.

'Good afternoon. I'm Belinda Kellscroft, chair of the parish council and the village hall fundraising committee.'

'Good afternoon,' said Lettie, feeling rather like she was standing in front of her old headmistress. The two women shared the same taste in grey bubble perms, elasticated trousers, and sensible sandals.

'I understand you're staying at Driftwood House. You're Rosie's first guest, I'm told.'

'That's right. I only arrived this morning.'

'I have my finger on the pulse of local news and not much escapes my attention. Are you here on holiday or business?'

Lettie raised an eyebrow at the woman's assertive tone and nosiness. 'I'm on holiday, mostly.'

'Mostly? What else are you up to?'

Lettie hesitated. There was something about inquisitive Belinda that put her teeth on edge but made it almost impossible not to give her a proper answer. 'Well, I'm kind of researching my family tree.'

'Are your family from around here?' Belinda enquired, her small brown eyes lighting up.

'Yes, I believe so.'

'What were their names?'

'Starcross.'

Belinda thought for a moment. 'That's a distinctive name, but I can't think of anyone called that in the area. Do you have any documents or clues to go on?'

'I know they lived at Driftwood House during the Second World War.'

'And now you're staying there?' Belinda clapped her hands together in delight. 'Ah, the circle of life. It's a mystery to us all.'

'It certainly is,' said Lettie, already hearing the Elton John song in her head. That was her earworm for the day.

'So what else do you know about their stay in our wonderful village?'

I know there was the whiff of trouble, maybe even scandal, thought Lettie, pushing the dainty key beneath the neckline of her T-shirt.

'Absolutely nothing at all,' she replied firmly, not about to share family gossip or Iris's mysterious letter with this overwhelming woman, even if she might be able to help her.

'That's a bit of a problem then. Oh!' Belinda began to gesticulate wildly at an older man who was walking past a small grocery store. 'Claude! Over here! Can I have a word? Claude!'

The man she was waving at kept on walking as though he hadn't heard Belinda's piercing voice. He was strange, thought Lettie. Tall and rangy with long grey hair past his shoulders and a bushy beard. The navy blue jumper he was wearing was baggy, with holes on the shoulders.

'Honestly,' huffed Belinda. 'He doesn't like outsiders but there's no need to be rude.' When Lettie raised an eyebrow, Belinda made strange smoothing movements with her hands. 'You might be an outsider, dear, but you're very welcome in Heaven's Cove all the same. Where would we be without tourists to boost our economy? Claude is just a little... old school.'

'Do you think he might know something about the Starcross family?'

'If anyone will, it's Claude. He's Heaven's Cove's unofficial archivist, with a cellar full of old documents and newspaper cuttings his family have collected over the years. I keep telling him to put them somewhere safer but he never listens to me, or to anyone else, for that matter.'

She tutted quietly while Lettie tried to hide her excitement. The thought of an old cellar filled with dusty old documents filled her with glee. Daisy was right when she said Lettie's head was often stuck in the past – sometimes it proved a welcome escape from the present. And the archive might provide an opportunity to find out more about Iris's life.

'Where can I find Claude? Presumably he lives in the village?'

'He does, but I wouldn't even attempt to see him at home. He doesn't take kindly to unexpected visitors, even people he's known for years, and he'd never let you through the door of his cottage. Which is just as well. He's never married and is a typical bachelor who's let his home go to rack and ruin, by all accounts. It's only got worse as he's got older and he's too proud to accept any help. The parish council offered only last month to—'

'Where else do you think that I might find him?' interrupted Lettie, not wanting to be rude but feeling uncomfortable about hearing gossip.

'He's been a fisherman all his life and still goes to sea when he can. He's an old sea dog and his experience is in demand. But you can often find him in the pub.'

Lettie had passed a pub earlier – a thatched white building, festooned with colourful hanging baskets.

'Is that The Smugglers?'

'The Smugglers Haunt, yes.'

'It looks very old.'

'It was built in the sixteenth century and once used to store various contraband.' Belinda leaned in close. 'Fred, the current landlord, bulk-buys cigarettes when he goes abroad and sells them under the counter to customers, including Claude. Just continuing the smuggling tradition, I suppose.' She gave a throaty chuckle. 'Fred also drinks too much and his wife is just as bad, though they keep a good pub, to be fair. They weren't able to have children – polycystic ovaries combined with a low sperm count – so they pour everything into their work.'

Lettie blinked, rather glad she hadn't over-shared any information with Belinda. Chances were it would have been all round the village by teatime.

'I'll look out for Claude in the pub, then. Thank you for your help. It was lovely to meet you.'

'Where are you from?'

'London.'

'Ah, I guessed as much from your accent. What job do you do there?'

Nothing, thought Lettie, feeling a pang of worry. Her savings would only stretch for a couple of months and then what would she do?

'Oh, this and that. I'm heading for the beach, actually,' said Lettie, keen to get away.

'You and every tourist in this part of Devon,' grumbled Belinda, but she pointed past the castle ruins. 'Cut through there and keep walking along the lane, past Liam's farm on the right and you can't miss the cove. You know Rosie who runs Driftwood House? Did you know that she and Liam—' She broke off and waved at a young woman in a bright red hoodie who was walking hand in hand with a small girl. 'I must catch Nessa, so I'll bid you goodbye, Miss Starcross.'

That was a shame. Lettie would quite like to have heard about Rosie and Liam. But Belinda was marching towards Nessa, who, Lettie noticed, had put her head down and seemed to be hurrying away. Perhaps Claude had been escaping Belinda, rather than avoiding an 'outsider'.

Lettie would track Claude down later, she decided, suddenly feeling more optimistic about her mission to reveal the truth behind Iris's mysterious letter and key. But for now, all she wanted was to relax and enjoy this beautiful village.

Ten minutes later, Lettie was nearing the beach. The lane was narrow and cars were parked along it on the grass verge. She went past a farmyard and a handsome farmhouse and could hear waves breaking against rock. The sound of the water made her shoulders tense, but she took a deep breath and tried to ignore familiar surges of panic.

Stay calm. Keep breathing. It happened a long time ago.

As she turned the corner, the beach was in front of her. Groups of people were scattered across the sand which had the same reddish tinge as the cliffs towering above it.

The small bay was a perfect semi-circle and gentle waves, tipped with white, were breaking on the sand. Children were running in and out of the water, watched by their parents standing in swimsuits at the shoreline.

With blue sky and sea, it looked like a holiday advertisement for an exotic location. Devon was absolutely stunning, Lettie decided, plonking herself down on the sand, as far from the water as possible. Near her, small children splashed in rock pools and dogs careered across the beach.

She shielded her face from the sun with her hand, her eyes drawn to a figure in the sea, slicing through the deep water with a confident front crawl. His dark hair was just visible above the swell of the water. He was farther out than everyone else so didn't have to dodge the people playing in the waves. He seemed totally at home in the water and full of confidence. Lettie watched him for a while, going back and forth, before rolling up her thin jumper, lying back on the sand and wedging it behind her head.

She started drifting off as the shouts of the children receded and the drone of a light aircraft overhead lulled her towards sleep. She imagined Iris on this beach as a child, paddling in the surf and sweeping rock pools with a net, searching for crabs. Ninety years before her life came to an end in a small flat in the middle of a noisy city.

Lettie pushed thoughts of Iris's death from her mind and instead imagined what fun it would have been if her great-aunt had brought her here as a child. She'd have loved it far more than the annual family trip to the Essex coast.

Daisy and Ed loved the coastal amusement arcades and fish and chip shops, but she preferred the history of this little village: the ancient cottages with doorsteps that dipped from centuries of use; the ruins of a grand castle that once housed lords and ladies; the narrow, winding lanes still paved with cobbles.

Her mind suddenly slipped back to that fateful Essex trip when she was eight years old. Daisy and Ed were playing football on the sand and her parents were reading. But Iris, brought along as an afterthought, was keeping an eye on Lettie as she splashed in the water. And it was Iris who saw her fall and sink beneath the waves.

Lettie had tried desperately to find her footing but the sand shifted beneath her feet. The waves had kept on coming, pushing her this way and that, and she couldn't stand up.

Lettie experienced again a surge of panic and tightness in her chest and forced herself to take in a deep breath. Air, not water, filled her lungs as she took in breath after breath, and she began to calm and settle, as the sun warmed her skin.

It happened a long time ago, she told herself again, as she closed her eyes. *I'm on dry land. I'm safe,* she repeated over and over in her head as she slipped into sleep once more.

Chapter Four

Lettie wasn't sure how long she slept. Losing Iris, followed by the shock of losing her job, seemed to have wiped her out, and she fell asleep at the drop of a hat these days. But she woke with a start when ice-cold water splashed over her.

'Hey.' She pushed herself up onto one elbow, feeling groggy and disorientated. 'Watch out. You're getting water everywhere.'

'It's a beach,' said a low, sardonic voice. 'And you're very close to my towel when there's a whole lot of beach to choose from.'

She peered up at the man, glistening wet, who was standing over her. He was the swimmer she'd watched earlier. When he picked up his towel that was lying flat, sand flew into her face.

'Urgh.' She wiped gritty sand from her lips with the back of her hand.

'Sorry,' he muttered, redeeming himself slightly, before ruining it by adding: 'You're going to get more sand in your face unless you move back a bit.'

He was good-looking in a tall, dark and scowling way, noticed Lettie. She averted her eyes from his abs.

'Perhaps you could move to the side a little while you dry off?'

'Only if I want to stand in the rockpool, which I don't.'

The man scowled some more while Lettie shuffled back slightly. He might be craggily handsome, but he had zero manners.

'Are you on holiday?' she asked, trying to improve the atmosphere between them.

The man rubbed at his hair with the towel before answering. 'I live here. You're a tourist, I presume.'

The way he said 'tourist', as though they were lower-class citizens, made Lettie cringe. Here was another local, like Claude, who didn't like outsiders.

'I'm visiting Heaven's Cove for a few days to research my family tree. My family used to live here.'

Why had she said that? She was almost offering excuses for daring to set foot in the village.

'Anyone I might know?' he asked, pulling a white T-shirt from a small backpack.

'I doubt it. It was a long time ago. Also,' added Lettie, still stung by the man's tone and remembering Belinda's words, 'I dare say Heaven's Cove would be in a sorry state economically without the tourists it attracts every year.'

The man regarded Lettie coolly, water dripping from his body onto the sand. 'I dare say, though I fish for a living so tourism doesn't much affect me.'

Lettie could imagine him on a fishing boat in a storm, doing whatever people do in boats in a storm, and building up his muscles. Maybe that was how he'd got the thin, silver scar that trailed from his side to under his rib cage. Lettie looked away, aware that she was staring.

'Where are you staying?' asked the man.

'At Driftwood House, up on the cliff.'

The man nodded. 'One of Rosie's first guests, are you?'

'That's right.'

'You can look down on the village from up there.'

Was he implying that she was a snob, or was his bristly attitude simply making her second-guess everything he said? Lettie got to her feet and shook off the sand, carefully. 'Much as I'd love to chat, I'd better leave you to dry off.' She draped her jumper around her shoulders, feeling bits of the beach trickle down her back. 'Enjoy the rest of your day.'

Then she walked off, as quickly as she could over the soft sand that squished between her toes with every step.

Rosie was weeding in the small garden behind the conservatory when Lettie got back to the guesthouse. She looked up from a pot bursting with lavender that she was tending and wiped the back of her hand across her forehead.

'Hello, there. Did you enjoy looking around the village?'

'I did, thanks. It's very old and quaint, and the beach is fantastic.'

'Isn't it lovely? I used to live in Spain, near the coast, and our cove measures up well to the beaches over there.'

'What did you do in Spain?'

'B&B work, selling apartments, this and that. I lived abroad for a few years and came home when my mum died earlier this year, and never left.' She didn't look unhappy about resuming her life in Heaven's Cove.

'I met a few of the locals while I was looking around the village.'

'Really? Who was that?'

'Someone called Belinda, first of all.'

'Ah.' Rosie sat back on her heels. 'She can be rather full on. Was she all right?'

Lettie grinned. 'She *was* pretty full on, but fine. She suggested someone called Claude might know about my family, when they lived here.'

'He might,' said Rosie, hesitantly, 'but he's not…' She paused, choosing her words carefully. 'He's not always the easiest person to talk to.'

'Has he lived here long?'

'All his life, I think.'

'And Belinda said he has some sort of archive of historic documents.'

'Apparently, though I've never seen it. His mother was a great one for collecting information, and Claude continued after her death.'

'Doesn't he show it to anyone?'

Rosie shrugged. 'Not as far as I'm aware.'

'I thought I might try calling at his house…' Lettie noticed Rosie's expression and bit her lip. 'Or maybe see if he's in the pub?'

'That might be a better idea. Claude guards his privacy rather fiercely and can be a little… abrupt when people knock on his door.'

'So Belinda said.' Going to Claude's home was seeming less enticing by the moment. Lettie stepped back as Rosie got to her feet and rolled her shoulders. 'I met someone else on the beach. A man who was swimming. He wasn't terribly friendly.'

Rosie frowned. 'What did he look like?'

'Tall, dark, um…' Lettie wasn't going to say 'handsome'. She wouldn't give him the satisfaction. 'He said he was a fisherman, and he was a bit, well, bad tempered, to be honest. He had a scar here.' She traced a finger across her middle.

'Oh, that'll be Corey. He can be a bit prickly with grockles, and he's got a lot on his plate at the moment.'

'Grock-what?'

Rosie grinned. 'Grockles. The Devon word for tourists. Take no notice of Corey. He has a good heart. He looks after his grandmother who lives at the top of the village.'

'Really?' That did imply a good heart. Lettie upgraded her opinion of Corey from obnoxious to simply unpleasant. 'What about his parents?'

'His mum moved away a couple of years ago to be closer to his sister who has a son with disabilities.' Rosie's mouth twitched in the corner. 'If you ask Belinda, she'll tell you all about it.'

'I bet.'

'And his dad died when Corey was small.'

'That's sad.'

'Yeah, it was. I was only a child but I can remember the upset in the village at the time.' She slapped her hands together to brush soil from her fingers. 'Anyway, that was a long time ago. Would you like a cup of tea? I seem to live on the stuff.'

'That would be lovely, if you're not too busy.'

'The gardening can wait, and my knees are killing me.'

Lettie followed Rosie inside, already feeling better after her bruising encounter with Corey. She would do her best to avoid him during her stay in the village.

The one person she did want to see again was Claude, with his stash of Heaven's Cove cuttings from the past. They probably wouldn't tell her what Iris had meant when she'd whispered, *Find out for me, darling girl.* Or if those final words were definitely linked to the mysterious letter hidden in her handbag. But surely discovering what she could about Iris and her family was the best place to start.

Chapter Five

The pub was packed and very hot, thanks to the low-beamed ceiling and the balmy evening. But it was charming. Lettie weaved her way to the bar and leaned against it, waiting for the barman to notice her.

History seemed to leach from the pub's stone walls. Lettie could imagine the people who had sat in here over the centuries, sharing their joys and sorrows. Drinking too much, sparking arguments, falling in love.

The walls were so thick, people were sitting in the wide windowsills that were topped with bright cushions. Others were grouped around dark wooden tables close to the huge fireplace, its hearth blackened by centuries of use. A back door was open, revealing a walled garden that also looked packed full. She assumed several customers – those with glowing sunburned faces – were tourists, but Lettie could also hear the soft Devon burr of locals all around her.

The atmosphere was so different from her London local, a brightly lit gastro pub with piped music and staff from all over the world providing table service. Here, it was horse brasses on the walls, and dog-eat-dog at the crowded bar.

After finally being served, she did a lap of the pub, looking for Claude. But he was nowhere to be seen and all she managed to do was annoy people and tread on a poor spaniel's tail as she made her way through the crowd. Eventually, she gave up and looked around for a seat. The only spare place was at a small table for two, where a young blond man was sitting with a pint of beer in his hand. Was he waiting for someone? The open laptop in front of him suggested not so Lettie weaved her way through the throng towards him.

He looked up when she got to the table, but didn't smile.

'Is this chair taken?' asked Lettie.

'No.'

He went back to staring at the laptop screen while Lettie slid into the seat with her gin and tonic. She pulled her history of London book from her bag and started reading about Celtic queen Boudicca burning the city, while stealing glances at the man opposite. He had a light caramel tan and was wearing a pristine white T-shirt that showed it off. Lettie watched his fingers tapping on the keyboard, noticing his gold signet ring and his square-cut fingernails.

An IT consultant, she decided. Or someone in finance. He had the look of an accountant, with his short, neat hair and clean-shaven face. He was good-looking, and probably knew it.

Lettie's phone suddenly beeped with a WhatsApp message from Kelly.

What the hell are you doing in Devon? Dirty weekend?

Lettie smiled. She and Kelly had been inseparable since school, until Kelly got married. Now she had a gorgeous little girl called Matilda, and the friendship had cooled. They were still good mates, and Lettie sometimes babysat so Kelly and Adam could have a night out, but their relationship had changed. Of course it had. Kelly had moved on to something new while Lettie's life had remained the same – basically, working (though not any more), fending off her mother's matchmaking efforts, and acting as an unpaid nanny for Daisy.

Sadly not, she replied. *Am taking a short break before I start job-hunting with a vengeance.*

When her phone pinged again almost immediately, the man opposite looked up from his laptop screen and cast her an annoyed glance.

Have you told your mum and dad yet that you've lost your job?

Not yet, Lettie replied, switching her phone to silent. *They'll go ape- shit.*

Not if you tell them what really happened, came back almost immediately. *I don't reckon they can legally sack you for doing that anyway.*

Kelly really didn't know her family very well. Telling them that she'd been 'let go' from her relatively new job for being rude to a customer would be a huge disappointment. And, to be honest, Lettie could hardly believe her behaviour herself. It was totally out of character, as was fleeing to Devon to unravel an ages-old mystery that was possibly all in her head.

Sometimes, these days, she wondered if she was having a bit of a breakdown.

I hated the job anyway but need something else to pay the bills, she fired back to Kelly, who replied immediately.

If things get too tight, maybe you could move in with your parents for a while.

Lettie hadn't even contemplated that scenario. If she moved back into her parents' house – which her mother would love – she'd be smothered by their well-intentioned interfering. And being tagged by her siblings as their parents' 'helper' would be even harder to avoid. While she was trying not to panic, a final message pinged through from Kelly.

Something'll come up. Gotta go cos Tilly won't settle down this eve. She's doing my head in. Take my advice and NEVER HAVE KIDS! x

Fat chance, thought Lettie, sitting back and wondering whether searching for a new job in customer care would ruin her evening.

At least the job she'd just lost had given her a chance to read. The work was sporadic and, in between calls, she'd surf the net, reading about people long gone and researching which historical exhibition she'd visit next. Staff at many London museums waved hello when they saw her because she spent so much time there.

But now she needed something new.

Glancing at the man opposite, who was clattering furiously on his computer keys, she typed 'customer care vacancies, London' into her phone and clicked on one of the first options that came up.

Join our Client Dream Team and take your ambitions to a new level. Immerse yourself in the world of farming foodstuffs and ensure our valued customers receive nothing but the best possible service.

Farming foodstuffs? That sounded only slightly less boring than glue. Lettie sighed before putting her phone away and picking up her book again. Searching for jobs could wait but Boudicca's sacking of London was getting interesting.

She'd only managed to read a couple of pages when the atmosphere in the pub changed. A group of men had gathered near the fireplace and the buzz of conversation around her faded when they suddenly started singing. The man opposite Lettie raised an eyebrow but kept on typing as their voices filled the old building.

It was an old song that spoke of life on the seas and empty bellies when the catch didn't come in. Lettie smiled, drinking in the atmosphere. This song must have been sung in this ancient pub for generations. There was something haunting about it, especially when a lone deep voice took up the verse. A man's voice, clear and strong.

The group of men, pints of beer in hand, joined in with the chorus before the man sang another solo verse. He turned as he sang and Lettie felt a sudden jolt of recognition. It was Corey from the beach. His eyes were closed as his voice filled the room and Lettie had to admit that, for such an unpleasant man, he had a very pleasant voice.

He was wearing jeans and a white shirt, and there was something about the way his dark hair curled where it hit his collar that made Lettie want to brush it away. She was watching him when his eyes suddenly opened and he stared straight at her.

She instinctively glanced away, back to her book, and was careful not to catch his eye again as the song ended and another one began.

'Oh, for goodness' sake,' said the man opposite loudly, before slamming his laptop shut, pushing back his chair and making his way to the bar.

A few songs later, the singing ended, much to Lettie's disappointment. Listening to the old songs had been soothing. She went back to studying her phone where a message from Daisy had just popped up.

*Date night is a disaster. Mum called us back from the pub early cos
kids being difficult about going to bed.*

Oh dear. More insomniac children. Was that meant to make her
feel bad? Daisy was a past master at making Lettie feel guilty. She was
considering her reply when a shadow fell across the table. She looked
up with a smile, determined to be cheery to the bad-tempered man
opposite, but her face fell when she saw it was Corey.

'Did you want something?' he asked, brusquely.

She folded her arms and stared at him. 'What do you mean? I was
listening to the songs.'

'You were staring at me.'

'Along with half the pub cos you were the one doing the singing.'

Corey looked at her for a moment before he shrugged. 'Yeah, fair
enough.'

'Are you always this unwelcoming to visitors to Heaven's Cove?'
asked Lettie, feeling annoyingly flustered.

'It depends why they're here. I assume you work with Simon.'

He tilted his head at the empty chair on the opposite side of the table.

'Do you make lots of assumptions about total strangers?'

Lettie knew that sounded rude but she was already fed up with
Corey. If a lot of the locals were like him, no wonder Iris and her family
had left Heaven's Cove and never returned.

The man opposite, presumably Simon, suddenly appeared with
another pint of beer and slid into his seat.

'Are you harassing this lady, Corey?' he asked levelly, taking a sip
of his drink and wiping froth from his upper lip.

'Surely harassment is more your style, Simon.'

'I wouldn't call going about my normal working day harassment.'

'I certainly would.'

The two men eyeballed each other while Lettie tried to work out what on earth was going on. When the macho staring contest continued, Lettie spoke up. The testosterone level was off the scale.

'No one is harassing anyone. I'm simply having a quiet drink and looking, without success, for a local man called Claude.'

'Corey's probably lived in this little village his whole life, so maybe he can help with tracking down the elusive Claude?' said Simon with what looked like a smirk.

Corey narrowed his eyes that were so dark brown, they looked almost black. 'What do you want with him? The only things he owns are a couple of ramshackle cottages.'

'Whoah!' Simon held up his hands. 'It's not me who's looking for the gentleman in question. It's this young lady, here.'

'That's right. Belinda told me he was a bit of an expert on the village's past. I'm… keen to do some historical research on the place.'

'Why?' asked Corey, turning towards her.

'My family used to live around here years ago and I thought Claude might have some information on them.'

'He might, if that's what you're *really* after.' Corey glanced at Lettie's book and frowned, as though trying to work her out.

'Of course that's what I'm really after.'

Simon smiled. 'Anyway, Corey, if that's all you wanted, best not be a gooseberry when this young lady and I are having a cosy tête-a-tête.'

What the hell? Simon had ignored her from the moment she sat down and now he was making out they were on some kind of date. But at least it got Corey off her back.

He shrugged. 'Claude won't be in tonight. He's out on a night fish with a crew from down the coast. A regular crew member went overboard last week and won't be back at sea for a while.'

Was Corey being serious or saying that for effect? It was hard to tell.

'Do you know where I might find him?' asked Lettie.

'Anyone'll tell you. He lives near the harbour, in Lobster Pot Cottage. But he won't thank you for calling round.'

'So I've heard. Thank you very much for your help.' Lettie was trying to sound level and grown-up, but it came out as though she was being sarcastic. Simon smirked and colour flared in Corey's cheeks. 'What I mean is…'

'I know exactly what you mean. Good luck with Claude, and have a very pleasant evening, both of you.'

Now, that *did* sound sarcastic. Simon whistled softly as Corey walked back to his friends near the bar. 'He's a charmer, that one.'

'You obviously know him.'

'I do, sadly. Like a lot of people round here, he's stuck in the middle ages and immune to progress.' He leaned across the table, showing off his bright white teeth when he gave a creepy smile. 'Here we are chatting and I don't even know your name.'

'It's Lettie.'

'And I'm Simon, as you obviously know by now. So tell me more about how you know Mr Corey Allford. You don't sound as though you're from around here.'

'I'm not. I live in London.'

'Me too, and quite honestly I can't wait to get back there. I've been working around here for a few days and it looks like I'll be stuck here for a while longer.'

'What do you do?'

'I'm a property entrepreneur,' he announced grandly.

'What does that mean?'

'It means I source land for building new homes and businesses and then snap it up.'

'Is Heaven's Cove expanding?'

'I certainly hope so. This area is prime for development, don't you think?'

'Maybe.'

Lettie wasn't convinced. She knew progress was inevitable, but she was already entranced by the olde worlde charm of Heaven's Cove. The village was much the same as Iris must have seen it, eighty years ago. It was like a living museum, a reminder of a way of life that was fast disappearing.

'So whereabouts in London do you hail from, Lettie?' boomed Simon, above the hubbub of conversation around them. 'Anywhere near my stomping ground, Kensington High Street?'

'I live a bit farther out,' said Lettie, being purposely vague. Her ex-council bedsit with its cemetery view was probably very different from Simon's home. She could picture him in an elegant Edwardian apartment that overlooked a garden square. 'Does your work focus on Devon?'

'God, no. My business sends me across the country, snapping up land in development hotspots.'

'And Heaven's Cove is a hotspot, is it?'

'Absolutely. Have you seen the views around here? People are desperate to escape to places like this. I don't get it myself. I'm more of a city boy, and some of the locals round here are batshit crazy.' He settled back in his chair, giving her all his attention. 'But tell me why *you're* here, Lettie.'

'In Heaven's Cove?'

'Yes, and in this pub on your own, reading a boring book. Did you really mean what you said to Corey, about wanting to find out more about the history of Heaven's Cove? Aren't you here with friends or family?'

'No, it's just me. I'm in the pub looking for Claude… and I'm in Heaven's Cove trying to find out more about my great-aunt who lived here a long time ago.'

'So how did you say you know our charming Mr Allford?'

'I don't really,' said Lettie, who hadn't expected Simon to be particularly interested in her search but still wondered how the conversation had come back round to Corey so quickly. 'I bumped into him on the beach this afternoon.'

'Poor you. What do you think of him, then?'

Why was he asking? 'I don't really know him but he's quite… abrupt.'

Simon laughed. 'You say abrupt, I say pig ignorant.' He suddenly leaned across the table. 'Do you know who might know about your great-aunt? Mrs Allford – Corey's grandmother. She's pretty ancient and will be needing care quite soon, I'd have thought. I've offered her a good deal on a piece of land she owns but Corey is trying to dissuade her from selling and using up the cash on a fancy care home. He's thinking of his inheritance when the old lady pops off.'

'Really? That would be terrible if he was doing that.'

'It would, and he is.' Simon brushed a few specks of dust from his shoulder. 'So, if you get to speak to her, maybe you could mention that you know me and I'm completely trustworthy.'

'I hardly know you.'

'Not yet. But we Londoners have to stick together when we're out in the sticks.' He sat back in his chair and stared at her until Lettie, feeling self-conscious, went back to her book.

Simon took a few sips of his beer and grimaced. 'Good grief.'

Lettie looked up from Boudicca again. 'Not good?'

'I imagine it's an acquired taste. It's a local brew, called Fisherman's Fungus or something.' When Lettie giggled, he smiled. 'Have you heard about what's happening around here tomorrow?'

He raised an eyebrow when Lettie shook her head. 'Then you're in for a treat because it's the day of the village fete, the only excitement the locals get all year.'

Lettie glanced around her, wishing Simon wasn't talking quite so loudly.

'Where's that happening?'

'It's on the green, next to the castle ruins, from two thirty onwards. I dare say it'll involve Morris dancers waving hankies, apple-bobbing, and sacrificing the odd virgin. You might find Claude there. Or Corey's grandmother.'

'I might. Thank you. I'll give the fete a go.'

Simon nodded, went back to his laptop and totally ignored Lettie for the next ten minutes.

Feeling rather dismissed, she finished her drink before looking round for Claude one last time, and leaving the pub. It wasn't very late but she couldn't stop yawning. They could bottle sea air and use it as a sleeping draught.

Outside the pub, the air was cooler and fresher, with a sharp tang of salt. Tourists in shorts were still milling about in the streets but they thinned out as she got to the edge of the village and started climbing the cliff path. The light was fading and throwing boulders on the path into shadow, but a full moon was rising and casting a silvery trail across the dark sea. As she climbed, she could hear waves hitting rock with a dull boom – a sound Iris must have heard as a child; a sound that thrilled and frightened Lettie in equal measure.

At the top of the cliff stood Driftwood House, with amber lamplight spilling from its ground-floor windows. A gusty wind was blowing through the potted flowers and swirling around the corners of the building. Lettie could almost imagine a younger Iris waiting to greet her, but no one was standing in the hallway when she opened the front door and walked inside. Iris was gone for good but the mystery of her final words, and the golden key around Lettie's neck, remained.

Chapter Six

Lettie squinted at the guide book that Rosie had lent her that morning and wished she'd remembered to bring her sunglasses. The sun seemed brighter here than in North London, especially when it was reflecting off the sea. She shielded her eyes with her hand and read that Heaven's Cove castle was built in the twelfth century to help fortify the coast against invaders.

It might have done a good job eight hundred years ago but today all that remained were tumbled-down walls and the grassy dip of an ancient moat. Lettie stood for a moment, drinking in the atmosphere and imagining herself in a long gown walking above a water-filled moat, towards the long-gone drawbridge. The past seemed so close in this place.

She was brought back to the present by the screams of an excited child who was running across a large green. The grass was dotted with stalls draped with brightly coloured bunting, and rope had been looped in a large circle to keep an area clear – though it was currently full of men wearing three-quarter-length white trousers, green hats and carrying sticks. Morris dancers. Simon had been right about them.

She started walking around the fete looking for Claude. Rosie had told her his surname and, when she'd googled him, she'd come across his photo in the local paper. Taken three years ago, it showed him and some fishing colleagues who had rescued a dolphin from their nets.

To Lettie, now she had a proper photo rather than a glimpse in the street, he looked like the stereotype of an old Devonian fisherman – weathered face, grizzled beard streaked with grey, and wearing a woolly hat, even though the photo was taken at the height of summer. He looked quite fierce in the picture but he and Corey's grandmother were the only leads she had to help find out information about Iris – and if her key opened anything at all.

Lettie wandered among the stalls selling local honey, jewellery, or offering children the chance to play hook the duck or whack a mole. In spite of Simon's misgivings, she realised she was enjoying herself. This fair must have taken place in the village for centuries and she was a sucker for tradition.

Just behind the apple-bobbing stand, Lettie spotted Rosie on the lucky dip stall and was beckoned over.

'Hey, Lettie, come and meet my boyfriend, Liam.'

Her eyes shone as she introduced the handsome man next to her and, as Liam stood with his arm around Rosie's waist, Lettie envied her being so happy. Lettie had missed out on Belinda's tale of his and Rosie's relationship, but the two of them seemed very much in love.

'What do you think of Heaven's Cove fete, then?' asked Liam, handing over a stuffed owl to a small child who presented him with a winning ticket. 'Not quite Notting Hill Carnival, is it?'

'It's a *leetle* bit smaller but it's lovely and it's traditional.'

'I remember it all the time I was growing up,' said Rosie. 'My mum used to make dream catchers and pots covered in shells for the craft stall. She was really creative, my mum.'

When she faltered suddenly, Liam put his arm around her shoulders.

'It must be hard with your mum not here this year,' said Lettie.

'It is. But you know what that's like. I'm sure life feels strange for you without your great-aunt around.'

'It does. Iris was always my champion, if that doesn't sound too daft. She loved me, whatever happened.' Lettie swallowed hard. 'Clearing out her flat was the worst. I kept expecting her to come through the door and tell me off for going through her private things – not that she had much left.'

'Why was that?' asked Rosie, reaching across the stall to pat Lettie's hand.

'There was a fire in her flat a couple of years ago and she lost all her paperwork and family photos and precious stuff.'

Everything except for the key she always wore around her neck, and the letter, stuffed into her handbag lining, that didn't make any sense.

'That must have been awful for her. Do you know what caused it?'

'It was an electrical fault, apparently.'

'At least she got out safely.'

'Hmm.'

Lettie nodded, remembering how Iris's health had nosedived after the blaze. Everyone said it was the shock, but maybe there had been a picture of the man who wrote the mysterious letter amongst the lost photos. The man – or the woman. Perhaps that was the 'scandal' that her mum had heard whispers of so long ago.

'Have you managed to find Claude?' asked Rosie, smiling at a young family walking past.

'Not yet, though I'm hoping he might turn up. So how come you've ended up manning the lucky dip stall?'

'We got press-ganged by Belinda.' Liam grinned. 'Speak of the devil.'

'Miss Starcross,' boomed a loud voice behind her. 'Have you managed to track down the elusive Claude yet?'

When Lettie spun around, Belinda was behind her. 'Not yet.'

The gold bangles on Belinda's arms clinked when she waved her hand. 'Oh, he's notoriously hard to pin down and, as I say, he doesn't like anyone who's not from here. It's taken him ages to get used to me and I'm Devon born and bred! I moved to the village from Exeter over twenty years ago.'

'Actually…' Lettie hesitated, weighing up her misgivings about involving nosey Belinda even more in her business. 'Someone suggested that Corey Allford's grandmother might be a good person to talk to.'

'Florence? Yes, that's a very good idea. She's lived here for donkey's years, since she was born, I think, and she must be heading for ninety. You're in luck because she's far more civil than Claude and she happens to be here at the fete. I saw her a while ago in the castle ruins. You might catch her if you hurry.'

'Thanks, Belinda.' Lettie smiled, glad of the older woman's help. 'That's kind of you.'

'You're welcome. And good luck with tracking down Claude. I've put him on the rota to help with clearing up the village hall after the whist drive next Saturday but I sometimes think he's avoiding me.'

Liam opened his eyes wide, making Lettie bite her lip so she wouldn't giggle.

Belinda, oblivious to Liam, carried on: 'Talking of the whist drive, there's Fiona, who I want to provide the food. It's definitely her turn but she's almost as hard to get hold of as Claude.'

With that, she bustled off.

'Gosh, she's a force to be reckoned with, isn't she?'

'Always.' Rosie laughed. 'But she knows her stuff, and the village would probably collapse without her. Florence is a good bet, actually, to find out more about your great-aunt. She's very petite, sometimes walks with a stick and has lots of white hair. You can't miss her.'

Buoyed by Belinda's assertion that Florence was more civil than Claude, Lettie walked across the wooden bridge that spanned the moat and stepped between the ruined walls of what must have once been a huge hall. Her imagination went into overdrive, picturing heroic knights in armour and ladies in elegant dresses, huddling around the fireplace on cold winter nights.

If only walls could talk. She brushed her fingers across the stone and felt a shiver go through her. The past was swirling all around this roofless hall that was now open to the elements. Had Iris felt it too when she'd played here as a child?

The sounds from the fete were muted in here. Lettie picked up a lolly wrapper that had been blown into a corner and placed it in her pocket. Its modernity seemed jarring in such an historic place.

'Visitors do leave their rubbish about, spoiling Heaven's Cove. It's good to see that you have more thought for the environment.'

When Lettie spun around, an elderly woman, with a shock of white hair, was leaning on a walking stick and watching her. Lettie would have mistaken her for a ghost from days gone by if it weren't for her trousers and the lifeline alarm on her wrist. The woman was short, curvy and rather frail-looking – the opposite of tall, angular Iris.

'Hello. Are you Florence Allford?'

The woman tilted her head and regarded Lettie inquisitively. Her eyes were such a pale grey, they held almost no colour at all. 'I am. Do I know you? You seem somewhat familiar.'

'I'm sorry to bother you. We've never met but I was told that you might be able to help me with some family history research. Belinda said you've lived here all your life.'

'Belinda's talking about *me* now, is she?' The woman smiled. 'Why don't we sit down and you can tell me what it is you're looking for.'

Lettie followed Florence to a low piece of the wall. The old woman settled down on it and sat with her hands resting on the top of her walking stick and her chin on top of them. 'Tell me more.'

'My family lived here a long time ago and I'm trying to find out more about them.'

'Did they, indeed? What was their—'

A man's voice suddenly boomed across the ruined room. 'What are you doing? Stop talking to her.'

Lettie glanced up in alarm and groaned when she spotted Corey hurrying towards her. That was the problem with tiny villages: it was impossible not to bump into the people you most wanted to avoid.

When Corey reached them, he stood protectively next to the elderly woman. A flush was rising on his cheeks, above the dark stubble covering his chin.

'How dare you ambush my gran like this? We've already told you and your colleague that we're not interested.'

Lettie vaguely registered that Corey was looking totally hot in tight jeans and a black sweatshirt before annoyance kicked in.

'Simon isn't my colleague,' she said testily.

'So you claim, but you were sitting with him last night and now here you are with my grandmother. I know what you're up to.'

'I'm not up to anything.'

'Don't you realise that man doesn't play by the rules? He's a cheat.'

'Calm down, Corey.' Florence put a steadying hand on his arm before addressing Lettie. 'I'm afraid my grandson has got the wrong end of the stick. This young lady isn't here to talk about land, Corey. She's asking about her family history.'

'So she says.'

'So I say? Why are you so suspicious, and why would I be lying about my family anyway?'

'You tell me.'

'I am telling you. You've got me all wrong.'

The colour in Corey's cheeks began to fade and he took a deep breath. 'Are you telling me that you don't work with Simon?'

'I definitely don't work with Simon. I work in customer services for... Well, I used to.' Lettie shook her head. 'My job doesn't matter. The fact is that I'm trying to find out more about my family when they lived here, and Si... someone told me that your grandmother might be able to help me piece a few things together, seeing as she's lived here for years.'

'I see.' Corey scuffed at the ground with his boots, but didn't apologise. Distrust was still etched across his face.

Florence tutted but gave Corey's arm a loving pat. 'Pay no attention to my grandson. He's a good lad and always looking out for me, Miss... what did you say your name was?'

'My name's Lettie.'

'That's pretty.'

'It's short for Violet. All the women in my family are named after flowers – my sister's Daisy, and my two paternal aunts were Alyssa and Hyacinth. It's a tradition.'

Florence's smile faltered. 'Is that right? And what would your surname be?'

'Starcross, I'm Lettie Starcross, and I'm trying to find out more about my great-aunt, who, it won't come as any great surprise, was also named after a flower.'

'Which flower?' whispered Florence, her mouth hardly moving.

'Iris.'

Lettie smiled but Florence's face had frozen. With the help of her stick, she pushed herself slowly to her feet. 'I have nothing to say to you,' she said coldly.

Lettie also stood up, shocked by the older woman's sudden shift in attitude.

'I won't take up much of your time,' she told her. 'I just wondered if you remembered my great-aunt and her family. They used to live at Driftwood House, where I'm staying now. They left Heaven's Cove towards the end of the Second World War, as far as I'm aware.'

'Corey, take me home.' Florence grabbed hold of her grandson's hand. 'I need to go home now, and you…' Her glare held such naked hostility, Lettie took a step backwards. 'Stay away from me. I need to go, right now, Corey.'

'Of course, Gran.' He put his arm tenderly around her shoulders and started leading her away. Just once, he looked back at Lettie, with a questioning glance.

'I'm so sorry. I didn't mean to upset you,' called Lettie.

But Florence and Corey were gone.

'What the hell?'

Lettie sank back onto the low wall as a gust of wind caught dust in the centre of the ruined hall and made it dance. What on earth was that all about?

Her mum thought Iris might have left Heaven's Cove after some sort of trouble or scandal. But what could possibly have been so bad that it still upset a local lady more than seventy-five years later? Lettie sat for a while, listening to the squeals of children having fun at the fete and wondering what she was going to find out about the Starcross family.

Chapter Seven

Claude

Lobster Pot Cottage was very small, squeezed between two larger cottages almost like an afterthought. It was made of whitewashed stone, with a black tiled roof, and it looked as though it had seen better days.

Claude had lived here so long, he rarely noticed what his home looked like. But sometimes, like today, when visitors were milling past and staring at the peeling paint on his front door, he imagined what they must be thinking. Especially if they spotted him peering out of the downstairs window. *Look at the eccentric old man of Heaven's Cove!*

To be fair, that was how some of the young locals perceived him, too. They never said as much to his face, but he'd heard them whispering when he went past, and children always clasped their parents' hands tightly when they saw him. Claude Creasey: bogeyman.

He sighed and was moving away from the window when a young woman stepped off the quayside and into his tiny front garden. He squinted at her. Tall, pretty, with striking red hair that fell in thick curls down her back.

He recognised her as the woman who'd been talking to Belinda a day or two ago. At least she'd distracted Belinda long enough for him to hurry past before he was nabbed.

The woman stared at the fraying lobster pot that was nailed to the wall, close to a stone trough of flowers, their blooms dehydrated and their leaves scorched by the salt wind. Then, to his surprise, she walked along his front path and knocked on his door. The sound echoed through the building as he drew back from the window, feeling confused. Why would she be calling at his home?

Claude decided to ignore her. Strangers never brought good news, and she would think he was out. But Buster suddenly bounded past him and started barking and scratching at the door.

'Shush, you daft dog.'

Buster shook himself and quietened down, but it was too late. The girl knocked again, more loudly this time as though she wouldn't easily be put off. He would have to get rid of her.

Nudging the dog out of the way with his leg, Claude pulled the door open and stood in the doorway. He almost filled the frame.

'If you're selling something, I'm not buying,' he told her.

He must have sounded quite fierce because the girl almost took a step back. He didn't like that. Frightening people wasn't something he was proud of. But she steadied herself and stood her ground.

'I'm not selling anything.'

Her voice was soft and her accent was different from the Devonian burr Claude was used to. She actually sounded a bit like that preening over-puffed property man, Simon, who was going round upsetting everyone. Perhaps she worked with him, in which case she definitely wasn't welcome.

'There's nothing for you here so you might as well move along.'

'I don't mean to be a nuisance,' said the woman, her pale cheeks flushing rosy pink.

'Then don't be and leave me in peace. This cottage is not for sale.'

'Oh.' Comprehension dawned in the woman's eyes which were a peculiar shade of pale brown with green flashes around the iris. 'I'm not selling anything and I'm not trying to buy anything either.'

'You don't work with that property man, then?'

'No, I don't and I'm not sure why people keep thinking that I do.'

When she patted Buster, who was snuffling his nose into her thigh, Claude frowned. His dog didn't usually take to strangers.

'What *do* you want, then?' he asked, gently pushing the dog away from her.

'I was hoping that you might be able to help me with some information.'

'I'm afraid I don't have the time to give out information. There's a perfectly good tourist information place in the village hall, near the café.'

'That's not the sort of information I'm after. I'm not a tourist. Well, I am, but my family come from around here.'

Claude tilted his head to one side. 'Is that right? What's your name?'

'Lettie Starcross.'

Claude stepped across the threshold into the garden, so he could straighten up. He was over six foot, which was rather too tall to be living in such a small cottage.

'Starcross, you say.' He looked Lettie up and down. 'That's an unusual name.'

'My family lived in Heaven's Cove decades ago and I'm trying to piece together some information about them. Belinda said you know a lot about the village.'

'Belinda says a lot of things to a lot of people.'

'I'm very interested in the archive I'm told that you've put together. I find history fascinating and I love materials that document the past.'

Hmm. It was hardly an archive, more a few battered old filing cabinets stuffed full with newspaper cuttings, photos and various other remnants of the past in these parts. But the girl's unusual hazel eyes had lit up at the prospect. She was a strange one.

Claude stroked his beard as she bent down to pat Buster again, who'd plonked down on the path next to her and was slowly wagging his tail.

'Belinda shouldn't go around telling people my business,' he told her firmly, stepping back into the hall. 'So my answer is no, and I'd thank you to leave my property.'

'I really wouldn't take up much of your time.'

'You have my answer.'

The girl looked sad but not surprised. 'In that case, I'm sorry to have bothered you. Have a good day.'

What a stupid American expression! Claude harrumphed quietly as she walked back down the path and across the quay. And he noticed that Buster was watching her go with a hangdog expression. Daft animal!

Claude whistled him back in, shut the door and sat at the small dining table next to the front room window. The girl's visit, though brief, had unsettled him. Would it have been so bad to have let her see what was in the filing cabinets? She'd seemed very keen to go through them.

He glanced at the silver-framed photo on the dresser before getting up to go and put the kettle on. Stirring up the past wasn't always a good idea. She'd learn soon enough and leave. He glanced again at the photo which had faded to sepia over the years. Everyone left in the end.

Chapter Eight

Lettie

Well, that hadn't gone very well. Lettie sighed. So far, in her bid to clear up the mystery surrounding her great-aunt's key, all she'd managed to do was cause Florence to rush away, and Claude to more or less run her off his property. She glanced back at Lobster Pot Cottage but the door was firmly shut and there was no face at the blank window. Claude was rather alarming, with his long salt and pepper hair and bushy beard. And he'd been less than welcoming. But there was something fascinating about him, and she was itching to get her hands on his archive.

Lettie had loved history ever since she was a child. She loved the fact that it was cut and dried and couldn't be changed. The future was shadowy and rather scary, but the past was fixed – a treasure trove of real-life stories that could teach those in the present so much.

Over years of poring over history books and visiting museums, Lettie had realised her favourite thing in the world was spotting fascinating human stories in historical tomes, and in objects that looked unprepossessing at first glance. There was something about Claude that gave her the same goosebumps, the same prickle at the back of her neck at hints of hidden depths just waiting to be discovered.

It was a shame she'd never found a way to spend more time doing what she loved, or turn it into something useful. Plans to do a history degree in Birmingham after leaving school had been 'put off for a while' when her dad needed heart surgery and her mum was uber-stressed. Lettie had stayed to help out and – she wasn't quite sure how – the degree had ended up being permanently shelved, even after her dad had recovered.

She walked to the edge of the quay and looked across the sea. Farther out, it was pale blue with darker stripes where the water deepened. But here, the gentle waves lapping against stone were clear. Tiny fish darted in and out of the rusted metal rings secured to the stone and a child's dropped sandal rested beneath the water, on the sand. Above her, a seagull was swooping and calling out as it flew towards a fishing boat coming into harbour.

It would be peaceful here, if it weren't for the excited shouts of children coming from the ice-cream parlour and the hum of traffic negotiating narrow streets. It must be so much calmer out of season, even when storms swept in across the sea and churned the dark water into towering waves. Lettie shuddered and moved away from the quayside.

She wandered through the village and bought an ice cream from the parlour that stood next to a fishmonger's, whose pavement outside was littered with shards of ice. The locally made ice cream tasted delicious, of bananas and cream.

In spite of her run-in with Claude and having no idea what to do next about the mysterious key, Lettie was feeling calm. This pretty, historic village was having a soothing effect on her, she decided. Everywhere she looked there were echoes of lives lived – old cottages, cobbled streets, fishing paraphernalia. She wondered how much the tourists thronging past her took notice or if they were too busy dragging reluctant children who'd rather be playing video games.

She walked on past what looked like an old church, an imposing building made of local stone with a pitched roof. A wide ramp led from its huge red doors into the sea. Intrigued, Lettie got closer and realised it was the local lifeboat station.

A laminated sheet pinned to the wall outlined the latest call-outs. Lettie was browsing through them when a woman ran past and disappeared into a small door in the side of the building. Then, she spotted Corey running hell for leather down the hill. His long legs raced across the cobbles and his arms pumped by his side, as his dark hair flew in the breeze. He didn't notice Lettie as he rushed into the building too.

Intrigued, Lettie sat on a stone wall and finished her ice cream, wondering if someone was in danger far out at sea. The thought of being lost with nothing around you but water made her shudder.

Suddenly, the red doors opened and a boat, painted blue and bright orange, rolled down the slipway and into the sea with a huge splash. The crew was dressed in yellow and Lettie craned forward to see if Corey was amongst them. She thought she saw him standing near the bow of the boat, but soon the vessel disappeared from sight around the headland.

'Be safe,' murmured Lettie, wiping drips of ice cream from her T-shirt. The thought of them all putting themselves in danger made her heart beat faster. For all his bad temper and bluster, Corey Allford was brave, rushing across the waves into the unknown. Whereas she was a coward, who could barely go for a paddle, let alone race across the sea to rescue someone else.

With a sigh, Lettie stood up and started wandering away from the busy front and up the hill. The cobbled street was steep, and Lettie had almost reached the top when she spotted a woman struggling to pull a shopping trolley. It appeared to have lost a wheel and the three remaining ones were catching on the cobbles and making the whole thing unstable.

The lady was puffing and panting and, as Lettie watched, she stumbled.

'Hang on,' cried Lettie, rushing forwards. 'I'll give you a hand.'

It was only when the woman steadied herself and turned that Lettie realised it was Corey's grandmother, who'd given her such short shrift at their last meeting.

Oh, perfect.

Lettie approached her with trepidation, sure that her offer of help would be rebuffed, and Florence's face did nothing to allay her fears. The elderly woman glared at Lettie, her hands on her hips and her trolley listing at a drunken angle.

'You're the Starcross girl,' she said, accusingly.

'That's right, but I wondered if you might need some help.'

'I'm sure I can manage, thank you.'

When she turned and started hauling her recalcitrant trolley farther up the hill, Lettie caught a glimpse of her own great-aunt: self-sufficient, proud and bloody-minded. And so different from the shell of a woman she'd become in her final days. The memory of Iris in her prime made Lettie smile – the first time she'd smiled when thinking of Iris for a long time.

'Damn it!'

Florence watched helplessly as a cabbage escaped her listing trolley and started rolling down the hill. Lettie stopped it deftly with the side of her foot and picked it up.

'Here you go.' She placed the cabbage back in the trolley. 'You're going to lose more shopping if I don't give you a hand. And you seem to be limping.'

Florence stared at Lettie, her eyes lively against her furrowed skin. Young eyes in an old face. She gave a curt nod.

'That would be helpful. My cottage is that one.'

Without another word, Lettie started pulling the trolley towards the cottage Florence had pointed out. Standing near the top of the hill, overlooking the ocean, it was whitewashed with a thatched roof and small latticed windows. Vibrant flowers were growing in her garden. And roses were trained around the front door. The cottage looked idyllic, and Lettie suddenly longed to live somewhere as historic and beautiful. It must be filled with the ghosts of the past.

Florence followed her through the garden gate, still limping slightly, and made her way to the door. She fumbled in the pocket of her cotton jacket for the key and, after opening the door, stepped into a dark, narrow hallway.

'You can leave it there,' she said, when Lettie lifted the trolley over the doorstep.

'Are you sure you wouldn't like me to take your shopping into the kitchen for you?'

'I'm most definitely sure.'

'What happened to the trolley?'

'A wheel came off halfway up the hill and rolled away.'

'Would you like me to try and find it?'

Florence shook her head. 'There's no need to trouble yourself, Miss Starcross. I think it's time to buy myself another one.'

'I saw your grandson going out on the lifeboat,' said Lettie, trying to make polite conversation.

Florence frowned. 'Putting his life at risk for someone who doesn't respect the sea, no doubt. I won't rest 'til he's back.'

'I'm sure he'll be fine,' said Lettie, regretting her words as soon as they were uttered.

How could she possibly be sure? The sea was unpredictable and who knew what was lurking beneath the surface? An image of Corey floating in dark water, waves washing over his face, pushed its way into her mind and made her throat tighten.

'I didn't mean to upset you on Saturday, at the castle,' she said quickly, doing her best to push the image away.

Florence stared at her for a moment. 'You look like her, you know. The same strange-coloured eyes and hair with a mind of its own.'

'Did you know my great-aunt?' asked Lettie, self-consciously smoothing down her red curls. It was probably unwise to ask, after Florence's reaction at the castle. But since Claude had basically told her to get lost, she was running out of options for finding out anything at all.

'I knew her, all right.'

'Can I ask how?'

Florence narrowed her eyes. 'We lived in the same bloody village, of course.'

Lettie gulped. 'Of course. I just thought you must have been quite a lot younger than Iris.'

'I was only a child when she left Heaven's Cove for good. But she knew my brother.'

This could be her last chance and Lettie was determined to grasp it. 'Would it be possible to speak to him, perhaps, to find out more about Iris?' she asked gently.

But Florence's gaze hardened. 'Cornelius is dead,' she said abruptly, slamming the door shut in Lettie's face.

Chapter Nine

Two hours later, still feeling unsettled by her latest run-in with Florence, Lettie was surrounded by the dead. People often found it ghoulish but there was little she enjoyed more than an ancient graveyard. She'd passed many an afternoon reading inscriptions on the stones, each one a tantalising snapshot into a complete life.

All those people who'd lived and loved and argued and worried and laughed. All those hopes and dreams now brought to an end.

She ran her fingers across a tilting gravestone. Each of these people had helped to make Heaven's Cove what it was today. The village's history was built on their stories – on the stories of people like Cornelius.

Several of the stones were so old the names had been obliterated by rain and salt winds. But Lettie walked around studying them all closely, looking for Florence's brother. She couldn't find anyone called Cornelius. But in the shadow of the red-stone church, at the very edge of the graveyard, she found a stone for an Elizabeth Allford, who was born in 1895 and died in 1942. The words beneath her name in curly script said: *Sheltered in the Lord's hands from the crushing trials of this world.*

Could she be Florence's mother-in-law or maybe sister-in-law? Lettie was doing the maths in her head when her concentration was shattered by her phone ringing. It was her own mother, and Lettie immediately felt a surge of guilt for not being there to help her with the shopping.

'Lettie, there you are. I hope you're having a good time.'

'I am, thanks. How are you and Dad?'

'Oh, you know. Missing you and looking forward to you being back. I've got lots of little jobs for you to do.'

'Can't Daisy help you, or Ed?'

'I don't like to ask because they're both so busy.'

Guilt wrapped itself around Lettie's heart, along with a stab of resentment that she tried so hard to dampen down.

'I'm only away for a couple of weeks at the most.'

'It was all rather unexpected but you'll have to come back soon for work, won't you.'

'Hmm.'

Lettie began to wish her mum hadn't rung. She couldn't tell her over the phone that she had no work to get back to. Even if she softened the circumstances around losing her job, if she told her mum she was unemployed, a list of 'suitable' – a.k.a. boring – jobs to apply for would be emailed to her before the day was out.

'So tell me what the village where you're staying is like?'

'Heaven's Cove is gorgeous. Full of character and history.'

'And what made you choose that village in particular?'

'It's a lovely place.'

'And…?'

'And… well, the house where I'm staying is where Iris and her family lived many years ago, when she was young. I found the address in her belongings.'

'Is that right?' Her mum paused before saying gently, 'I know your great-aunt's death hit you hard, Lettie, but do you think it's healthy to chase after her now she's gone?'

'I'm not chasing after her. I'm trying to find out more about the key necklace that she left me.' Lettie hesitated. 'And the letter I found.'

'What letter?'

'I found an old letter to her that says she's a "darling girl" and mentions "the key to my heart", which possibly refers to the necklace.'

'And you're only telling me this now, more than a month after her death?'

'It seemed a bit too private to talk about at the time.'

'Hmm.' Her mum sounded annoyed. 'Nothing is too private to share with family, Lettie.'

Lettie felt told off, and suffocated. She was already regretting telling her mum about the letter, even though talking about it might be the only way to discover what it meant.

When she stayed quiet, her mum jumped back in. 'Anyway, I'm sure you're reading far too much into this old letter you found. It was probably sent to Iris by some man who was infatuated with her when she was younger and she never completely forgot him. That's all.'

'Has Dad ever mentioned anything about any of this?'

'Your father?' Her mum laughed. 'Of course not. He's a lovely man but he goes through life oblivious to what's happening around him. Always has.' She paused to draw breath. 'Anyway, Iris never talked about whoever wrote this letter, so how important could he have been?'

'Sometimes talking about painful things is difficult.'

'That's very true, which is why it's often better to sweep things under the carpet and get on with life.'

Lettie winced. Her mother, like Daisy, was ever pragmatic and practical. The past was gone, so move on…

'Possibly, but…'

Her mum sighed down the line. 'It's ancient history, Lettie, and you've always been obsessed by the past, I know. But don't let your feelings for Iris lead you on a wild goose chase. We need you back home. Daisy's desperate to see you. She and Jason have got tickets to some concert at the O2 so she needs you to look after the children. I can't be trekking across London at the dead of night to babysit, and I don't want to stay over because their spare bed is so lumpy.'

'Tell me about it.'

'Your young back can take it. Unlike mine.'

Lettie sat down on a bench and stretched out her legs as her mother launched into a long list of her ailments, followed by an update on her grandchildren. The sun was warm on her face and she closed her eyes.

'Lettie, are you listening to me?'

'Absolutely.' Lettie sat up straight and blinked. 'I'll be back soon.'

'Good. Well, enjoy your break now you're there, but don't get caught up in silly stuff.'

'OK. Give Dad my love.'

'I will. Bye, and see you in a few days.'

Pushing her phone back into her pocket, Lettie sighed. She could see the future that her family had mapped out for her – unpaid nanny to Daisy's kids, marriage to a 'safe' man who was happy living close to her parents and, eventually, as her mum and dad got older, becoming their carer. Daisy wouldn't do it and Ed only visited intermittently.

'Hey, I was hoping to catch up with you.'

She was surprised to see Simon pushing open the churchyard gate. He veered from the path and walked straight across the grass towards her.

'What are you doing sitting in a graveyard?' he asked, turning up his nose at the historic stones. 'Looking for ancestors?'

'Something like that,' said Lettie, realising that she hadn't seen a single Starcross in the graveyard. It was as though her family had been expunged from the village.

'Have you seen the old Allford woman yet?' Simon sat down beside her and pushed his blond hair behind his ears.

'Only briefly. I helped Mrs Allford with her shopping earlier.'

Simon leaned towards her, to hear more, but there was no way Lettie was going to tell him how their conversation had really gone, or why it had led her to this graveyard.

'Nice. It's good to gain her trust.'

He winked as Lettie twisted round towards him.

'I was being helpful, and I'm only interested in finding out more about my great-aunt. I'm not buttering her up so you can move in and make a deal with her for the land.'

'Of course not.' He laughed, before leaning even closer. 'But you could always drop me into the conversation to, you know, keep me and my very generous offer at the forefront of her mind.'

'I don't know enough about you or your offer to do that.'

'What do you want to know about me? I'm a bona fide businessman with plenty of irons in the fire.'

'Hmm. So what else are you working on while you're here?'

'I've got a meeting with a local landowner tomorrow, though I'm not sure the land he has for sale will be suitable for development. There's no sea view and a history of flooding because it's so close to the river. It's a shame because he's keen to sell. Whereas, the land I really want to get my hands on isn't for sale.' He winked. 'Not at the moment, at least.'

'What's so special about Mrs Allford's land?'

'It all comes down to location, location, location. The land juts out into the sea, a little peninsula, and it has the most amazing views. We could build a tiny holiday village – a holiday hamlet, if you like. Just two or three houses, and get top-dollar prices from visitors. Look, if you stand up you can probably see it from here.'

Lettie got to her feet and followed the line of Simon's pointing finger across the village.

'There! If you look out to sea and then to the right, can you see the land I'm talking about?'

Lettie squinted at the flash of blue ocean that she could glimpse between the cottages. Just visible to the right, the land pushed out into the sea, forming a headland with high, red-stoned cliffs. Simon was right that the views must be amazing from up there, in all weathers.

'It's officially called Cora Head but it's known locally as Lovers' Link because it links two coves and I daresay lovelorn locals used to throw themselves off it. They're quite literal around here.'

'Does the whole of it belong to Mrs Allford?'

'The slice of it that I'm interested in does. Though she's getting on a bit so it'll be the singing fisherman's soon enough.'

Anticipating Florence's death so callously seemed rather off, but Lettie let it go.

'Does she have plans to build on it herself?'

'No, she wants to leave it as it is. Land that's perfect for development! It's selfish really, to deprive holidaymakers of that view.'

'Is the headland open to visitors at the moment?'

'There's a footpath that runs right across it, though I bet grumpy Allford would do his best to stop that, if he could.'

'So holidaymakers can still enjoy the view.'

'They can, but think of waking up with that vista before you. It's not my kind of thing, endless sea and sky. But marketing the holiday lets to stressed city types would be a piece of cake. I can't believe the old lady has turned me down, especially with the price I'm offering.'

'Not everything comes down to money, I suppose.'

Simon looked at her as if she was mad. 'Absolutely everyone has their price, I've found. But I'm sure her grandson is pressuring her not to take the money, even though it would make the end of her life much more comfortable.'

'Why would he do that? He seems to love his grandmother.'

'He's a bit of a Green warrior, very into preserving the village and stopping progress.'

Perhaps that was one thing she and Corey might have in common.

Lettie gave Simon a tight smile. 'I guess he's used to things being the way they are. The headland must be wild and amazing. It seems a shame to blight it with development.'

'Blight it?' If looks could kill, Lettie would be stone dead. Simon got to his feet. 'I'd improve it, and more visitors would boost the local economy. It would be good for Heaven's Cove.'

'Maybe in some ways. So where would your holiday hamlet be?'

'Right there, in the middle. Look.'

He moved towards her and that was when she caught sight of Corey hurrying past the church.

She smiled, glad to see that he'd returned safely from his mercy mission out at sea. But he scowled after catching her eye and hurried on.

That was when she realised that Simon had his hands on her shoulders and was positioning her so she could see the location of his proposed holiday hamlet.

Great! Spotting her and Simon together wouldn't do anything to allay Corey's suspicions. Lettie wasn't sure why she cared so much about the opinions of a grumpy singing fisherman in the depths of Devon, but she did.

Chapter Ten

Sitting on her bed the next morning, Lettie studied the letter that had brought her to Heaven's Cove. *Sit where I sat, darling girl, with the key to my heart and all will become clear.*

The words held an echo of what Iris had whispered on her deathbed. *Find out for me, darling girl.*

'What does it mean, Iris?' she muttered out loud into the early morning air. 'How am I supposed to know what you wanted me to find?'

She'd searched online for the Allford family in Heaven's Cove but there was little there of note, though she had read a brief history of the village, which was fascinating. And she'd dreamed last night of being a child in Heaven's Cove – which had been idyllic until she found herself immersed in the ice-blue waters of the cove and it turned into a nightmare that woke her in a cold sweat.

Lettie grabbed her phone and looked again at the message that had arrived at an ungodly hour from Kelly, who didn't sleep much these days.

Tilly has more teeth. Look! Isn't she adorable? Just wish the little bugger would sleep.

Matilda was giving a toothy grin from the screen, her tiny face gurning at the camera and her pudgy hands waving. She really was adorable and Lettie loved her but the photo made her feel jittery, as though life was moving on and she was being left behind. No job, no proper career, no love life to speak of, no hope.

Giving herself a mental shake, she gathered up her handbag and sunglasses and slipped out into the morning. The air smelled sweet and fresh and the sun was peeping from behind white banks of cloud. Fishing boats were splashes of colour on the pale blue sea and Lettie suddenly felt a surge of contentment wash over her. Her great-aunt and her job were gone but this would always be here. And the beauty of it spoke to her soul more than the glass and concrete of London.

Did that make her sound ridiculously pretentious? Iris would probably say so. Smiling to herself, Lettie walked down the cliff path and into the village. Claude and Florence were both refusing to speak to her, but she had one more idea.

The village hall was in a cobbled street at the heart of Heaven's Cove. It looked as if it had once been a church, with its pillars outside the front door that seemed rather too grand for what was once an insignificant fishing village, before it was discovered by tourists who now thronged the streets.

To the side of it was a low whitewashed building that housed the Tourist Information Office. Lettie pushed open the door and went inside. A middle-aged woman was on her knees, unloading a cardboard box of leaflets.

'Can I help you?' she asked, pushing her glasses into her hair. She sounded harassed.

'I'm trying to find out about the history of Heaven's Cove. Specifically about my family who come from around here.'

'Really?' She got slowly to her feet and wiped her hands on her smart black trousers. 'What was their name?'

'Starcross.'

The woman frowned. 'That's not a name I'm familiar with.'

'They lived at Driftwood House in the 1940s.'

'Ah, that's such a wonderful location.'

'It certainly is. I'm staying there at the moment.'

'That's good. I'm hoping that Rosie's guesthouse will be a great success.' She smiled. 'You're welcome to have a browse around and take whatever information you'd like.'

Lettie looked around the office with its leaflets stacked in Perspex dispensers on the walls and piled up on the shelves. They highlighted attractions nearby, National Trust properties, Dartmoor, a pony sanctuary and a list of shops in the village selling local produce. A door was open to a side room that was stacked with more cardboard boxes.

Lettie picked up a leaflet that gave a brief history of the village but a quick skim through showed it was similar to what she'd read online. That was all the historical information there seemed to be.

'What about the people who used to live here?' she asked. 'They must have had interesting stories. What about the people lost at sea or the men who went to war? Is there a local museum around here?'

The woman stopped delving into the large cardboard box. 'I'm afraid not, though you're absolutely right that this place – a village so rich in local history – is crying out for something like that. There's Claude, a local man who's collected lots of information about the village's past, but sadly it's not on public display. And I'm not sure he'd be very helpful, to be honest.'

'I went to his cottage and asked to see the information he has but he said no.'

'I'm not surprised. He's a rather solitary man.' She thought for a moment. 'The museum in Exeter might have some local information and there are church records. But we share a vicar with three other parishes so she's not here that often.'

'I can't imagine that my family were ever terribly involved with the church.'

Hadn't Iris said that she'd given up on God?

'Then Claude was your best bet, I'm afraid. You're welcome to take any of our information with you.'

She went back to unloading her leaflets while Lettie selected pamphlets about Dartmoor and a local pottery and stepped back outside into the salt air.

She walked on through the village and sat on a bench by the side of the crystal-clear stream that ran down to the sea. A child in yellow wellingtons was paddling in the water and laughing when splashes hit his face.

A few days had gone by already and all she'd learned about Iris was that she'd once known Florence's brother, who was now dead. The riddle of the key and letter remained, and another mystery had been added – why did Florence hate Iris so much?

Lettie sighed because soon she'd be back in London, looking for a job. She really should be looking for one now. Little flutterings of panic clutched her heart when she thought of her savings running out, but everything felt rather unreal and detached here. Heaven's Cove was like a little bubble where the real world couldn't catch up with her.

But it would catch up soon enough before she found out more about Iris. And she'd have let her great-aunt down. Iris hadn't asked much from her when she was alive. Lettie's company was enough.

Find out for me, darling girl. Iris's whisper sounded in her ear.

Lettie got to her feet and brushed dust from the back of her summer dress. There was nothing else for it. She would have to go back to see Claude, and try to persuade him again to help her. She owed Iris at least that.

She'd almost reached the quay when Belinda stepped directly in front of her. The only way to avoid the woman was to step around her and the way was blocked on one side by café tables on the pavement, and on the other by milling tourists.

'Did you find her?' demanded Belinda. 'Mrs Allford. Florence,' she clarified when Lettie gazed at her blankly.

'I did, thank you.'

'And was she helpful?'

'As much as she could be.'

When Belinda stayed stock still, waiting for more information, Lettie did her best to change the subject. 'I've just been to the tourist office and I saw the village hall. What a lovely building.'

Belinda almost purred. 'It is, isn't it, though it's such an old building, it's often in need of repair. I don't want to be too big-headed but I doubt it would have survived without all of the fundraising I've organised.'

Lettie had a sudden thought. 'It's great that the hall houses the tourist office. It's just a shame that there's no museum in the village that celebrates local history and culture.'

'Mmm.' Belinda's eyes narrowed. 'That would be a good idea, if we had enough information and objects to fill it.'

'If anyone could set up something like that, it would be you, by the sound of it.'

Flattery got you everywhere and, to be fair, with Belinda involved in so many parts of village life, it was probably true anyway.

The older woman smiled. 'I do believe you're right and perhaps it's something I should be looking into. You've certainly given me food for thought. What made you think of it?'

'I love history and this village is a little like a living museum anyway. Its rich past should be properly celebrated so it's never lost to progress.'

'Well said.' Belinda gave Lettie a searching glance. 'And you're more interested than most in Heaven's Cove history, of course, because of your ties to the village.'

Ties that were still unclear. Lettie nodded, keen to get away and Belinda stepped to the side.

'Well, I mustn't keep you. Where are you off to?'

'I thought I'd call in on Claude.'

Belinda's parting words, 'Good luck,' didn't fill Lettie with confidence.

Chapter Eleven

Claude

The girl was persistent, he'd give her that. Claude watched her march purposefully along his path and waited for the knock on the door. When it didn't come, he peeped out of the window.

She was standing there, with her fingers wrapped around the tarnished door knocker, as though she was deliberating what to do. She was building up the courage, he realised in a flash of shame. What would his mother think of him becoming so frightening? What would Esther say?

His thoughts were stilled by her heavy knocking which reverberated through the tiny cottage. Buster, sitting at his feet, got up slowly and wandered out of the front room.

Sighing, Claude walked into the hall, ignoring the fatigue that dogged him these days, and opened the door.

'Yes?' he asked slowly, deliberately trying not to snap.

The girl – Lettie, wasn't it? – gave him a nervous smile. She was wearing a bright cotton sundress today and neat brown sandals but her red hair was still untamed and falling in waves down her back. She looked like a woman from the Pre-Raphaelite paintings that his mother had loved so much.

'I'm sorry to bother you again,' said the girl hesitantly. 'I know you were quite… definite when we last spoke that you didn't want to help me, but I'm not quite sure where else to try.' She started gabbling, her words tumbling out. 'I need to go back to London soon and I haven't got to the bottom of what happened to my great-aunt when she lived here, and I don't want to let her down. She would understand. She was always lovely to me. But it's the last thing I can do for her. She died, you see.'

Her bottom lip wobbled at that and her eyes glistened as though she was about to cry. Oh, hell. Claude was never good with women's tears. They were unsettling and, these days, made him want to cry himself, which would never do.

'What exactly is it that you want?' he asked, giving a curt nod to local postmaster Marcus, who was passing by and craning his neck to see what was going on. Claude talking to an attractive young woman on his doorstep! It would be all around the pub by this evening.

'If possible, I'd like to have a look at local photos and documents from the 1930s and 40s. Is that the kind of thing you might have?' Lettie smiled when Claude nodded. 'That's great. It might tell me more about my great-aunt. All I know for sure is that she knew Florence Allford's brother so I'm trying to find out more about him too.'

'Why don't you ask Florence?'

'I tried but she doesn't want to speak about it.'

'Perhaps it's best left unspoken then.'

'You might be right, but I won't know until I find out what's going on.' She shook her head slightly. 'What *went* on in the village so long ago. It's in the past, but the past can have such a bearing on the present, don't you think?'

It certainly had a bearing on his present these days. He spent hours thinking back to what might have been.

Claude suddenly noticed that Lettie looked done in, with smudges of dark shadow beneath her eyes.

'What are you expecting to find?'

The girl shrugged. 'I don't know, but something happened back then. Something that made the family leave Heaven's Cove and never come back. Something that still affected my great-aunt eighty years later, even though that sounds daft.'

It didn't sound daft to Claude. The past weighed heavily on him, and this girl who'd appeared out of nowhere somehow felt like a link to what he'd lost. He hesitated before stepping aside. 'You're being very mysterious, but you'd best come in.'

He was giving the girl what she wanted, but she still hesitated on the doorstep. Claude suddenly caught sight of himself, reflected in the tarnished mirror hanging on the hall wall. His hair was wild today, frizzed out around his leathered face, and his beard was bushier than ever.

'I daresay Belinda would have informed you if I was a serial killer on the quiet,' he said, raising an eyebrow, and ironically, the girl seemed to relax at that. Her shoulders dropped.

'Belinda does seem to know a good deal about the people who live around here.'

'Too much,' muttered Claude, grateful that she hadn't yet picked up on his latest news. His visits to the hospital had gone unnoticed.

He opened the front door as far as it would go. 'After you, if you *are* coming in.'

With a nervous smile, the girl walked into his cottage and he followed, leaving the front door wide open. Buster wagged his tail and nuzzled up to her leg.

The hall – more of a tiny passage, really – led into a little sitting room with a low ceiling and small windows with deep stone windowsills. It was gloomy in here, even on the brightest of summer days, and the girl's features were thrown into shadow.

Claude gestured for her to sit on the two-seater sofa, after moving Buster out of her way with his foot. He took a seat at the table, next to the window, and stared at his unexpected guest.

'What did you say your name was again? Something Starcross?'

'Lettie.' She smiled and shifted on the sofa that he remembered was so uncomfortable, he usually left it to Buster. The fabric was covered in long brown dog hairs. Perhaps he should have made her sit at the table. He wasn't used to having strangers in his home and began to regret asking her inside. It was ridiculous to think she was any kind of link to his past.

'What's your dog called?' she asked, patting him on the head.

'Buster.'

'Have you had him long?'

'Eight years, since he was a puppy.'

'What breed is he?'

'No idea. A mongrel. I found him shivering on the quay in a storm and took him in.'

'That was kind of you.'

Claude shrugged. 'Not really. He's no trouble.'

Truth be told, Claude had saved Buster that night, as the rain lashed down and the shivering stray risked being swept away by the waves breaking over the quay wall. But then Buster had saved Claude, in return, from the loneliness that often threatened to overwhelm him. Everyone had someone in Heaven's Cove, it seemed. Even Florence, a widow for ages, now had her grandson living with her. But Claude had been on his own for forty years, ever since Esther had walked out of his life. His parents, though loving, could never fill the gap she'd left behind.

He brought his attention back to the stuffy room.

'You'd better tell me what you do know about your family, then, Miss Starcross.'

'My grandfather, great-aunt Iris and their parents lived at Driftwood House during the early 1940s, as far as I know, but they moved away during the war.'

'They moved away from Heaven's Cove?' Claude slowly shook his head, hardly able to believe their folly.

'They did. The whole family uprooted and never came back to Devon again. I was just curious about what their life was like here and why they moved. I'm particularly interested in Iris, who died recently.'

'Close, were you?'

'Yes.'

To Claude's alarm, tears filled Lettie's eyes this time and she blinked furiously. Should he offer her a tissue? He didn't have any tissues. He was contemplating offering her the hankie in his pocket, and trying to remember when it was last washed, when she sniffed and tried to smile.

'I'd like to know more about her, if possible.'

'Why didn't you ask her about growing up in the village?'

'I tried but the rest of the family from that time are long gone and Iris didn't want to talk about it.'

No one, it seemed, wanted to talk about it, and yet this young girl still seemed determined to blithely turn over stones when who knew what lurked beneath them.

'I've tried looking online,' she continued, 'but there's nothing concrete.'

'Online!' Claude spat out the word, making Lettie jump. 'You young-sters spend far too much time searching for fulfilment in your phones and computers. All I ever had was a clear sky and the north star to guide me.'

'I don't suppose they could tell me much about my great-aunt though.'

Lettie bit down on her lower lip and started running her fingers across the pretty gold key hanging around her neck.

'I don't suppose they could.'

Lettie's attention was caught by the dresser and Claude got to his feet and shoved the NHS letter on top of it into a drawer. Then he turned the small silver frame next to it face down. He cursed the nostalgia that had prompted him to take the photo from the drawer a few weeks ago. It didn't usually matter because the only person who could see the picture was him, but now Lettie was looking at it with curiosity. This was why he didn't usually invite people into his home. They were nosey.

'Come on then,' he said quickly, before she could start asking questions.

'Come on where?'

'Down to the cellar, to see what I can find out about your great-aunt and the mysterious Starcross family.'

'The cellar?'

She sounded nervous and Claude briefly wondered about the sense of taking a pretty young woman into his basement, but she'd got to her feet.

'Are you going to keep repeating what I say? The cellar is where I keep the information. It's this way.'

Lettie followed Claude through his tiny kitchen with its ancient cupboards and narrow cooker with its grill above the electric hob. He opened the door to the cellar and a waft of musty air hit his nose.

'I'll go first. Make sure you don't slip.'

He flicked on the light and the bare bulb turned his shadow into a looming mass on the walls as he descended the stone steps, with Lettie behind him.

At the bottom of the stairs, he clicked on a brighter lamp that illuminated three large black filing cabinets in the middle of the room, next to a rickety trestle table. Whistling softly under his breath, he pulled open the top drawer of the nearest cabinet and started rifling through the files inside. 'What years are we looking at?'

'The 1930s and 40s, I suppose. My family moved away from Heaven's Cove during the war and I'd love to know why.'

'There's a fair bit of information in here from that time.'

Claude started to spread pieces of paper, photos and old newspaper cuttings across the grubby table. It was cold down here, and damp, and Lettie was shivering. Though whether from the chill or from being in a cellar with the bogeyman of Heaven's Cove, he couldn't be sure.

'Do you want something around your shoulders?' he asked gruffly, making sure to keep his distance so as not to spook her.

She shook her head, already studying the documents.

'No thank you. These are fascinating. Did you collect all of this information yourself?'

'No, I collected some of the newer stuff, but it was mostly my mother who was born and bred in Heaven's Cove and loved this village.'

She'd been quite a hoarder, his mother. Claude thought back to when she'd lived in the cottage next door to his. It had been full to the brim with her 'collections' of everything from local history and *Good Housekeeping* magazines, to felt hats and china ornaments of parrots. Why parrots, he'd never discovered.

Much of it had gone to charity shops or the tip after her death, but he'd kept a few mementos, including her newspaper clippings, documents and photos from the past.

He could have moved into the cottage next door after his mum had died but he'd been happy here, in his smaller home. Though he often regretted his decision to rent out her cottage to tourists through a holiday lettings agency. They did all the work and he got an income from it. But the agency didn't always do a very good job of vetting the people who stayed, and he'd been kept awake many a night by loud music or people singing after drinking too much. At least this girl didn't seem the sort of outsider to cause trouble.

Lettie, her face a picture of rapt concentration, was working her way through many of his 1930s and 40s photographs, some of them black and white, some in faded colour. There were pictures of the village, Land Girls in fields, and a panoramic view of Heaven's Cove, with Driftwood House visible on top of the cliffs.

Perhaps the girl's great-aunt had been in the house when the photo was taken, thought Claude, listening to Buster whimpering upstairs. He didn't like being excluded.

'This is all amazing,' said Lettie. 'I'm sure local people and tourists would love to see it. I was only just saying to Belinda that a museum dedicated to village history and culture would be a brilliant addition to Heaven's Cove.'

'Maybe, but it's not for show.'

She rifled through dozens of photos, holding them up to the light and studying the faces of people long gone, lives lived and now ended, while Claude stood in the corner with his arms folded.

'This is wonderful.' She grinned, her face pale in the beam from the bare lightbulb. 'It's an absolute treasure trove of local history.

So many life stories. It's such a shame that it's all hidden away down here.'

'Who'd want to see it?'

'Lots of people. Locals, and tourists like me who are interested in what happened over the years to make the village how it is today.'

'I guess, but it would need to be sorted out and I don't have the time.'

'It's a shame I don't live nearer or I'd offer to help you. I'd love going through all of this properly. Oh!' She smiled and waved a photo at him. 'I think I've found her! I'm pretty sure this is Iris from other photos I've seen of her when she was younger. Look!'

Claude moved to stand beside her and peered at the picture. A young woman, probably in her early twenties, with long dark hair, stood leaning against a cart with a handful of other people. Even though he'd never seen any photos of Iris, Claude could tell she and the young woman in his cellar were related. They were both tall with high cheekbones and big eyes, and the same long curly hair.

'Iris's hair was so thick back then,' said Lettie, smiling at the photo. 'It got thinner as she grew older.'

Next to Iris stood a young, dark-haired man with his arm around her shoulders. He was grinning happily, with Iris pulled tightly into his side.

'Do you know who these other people in the picture are? Iris and this man look very close.'

'I've no idea, but these photos belonged to my mother and she was always organised.' He turned the photo over and the sight of his mother's careful handwriting made the breath catch in his throat, even after all these years. 'Look, she's written down some of the names.'

He handed the photo back to Lettie, who squinted at the letters.

'*Iris Starcross* is written here, and next to her it says *Cornelius Allford.*' She frowned. 'That's the correct first name, but it can't be Mrs Allford's brother. He wouldn't have the same surname as her if she was married.'

'You don't know Florence. She used to be quite feisty in her younger days,' said Claude, noticing the girl's eyebrows raise at that. 'When she got married, according to my mother, she made her husband take on the Allford name so it wouldn't die out.'

'In which case, that man must be Florence's brother – he does look a little like her around the mouth. He and Iris look so young and carefree.' She leafed through the rest of the photos in her hand and paused when she got to the final one. 'Isn't that him, too?'

Claude peered over her shoulder. She was looking at a group of young men in army uniform. They stood in a line, their faces proud, and there, at the end, was a young man who looked very much like Cornelius.

Lettie frowned. 'I assumed that Florence's brother had died fairly recently, but if she needed to carry on the family name when she got married, he must have died a long time ago. Do you know when or how?'

Claude shrugged, distracted by Buster's whimpering, which was getting louder. 'Not that I remember. He wasn't around when I was growing up.'

Lettie leaned over and started scanning through the small number of newspaper clippings laid out on the table.

'Anything there?' asked Claude, after a while.

'I don't think so. I can't see a Cornelius mentioned, and there's definitely no mention of my great-aunt.'

'You could try the war memorial.'

'I haven't seen one in the village.'

'It's at the end of Weaver's Row, near the church.'

Lettie seemed upset again. 'I almost can't bear to look for Cornelius's name there. Not after seeing the photo of him and Iris looking so happy together. It must be awful to lose someone you love.'

Claude closed his eyes for a moment, swamped by bittersweet memories.

'I don't think I can help you any further. I'd like you to go now,' he told Lettie firmly.

He knew that he was being brusque, rude even. But he was suddenly overwhelmed by memories of his parents, long gone, and a woman he'd lost many years ago. It was also overwhelming simply having another human being in his home for any length of time. He wasn't used to it – usually it was just him and faithful Buster.

'Oh. OK. Of course. I'm sorry to have taken up your time.'

Lettie's eyes opened wider and she gathered together the information she'd been looking at and placed it back into the filing cabinet. He'd upset her.

'Thank you so much for your help,' said Lettie. 'I really appreciate it. Could I borrow this photo of my great-aunt for a day or two? I'll bring it back.'

Claude eyed her suspiciously. These outsiders came and went – here one minute and gone the next.

'I promise I'll return it,' she assured him, and her earnest expression suddenly reminded him of Esther.

'Take it,' he said, switching off the lamp and leading her back up the cellar steps. 'I'll trust you to bring it back.'

*

According to Google Maps, the lane she was looking for was right about... here. Lettie looked around for a road sign and eventually spotted one, screwed to the side of a stone cottage. *Weaver's Row.*

The row was narrow, cobbled and lined with ancient cottages with tiny windows and shiny front doors. They looked like workers' homes from centuries long gone. Lettie peered through the latticed panes as unobtrusively as she could as she passed by and spotted stone hearths and beams. How wonderful to live in a house with such history. Her flat was ex-council, erected in the 1970s, and didn't have a single interesting feature to redeem it.

The end of Weaver's Row opened onto a small green and there, in the middle, stood the war memorial. The memorial was formed of a stone cross standing on a stone plinth and both were pitted and weathered. Someone had planted flowers around the base of the plinth and the bright blooms swayed in the breeze as Lettie approached.

Depressingly, there were lots of names for such a small village. Some were from the 1914-18 conflict, while others were from World War II. Lettie ran her fingers across the indentations of the names of men long gone and scanned down those lost in the 1939-1945 conflict. In her heart, she hoped he wasn't there but she suddenly saw his name: *Cornelius J. Allford, 1915–1941.*

He was only twenty-six years old when he died, and Iris would have been in her early twenties. *How deep was their relationship?* wondered Lettie. If they were good friends, his death would have shattered her great-aunt, and if they were more, as the photo suggested...

Lettie suddenly felt near to tears. There was so much she wished she'd asked her great-aunt. So much she wished that Iris had told her.

An old flyer advertising the village fete fluttered by and Lettie watched it twist across the grass. The blue of the sea sparkled in the distance and there, to the right, was the Allford headland jutting out into the ocean.

Sit where I sat, darling girl.

Was the letter written by Cornelius? He must have sat up there on the headland, high above the village and the ocean. He and Iris might even have sat there together, making plans and dreaming of a future that was about to disappear in a rattle of gunfire. If only Lettie knew for sure.

She sighed, longing to know the truth. But both Cornelius and Iris were now gone and all she had was a letter that made little sense and the key that was hanging around her neck, glinting in the sunshine.

Chapter Twelve

Lettie

Lettie started walking. She headed to the edge of the village, where a shallow river had cut its way through the land and was flowing towards the sea. After crossing over a pretty wooden bridge, she climbed higher.

The heat was rising and she took off her cardigan, exposing her shoulders to the sun. She'd have to be careful not to get burned. In London, she sometimes went to the local park but still spent far too much time indoors, either at work or in her flat.

She finally reached the headland – Cora Head, or Lovers' Link as the locals called it. She was exposed here, high above the sea which rippled in the sunshine to the horizon. Closer to shore, the waves were more defined and filled the air with salt spray that split the sunshine into rainbow colours.

Farther round the bay stood Heaven's Cove and Lettie noticed how small the community was. It looked like a toy town from up here, with tiny boats bobbing at the quayside, dozens of pretty houses including Claude's cottage, winding narrow streets and, where the land began to rise, the castle ruins.

The people who lived in the castle centuries ago would have had a view across the village and down to the sea where invaders might arrive at any time. A little like the influx of new holidaymakers if Simon had his way, thought Lettie, before catching herself. That was how Corey and his grandmother thought, but maybe Simon was right and more people would mean more income for the village.

Lettie moved closer to the edge of the cliff to take in the vista and immediately regretted it. She could imagine falling through space into the water below. A familiar sensation of suffocation clamped its way through her chest until she could hardly breathe. If she closed her eyes she would be back there, in the cold Essex sea, being dragged under the waves, her chest burning and water flooding her mouth. She was about to die. She was only eight years old but she knew without doubt that her life was over. No oxygen meant no life, and she couldn't breathe.

Step back, ordered a voice in her brain, so loudly that she almost fell backwards.

Still shaking, she sat on the grass and pulled her knees up under her chin.

Come on, Cornelius. Did you write the letter? 'Sit where I sat with the key to my heart and all will become clear.' Was this where you sat? What did you want Iris to see?

Perhaps there was nothing to see other than the view they had shared, and Lettie really was here in Heaven's Cove on a wild goose chase. Iris had escaped from the village after the man she loved had died. That was all there was to it. And now, ironically, Lettie was here escaping from a life in London that seemed hollow and empty.

Lettie's reverie was shattered by the shrill ring of her mobile phone, and she groaned when she saw Daisy's name on the screen.

She was tempted to ignore it, but it could be an emergency. *A childcare emergency*, thought Lettie, raising her eyebrows as she clicked on the call.

'Lettie, there you are. Are you all right? How's Devon? And when are you coming home?' Daisy was nothing if not to the point.

'I'm all right, thank you. How are you, Daisy?'

'Absolutely knackered, if you're interested. Mum is doing my head in. Honestly, if she asks me to take her shopping one more time I'm going to crown her. I've got better things to do on a Saturday than traipse around Poundstretcher.'

'So have I,' said Lettie, but Daisy was too busy complaining to listen. Not that she would rate reading or going to museums as 'better things to do' anyway.

'So what are you actually *doing* in Heaven's Cove?' asked Daisy peevishly.

'I'm having a rest and trying to find out a bit more about Iris when she lived here.'

'That was decades ago.'

'I know but being here makes me feel closer to her.'

Daisy was silent for a moment. 'I know you were close to Iris and you miss her, Lettie. Is that why you suddenly took off? You're not suffering from complicated grief disorder, are you?'

Her sister was a would-be psychotherapist. Lettie thought for a moment. 'I don't know. Isn't all grief rather complicated? But I don't think I have a disorder.'

'Have you fully accepted the reality of losing Iris and allowed yourself to experience the pain of no longer having her in your life?'

'I think so,' answered Lettie, thinking of the tears she'd already shed.

'I expect you're all right, then,' decided Daisy briskly. 'And she was a very old woman, almost a hundred.'

Lettie flinched. Several people had said that to her, as though the fact that Iris had had a long life meant she should miss her less.

'So what have you discovered about her? Did Iris have a racy past?'

'I doubt it,' said Lettie, bristling at Daisy's jocular tone. This was exactly why she hadn't told her about their great-aunt's final words, or finding the letter in her handbag. 'I'm just interested in what she was like as a young woman.'

'Why? What's the point?'

'Does there have to be a point?'

'There's always a point.' Daisy sighed. 'Is it nice down there?'

Lettie looked across the ocean and back towards the village with its tiny cottages and winding lanes. 'It's absolutely gorgeous. A bit more picturesque than suburban London.'

'Quiet though, and deadly dull, I expect.'

'Not really. It's quite busy, with lots of tourists and I've met some' – she paused – 'interesting people.'

'Well, I must admit that I'm slightly envious. The kids are bickering and Jason's got the day off and is sitting on his arse reading the paper.' That was the closest Daisy had ever come to admitting her marriage was anything less than perfect. 'Talking of the kids, don't forget it's Elsa's birthday later this month and I was going to ask you to make her cake 'cos I don't have the time and she's desperate for one of those rainbow cakes with lots of different colours when you cut it.'

'You won't mind, will you?' asked Daisy when Lettie said nothing. 'You'll be back by then, won't you?'

Yes, was on the tip of Lettie's tongue, but Iris's voice suddenly sounded in her head. *You're too obliging for your own good and your family take advantage.* Lettie looked out across the village below her.

'Maybe, maybe not.'

There were a few moments of silence before Daisy replied. 'What do you mean, maybe not? You are coming back, aren't you?'

'Probably.'

As the word left her mouth, Lettie regretted it. Of course she was going back to London. She just got tired of being taken for granted sometimes.

'Probably?' spluttered Daisy. 'What the hell does that mean?'

Lettie sighed, having learned the hard way that winding Daisy up invariably backfired. 'It means that I haven't made up my mind yet when I'll be back, but I daresay it'll be in time to make Elsa's birthday cake.'

Daisy's voice softened at that. 'Good. So what are you doing right now?'

'I'm sitting on a headland in the sunshine, looking out over the sea.'

'That sounds nice.'

'It is. Growing up here must have been amazing, Daisy. The air smells clean, and, even though the place is crammed with tourists, the pace of life is less frantic. And the history of the village is fascinating.'

'History, schmistory,' groaned Daisy. 'It all sounds very lovely but if you go AWOL for too long, you'll lose your job.'

Lettie hesitated. Now was the perfect time to let her family know that she was officially unemployed. But the moment passed and Daisy started burbling on about her training course and the children.

'Anyway,' she said eventually, after describing the ins and outs of child rearing, most of which seemed to involve praying for sleep and bribing them with biscuits. 'Just get back to London soon.'

'I will as soon as... oh.'

Lettie paused, the breath catching in her throat. Corey had just appeared in the distance. He spotted her and stopped walking. Then he turned as though he was about to flee before turning again and walking briskly towards her.

'Oh, what?' demanded Daisy.

'I've got to go.'

'Why?'

'Someone's coming.'

'Who's coming?'

'A local man I know.'

'What do you mean, *know*?'

'He's a fisherman I've met.'

'What fisherman? What exactly are you getting up to in Devon, Lettie? We need—'

'Gotta go. Bye.'

Daisy would never forgive her for cutting her off, thought Lettie, switching her mobile to silent. But she couldn't deal with her inquisitive sister *and* grumpy Corey at the same time.

Chapter Thirteen

Corey walked towards her, his face set and a warm breeze ruffling his hair which just reached the neckline of his grey Aran jumper. He looked ruggedly handsome and, for a brief moment, Lettie wondered what it would feel like to be held against his chest, before giving her head a shake.

Yes, he was good-looking and charismatic, but he was also bad-tempered and suspicious of her. It didn't help, she realised, that he'd come across her here on the very land that Simon was trying so hard to get his hands on.

'Good afternoon. I thought I'd come up here for a walk because I understand lots of tourists do.'

She winced. That sounded far too formal and defensive.

'Good afternoon,' he answered with the slightest raise of an eyebrow. 'I didn't mean to interrupt your phone call.'

'That's all right. It was only my sister and I was quite glad to say goodbye.'

'Is everything all right?'

'Absolutely fine.'

'That's good.'

He gazed across the sea, his face in profile.

'Though I seem to be letting my family down by daring to be away for a few days.'

Why had she said that? She seemed to be the queen of unnecessary comments today, but Corey's mouth quivered as though he might actually crack a smile.

'Do they rely on you?' he asked, turning to look at her.

'Yep, my sister relies on me for childcare and my mother for shopping trips. And my brother relies on me to do all these things so he doesn't have to.'

'Happy families.' He shuffled his feet. 'I've been hoping to see you, actually. I wanted to thank you for helping my grandmother yesterday.'

This was surprising. If anything, Lettie had expected to be told off for pestering Florence again.

'I was happy to. She was in danger of losing her shopping.' Lettie paused, wondering if it was wise to bring up their subsequent disagreement. 'I'm surprised she mentioned me at all. I don't seem to be her favourite person.'

It was Corey's turn to wince. 'Was she abrupt?'

Lettie remembered the front door slamming in her face. 'You could say that.'

He frowned slightly. 'Gran's not usually rude. I'm not sure what's going on.'

'Me neither. It's all a bit of a mystery.' She hesitated. 'I saw your great-uncle's name on the village war memorial.'

'Cornelius?'

'Yes. Your gran mentioned him to me. Briefly. It's so sad that he died in the war.'

'That was way before my time, obviously, but I know the family were devastated. He's buried in some foreign field.'

'I suppose he used to walk here a lot on the headland.'

'I expect so. Gran said he loved it up here.'

'I expect he'd sit for ages, watching the sea.'

Corey gave Lettie a sideways glance. 'I don't know. Probably.'

'Your gran must have been heartbroken when he died.'

'It must have been awful. She was only ten at the time and her mother died quite soon afterwards.'

Lettie gasped at the thought of so much heartache landing on one poor child. To lose your beloved older brother would be dreadful, but your mother too? She shook her head, feeling a sudden fondness for Florence, who had managed to survive such tragedy.

'That's really terrible. I saw a headstone for Elizabeth Allford in the village graveyard.'

'Did you now?' said Corey, fixing her with a stare that made her legs wobble.

'Was she your gran's mum?'

Corey ignored her question, posing one of his own instead. 'Why *are* you so interested in what happened in Heaven's Cove so long ago?'

'I… I miss Iris.'

He tilted his head, still staring into her eyes. 'There's more to it than that. I can tell. Why are you so interested in my family?'

What could she say? That she was on a wild goose chase, trying to understand her great-aunt's final words? That she was trying to discover who had written a letter decades earlier that made no sense at all? He'd think she was crazy and his already low opinion of her would plummet even further. And yet…

For some reason she didn't quite understand, Lettie wanted to tell Corey Allford the truth. Even though she'd deliberately kept it from her family and was wishing she'd never mentioned the letter to her mother yesterday. Even though Corey and his grandmother might think she was obsessing about nothing at all.

'What's really going on?' urged Corey, taking a step towards her. There were dark shadows beneath his eyes, she noticed, and stubble across his jaw. He looked tired.

'It's all to do with Iris.'

'Who sounds very important to you.'

'She is.' Lettie swallowed hard. 'She was. My family are quite…' She felt around for the word. '…overwhelming sometimes. They're louder than me, more confident. But Iris always understood. Sometimes I'd go to her flat and we'd hardly speak. I'd sit and read a book for ages or we'd go to museums together. I love history. Iris was an amazing woman, but she was sad. Just like your gran. Underneath it all – all the years of experiences and life – she was sad. There was something from her past that never left her. Some heartbreak that I think may have happened in Heaven's Cove, and I want to find out what.'

She thought Corey might be dismissive, sarcastic even. But he grimaced, sympathy in his eyes. 'I'm sorry. Losing someone you love is painful.'

Lettie nodded.

'But I don't see how you can find out what happened so long ago. What do you have to go on?'

Lettie took a deep breath, reached into the small bag slung across her body and handed him the letter.

'I found this among Iris's possessions and she left me this necklace that she always wore.'

Lettie automatically took hold of the key around her neck and began to run it back and forth along its gold chain. As usual, it made her feel comforted and safe.

'I still don't understand why you're so interested in my family, unless…' Corey paused, reading the cryptic words for a second time. 'Unless you think this was written by Cornelius?'

'It's my best guess. I think your great-uncle and my great-aunt were sweethearts.'

He handed back the letter. 'That's quite a stretch.'

'Not really. Look at this photo.' Lettie pulled the old photograph from her bag and gave it to Corey. 'The woman on the right is Iris and the man standing next to her is Cornelius. It says so on the back.'

Corey peered at the photo. 'That's him, all right. There's an old photo of him in Gran's bedroom.'

'And they look pretty close.'

'Where did you get this picture?'

'From Claude. I found it in his archives.'

'Claude let you into his cottage?' When Lettie nodded, Corey breathed out slowly. 'That's impressive. He doesn't usually trust outsiders. He's quite…'

'Distrustful?' asked Lettie, giving a small smile.

Corey regarded her with his dark brown eyes. 'You could say that.' The corner of his mouth lifted slightly. 'What does the key open?'

'I have no idea. Maybe nothing. I think Iris wanted me to find out, but I don't know anything about her past here. That's why I wanted to talk to your gran.'

'And is that definitely the only reason you're so interested in my family? You're *not* working with Simon, are you?'

Lettie sighed. What was it about Corey and Simon, two men who apparently disliked each other intensely but couldn't resist bringing one another into every conversation?

'No, I'm definitely not working with Simon. I only met him a couple of days ago.'

'I saw you with him in the churchyard yesterday.'

'I bumped into him by chance and he was pointing out this headland. He seems quite determined to buy it.'

'Then he'll be disappointed,' said Corey, his gaze hardening. 'Gran could never part with it because of what it meant to her brother and she, like me, doesn't want it to be spoiled.'

'If your gran needs the money, maybe Simon would agree to keep this part of the headland untouched and build farther back.'

'I imagine he would agree but I don't trust him. Once he's got the land, he can do what he likes with it.'

'Surely there are planning rules he'd have to follow?'

'A man like him will get round them, or stretch them to their limits.'

Lettie turned towards the sea, keen to change the subject and stop talking about Simon. The headland was deserted and all she could hear was the soft whoosh of the waves below them. Even the circling gulls had stopped their screeching.

'You can see for miles from up here.'

She moved as close to the edge as she dared and looked across the sea. The shade of the water had deepened to the kind of blue you see in adverts for continental Europe, and the clouds in the sky had melted into wispy trails. The view was stunning and the fresh air carried the salty tang of the sea.

'My grandmother once mentioned that Cornelius used to sit up here and write poetry,' said Corey, folding his arms and looking towards the horizon. 'Apparently he was an artistic kind of man. Was your great-aunt artistic?'

'I guess so,' answered Lettie, remembering sitting still as a child so Iris could draw her likeness. 'She didn't write, but she liked to sketch me sometimes.'

Corey smiled. 'I'm not surprised. With your striking red hair and pale skin, you look like one of the women painted by Millais or Rossetti.'

Lettie self-consciously ran her auburn curls through her fingers, surprised by the compliment out of nowhere.

'Does your gran write poetry as well? Does it run in the family?'

'No, she's not into poetry but she enjoys art too. She used to take me to art exhibitions when I was younger.'

'You went to art exhibitions?'

Corey raised an eyebrow. 'I'm not the uncultured barbarian that you, coming from London, might imagine. We have electricity and running water and everything in this neck of the woods now.'

'I didn't imagine anything of the sort,' said Lettie, colouring at his accurate appraisal of her first impression of him.

'Hmm.' He stood with his hands in his pockets, gazing out to sea. He looked strong and solid and a part of this amazing land. Lettie could hardly take her eyes off him. 'So what are you going to do next in your quest for the truth?' he asked.

'I'm not sure. I was rather hoping to speak to your gran but that's a bit tricky seeing as she hates me.'

'I wouldn't say she hates you. Dislikes you intensely, maybe?'

When Corey raised his eyebrows again and grinned, Lettie couldn't help but smile back. Maybe he wasn't quite so grumpy after all. His face was very close and she could see the feathery lines around his eyes and the soft curve of his upper lip. *You're in trouble,* said a little voice in the back of her mind as she suddenly felt off-kilter.

The distant sound of an emergency services siren brought her back down to earth.

'Anyway,' she said quickly, using the no-nonsense tone of voice Daisy usually reserved for her. 'I'd better head back into the village. There are lots of local places still to see and lots of history to take in.' She waved the guide book at him, still feeling flustered. 'I'd particularly love to see Dartmoor which is an ancient landscape and well worth a visit, according to… this.'

She waved the book again, wincing inside. She sounded like a head-mistress turned tour guide, talking to a class of truculent ten-year-olds.

'O-K,' said Corey slowly, with a look that made her feel even more foolish. 'Well, thanks again for helping Gran, good luck with your search, and I might see you around before you leave the village.'

'Mmm, probably.'

Lettie waved and walked off, her face screwed up into a mask of embarrassment.

Chapter Fourteen

Rosie looked up from her computer when Lettie got back to Driftwood House. She'd given up any thoughts of exploring the village further, in spite of what she'd said to Corey. She felt too flustered.

'Hello, there.' Rosie closed the lid of her laptop.

'Hello. Sorry, I don't want to interrupt you.'

'Don't worry. The internet connection is playing up again so I can sort out my marketing some other time. Did you have a good day?'

'Yes, thanks. I walked up to Cora Head – or Lovers' Link, do you call it? – and before that I spent some time with Claude.'

'Really? Did you see him in the pub?'

'No, he let me into his cottage to see his photos and cuttings about old Heaven's Cove.'

Rosie got to her feet, her mouth open. 'Wow, you're honoured. Not many people, particularly people Claude doesn't know, ever get over his doorstep. He must have taken a shine to you. What did you think of him?'

Lettie thought back to the slightly odd, but quietly endearing man she'd spent time with that afternoon. He'd suddenly been so keen to get her out of his house, almost as if he was frightened of her.

'He's rather eccentric, but he seems like a nice man. A bit lonely maybe.'

'I think so. We try to involve him in village life but he tends to keep himself to himself.'

'Do you know much about his past?'

Rosie shrugged. 'Not really. He's always lived in the village, as far as I know.'

'Has he always been single?'

'I think so. He's never been married and I've never heard talk of him having a partner. It's just him and his dog, Buster. They go everywhere together. Was Claude helpful with your search for family info?'

'Really helpful. Look!' Lettie pulled the photo of Iris and Cornelius from her bag. 'That's my great-aunt Iris over seventy-five years ago, with Cornelius Allford next to her.'

'Allford?' Rosie took the photo and studied it closely. 'Is he related to…?'

'He was Florence's brother, Corey's great-uncle, who died in the war.'

'That's sad.' Rosie handed the photo back. 'Did you find out any more about Iris or her life here?'

'No, not yet.'

Lettie hesitated. Should she tell Rosie about the run-in with Florence? She decided against it and changed the subject. 'I bumped into Belinda again in the village.'

Rosie grinned. 'She's involved in everything and is quite hard to avoid.'

'So I'm discovering – I keep bumping into her, and Simon too. I saw him in the pub on my first evening here, and in the churchyard yesterday.'

'Is that the property guy?' When Lettie nodded, Rosie took off her reading glasses and sat back in her chair. 'He's quite a smooth talker and presumably a good businessman, but he's not making many friends in the village. He doesn't want to buy the land that people have for sale, but he's keen on buying up Cora Head for holiday housing.'

'What do you think about it?'

'Me?' Rosie frowned and sucked the end of her pen for a moment. 'I think it would be a shame to spoil that land with development, but I can see that people would love to wake up to that view, and I wouldn't blame Florence for taking the money. I'm lucky because I wake up to a fabulous view every day.'

'I'm surprised Simon hasn't called on you to see if you're up for selling. Oh,' said Lettie, seeing Rosie's expression. 'He has tried to get you to sell?'

'He had a chat to me about whether I'd be willing to sell Driftwood House so he could knock it down and build some holiday lets instead.'

'What was your answer?' asked Lettie, hoping against hope that this attractive, historic house was safe.

'No way,' answered Rosie with a grin. 'I've not long taken this house on and it means too much to me to let it go. I understand why Florence is so against selling Lovers' Link.'

'I saw Florence's grandson today, too. Up on the headland. Oh, I forgot to ask him about his call-out on the lifeboat yesterday afternoon.'

'That was just a false alarm but word in the village is that the lifeboat got a call after midnight and didn't return until almost dawn.'

No wonder he'd looked tired. Lettie tried to imagine surging through towering dark waves to come to someone's rescue, but even the thought of it made her shudder.

'Corey's brave, working on the lifeboat.'

'He's one of the volunteer crew members. Hold on.' Rosie rummaged in a pile of papers under her desk and pulled out a newspaper. 'They had their photo in the local paper last week.'

The picture Rosie thrust under her nose showed a group of men and women lined up on the deck of a lifeboat, all wearing the same yellow and black weatherproof uniforms and matching boots. She looked along the line until she spotted Corey, taller than the rest, with his coal-black hair blowing in the breeze.

'Did last night's call-out go OK, do you know?' she asked.

'I think so. They went out to a boat that had got into trouble in rough seas and towed it back into harbour.' When Lettie shivered again at the thought of deep, dark water, Rosie gave her a sideways glance. 'And I agree he's very brave.'

'Anyone who goes out on the sea in a storm to help someone else is brave in my book.'

'And he's good-looking.'

Lettie glanced back at Rosie, who was putting her papers into a pile and didn't catch her eye.

'Yeah, I guess so. How long has he lived here?'

'Not that long. He moved away for a while and his marriage to Grace ended badly and he moved in with his grandmother about twelve months ago because she needed his support.' Rosie shrugged. 'That's all I know. I'm not much into gossip.'

'Me neither,' said Lettie, though she was itching to know more. Singing fisherman Corey, who was grumpy one minute and being heroic the next, was almost as much of an enigma as his great-uncle.

Chapter Fifteen

Claude

'Buster, come here, boy.'

What was the daft dog doing? Claude called him again but Buster was pushing his nose up against a woman sitting with her back to him. She was sitting on the bank of the river, with her bare feet in the shallow water.

'Sorry,' said Claude gruffly, pushing his fingers through Buster's collar and pulling him away. When the woman turned, he realised it was the girl who'd called at his cottage a couple of days ago. 'Lettie Starcross.'

'That's me.' Claude knew he should have recognised her immediately. There was no mistaking her striking auburn hair which shone red-gold in the sun as she pushed it over her shoulder. 'It's Buster, isn't it?' She patted the dog before turning her face towards Claude and smiling. 'How are you?'

'All right.' Claude pushed his hands into the pockets of his trousers, unused to making small talk in the street with a woman young enough to be his granddaughter. 'Um, how are you?'

Lettie gave him a sympathetic smile, as though she could feel his discomfort and got to her feet, shaking water from her toes. 'I'm OK, thanks.'

'Really?'

There was something about the girl that bothered him. She was smiling but there was a sadness about her, a loneliness. And he knew what that was like.

As Lettie nodded, Claude was aware of Belinda staring at them from the doorway of the village post office.

'That's good then. How are you getting on with tracking down information on that local lad you were interested in?' he asked, suddenly determined to prolong their conversation, if only to confound Belinda's opinion of him. She'd never said as much but it was obvious she considered him a recluse. Lots of people did, and it was true he preferred the company of Buster and didn't much like socialising. But he disliked being gossiped about even more.

'I've come to a bit of a halt to be honest, so I've just been enjoying the village for the last day or two. It's a wonderful place.'

'I wouldn't want to be anywhere else. So have you given up your search?'

'No. I still want to know more about Iris's young life.'

'It won't bring her back, you know.'

Lettie's bottom lip wobbled at that and he wished he hadn't been so brusque.

'I know. That's not why I'm doing it.'

'People disappear from your life but they always leave an echo,' said Claude quickly. He remembered the woman who left so long ago but still haunted his dreams. Once upon a time they'd been comforting, but more recently Esther had visited his dreams to stare at him mournfully with her big blue eyes and berate him for becoming such a loner. This wasn't how his life was supposed to turn out. He turned to go – damn Belinda and her stupid opinion – but Lettie touched his arm lightly.

He had to stop himself from flinching. It had been so long since he'd been touched by a woman. The men on the boats were always bumping into him, and they shook hands with him in the pub. But women tended to give him a wide berth. Perhaps they found his good looks and sparkling personality overwhelming. Claude allowed himself a sardonic smile at the thought, because he knew exactly what he'd become over the years – a grizzled, grumpy old bugger who preferred his dog to human company. A loner. The local eccentric.

That's why he was particularly surprised by Lettie's next words.

'Can I buy you a cup of coffee?'

'Why?' he asked, narrowing his eyes.

'To say thank you for helping me find the photo of Iris and Cornelius.' Lettie shrugged. 'And, to be honest, I don't really know anyone around here and I'm getting fed up with my own company.' Claude hesitated as Lettie bent down and patted Buster on the head. 'I saw a nice café in the street near the church – The Heavenly Tea Shop or something like that? – and I quite fancied giving it a go.'

'I've never been in there.'

'Really? How long have you lived in Heaven's Cove?'

'All my life.'

'And how long has the café been there?'

'Ten years, maybe? Pauline runs it with help from her husband when he's not on the boats.'

'Why haven't you ever been inside?'

Claude shrugged. 'I can make a perfectly good coffee at home.'

'Good point, but I've got a craving for a cream tea. I can't go back to London without having one. So will you join me?'

He was about to refuse, but there was something about this young woman that made him want to spend time in her company. Her youth made him feel old and she talked too much, but her interest in the old days was intriguing, and what was the alternative? Another afternoon in his cottage with faithful Buster while tourists screamed and squealed on the quay outside. If he sat outside smoking his pipe, people tried to take photographs of him.

'I suppose that would be acceptable,' he said, before he could change his mind.

Pauline's tea shop was rammed with braying tourists and noisy children and Claude regretted his decision the minute he saw them. He steeled himself, getting ready to weave his way past the pushchairs, rolled-up windbreaks and backpacks littering the café floor.

But Lettie took one look inside and led him away from the front door to the only empty table on the pavement outside.

'Shall we sit outside instead? It seems a shame not to on such a nice day.'

Claude sank thankfully onto the metal fold-up chair which was surrounded by an array of flowers in bright pots and stone troughs.

Pauline had done a good job out here, giving it the feel of a Mediterranean street café. Not that Claude had ever been farther than Dieppe. He and Esther had had plans to travel but those had all fallen through. And if you were going on holiday on your own, you might as well stay at home, really. And who would look after his dog while he was off gallivanting? Buster was the latest in a long line of canine companions. You could rely on a dog not to let you down, far more than a human.

'It's much nicer out here,' said Lettie, scanning down the menu on the table. Claude nodded though it was like being in a goldfish bowl. People were staring at them as they went by and several of the locals were doing a double-take when they spotted him sitting there.

'Claude, fancy seeing you here!' Pauline stood in front of them, her ash-blonde hair frizzed out around her flustered, red face. She fanned herself with the notebook she was carrying. 'This hot weather is good for business but it's about a hundred degrees in the café so you've made a good choice to dine al fresco. I don't reckon our new fans do much except waft the hot air round in there. Anyway.' She stopped fanning. 'What can I get you and your lady friend?'

Lady friend? Claude didn't like the term, especially when Lettie was so young. He was mid-seventies and she must be, what, about thirty? Judging women's ages wasn't his strong suit. But Lettie didn't seem at all put out.

'I'll have one of your cream teas, please. And Claude will have…?'

He shrugged. 'A coffee'll do.'

'Are you sure that's all? My treat.'

'I'm not hungry. Just a coffee will be sufficient.'

Pauline drew in a breath. 'Latte, flat white, macchiato, espresso, or Americano?'

When did having a coffee become so complicated? This was why he didn't frequent cafés. Nothing was simple any more. The modern world was encroaching more and more on Heaven's Cove. There was a mobile phone mast on the hill he could see from his window, some of the cottages away from the front sported satellite television dishes, and tourists wandered round with mobile phones snapping interminable photos of anything that moved – including him. They didn't enjoy the beauty of the place because they were too busy adding to their photo collection. Photos they probably never looked at once when they returned home.

Claude ran a finger around the neckline of his old T-shirt. Although he was a local, he felt out of place here.

'Just an ordinary coffee,' he said, and Pauline scribbled in her notebook.

'OK. Flat white it is. Cow's milk, oat, soya or—' She looked at the expression on Claude's face and stopped scribbling. 'Ordinary milk,' she muttered, before scurrying off.

The cream tea and coffee took a few minutes to arrive and, all the while, Lettie chattered – about her family and the fabulous view from Driftwood House and re-tracing her great-aunt's footsteps. She'd obviously loved her great-aunt and it struck Claude that no one would bother to retrace his footsteps when he shuffled off. The only person who would really miss him – rather than just note the passing of a Heaven's Cove stalwart – would be Buster. That was a shame. He'd have liked a young person like Lettie to give a damn about him.

'What about you, Claude?' asked Lettie, as she cut into her warm scone and the smell made his stomach growl. Lunch had been one slice of toast and a small tin of baked beans because his food cupboard was almost bare.

'What about me?' he asked gruffly, before taking a sip of his coffee. It tasted good and he relaxed back into his chair, while keeping an eye on the seagull sitting on the wall nearby that was eyeing up Lettie's scone. Those scavengers would go for anything, given half a chance. Claude had lost track of the number of tourists he'd seen dive-bombed for their fish and chips.

'Were you actually born in Heaven's Cove?'

Lettie was still looking at him, her knife poised above the clotted cream.

'I was, seventy-five years ago, in the cottage next to mine.'

'You must have been born soon-ish after Iris and her family left the village.'

'I guess so.'

Lettie glanced down at her plate. 'Is it cream or jam on the scone first in Devon? I don't want to upset the locals.' She grinned.

'You can eat it how you want. It's a free country.' He paused. 'But Belinda would tell you that it's cream first because we're not barbarians.'

Lettie grinned and Claude felt pleased that he'd amused her. Buster was a wonderful companion but he didn't appreciate the odd flash of humour that Claude displayed. Esther had once told him his sense of humour was one reason why she liked him so much.

He took another sip of his coffee, which definitely tasted better than the instant he made at home. Why was he thinking of Esther so much these days, particularly since meeting Lettie? Raking up the past, as she was doing, wasn't always a good thing. It was unsettling. He shuffled his feet under the table, suddenly wanting to get away.

'You'd better eat up because I haven't got all day,' he said, and then felt awful when Lettie's face fell. He should never have accepted her invitation. Belinda was right. He was an eccentric loner. Wasn't that what she'd once called him, when she hadn't realised he was listening? He took a huge gulp of his coffee and waved away a bluebottle that was buzzing nearby. 'I apologise. I don't mean to be ungracious.'

Lettie slightly raised her eyebrow, as though she would never have described him as gracious in the first place, but she smiled.

'That's all right.'

'I've found some more newspaper clippings about the village in the war,' he blurted out, before thinking it through. 'They'd fallen to the back of the filing cabinet.'

'Really? That sounds fascinating.'

'Mmm. You can come and look at them if you'd like.'

Her face lit up. 'Definitely. When's good for you?'

'It doesn't matter. If I'm in, you can see them.'

'OK. Thank you.'

'Whatever.'

That was a stupid thing to say – Claude had heard youngsters saying it to each other outside his cottage, and heaven knew why he'd used it now. It made him sound even more rude.

He smiled at Lettie in a bid to soften the word, wondering why he'd invited her back round at all. Looking into the past was like opening a can of worms.

Lettie sat back and wiped a smudge of cream from her lips with a paper serviette. 'That cream tea was epic, though my hips don't approve. I'll just go and pay.'

'That's all right. I can pay for myself,' said Claude gruffly, but Lettie waved his words away.

'No, it was my treat after you helped me with your archive. And you only had a coffee anyway.'

She was searching in her bag for her purse when Florence Allford walked past, then stopped and retraced her steps.

The elderly woman Claude had known since he was a boy marched towards them, looking overdressed in a long-sleeved dress and tights, her white hair glinting in the sunshine.

'Afternoon, Claude. I'm surprised to see you sitting here.' She nodded at him while he grunted a greeting. Then she turned to Lettie, who had stopped scrabbling for her purse. 'I saw you, Miss Starcross, and wanted a word.'

'Of course,' said Lettie, her cheeks blazing pink in the heat.

'My grandson says it might be a good idea for me to meet you. He tells me you have some things from the past that might be of interest to me.'

'That's right. I do,' stuttered Lettie.

'Then, you'd better come round to see me tomorrow morning at eleven. Is that acceptable?'

'Absolutely acceptable. Yes. Thank you.'

Florence leaned closer. 'Don't thank me, Miss Starcross. Thank my grandson for persuading me against my better instincts.'

With that, she gave Claude a curt nod and strode off again.

Lettie swallowed hard. 'Crikey. Is it just me or is Florence Allford a bit scary?'

Claude laughed out loud at that and several people turned to stare at him. 'Florence has always been rather fierce and not great with people.' He felt his cheeks redden, seeing as he was far less sociable than Florence. 'I'd better get home, Miss Starcross... Lettie.' He got to his feet and Buster ambled to his side with a wide yawn. 'Thank you for the drink.'

'No, thank you. I enjoyed your company.'

Had she really? Claude nodded self-consciously and mumbled, 'Me too,' before walking off.

'Why did I invite her back round, Buster?' he muttered, when he was far enough away not to be overheard. But in his heart of hearts he knew exactly why he wanted a private word with Miss Starcross. A plan had come into his head as he'd sipped his expensive coffee. 'I'll live to regret it... that is if I live long enough,' he said out loud, with a mirthless laugh. He ran his calloused hands gently across his dog's flank before sloping off home over the cobbles, ignoring the pull of a pint or three in The Smugglers Haunt on the way.

Chapter Sixteen

Lettie

Lettie smoothed down her summer dress before knocking on Florence's front door. After making such bad first impressions on the elderly lady, Lettie had made an effort with her appearance in the hope that later impressions would be better.

Her hair had been tamed into submission and was pulled into a ponytail and she'd put on a little make-up to hide the shadows beneath her eyes. The fresh sea air had put colour into her cheeks, but she'd slept badly last night. A strong wind had blown through the open Velux window, bringing with it the sound of waves crashing into the cliffs. It had sounded like the roar of a malevolent beast and Lettie's mind had strayed to the lifeboat.

Were Corey and his crew out on the roiling sea, battling through the waves? When she did sleep, she'd dreamt of strong currents pulling her and Corey under, her hair trailing behind them like seaweed and their limbs entangled.

The storm had blown itself out by morning and the sun today was blazing from a blue sky that looked as if it had been washed.

Lettie took a deep breath. At least Florence was willing to see her, thanks to Corey's intervention. She hadn't been sure that he'd tell his grandmother about their meeting but was glad he had. She'd stayed close to Driftwood House all morning, spending time wandering across the cliff top – never too close to the edge – in case Corey rang to say Florence had changed her mind. But there had been no call, so here she was.

Lettie raised her hand to knock again but the door was pulled open before her fingers could tighten around the gleaming brass door knocker.

'Are you trying to raise the dead? I may be old but I'm not deaf.'

Florence and Claude had a lot in common, thought Lettie, watching the elderly lady, in a brown tea dress with cream spots, walk with her stick along her narrow hallway. With the slightest of hesitations, Lettie stepped inside, closed the front door and followed her into a sitting room.

The room was small but homely with a standard lamp in the corner with a fringed shade, similar to one in Iris's flat. There was a large stone fireplace with a brass coal scuttle in the hearth, and silver-framed photos on a dark-wood dresser that looked ancient.

The paintings on the wall were all of the sea, except for one in a gilt frame that caught Lettie's eye. The scene, of trees in full leaf next to a tumbling stream, looked strangely familiar and she stopped to have a closer look. In the corner of the painting, a waterfall fell in a single gushing torrent before breaking into a white, churning mass of water.

'What are you staring at?' demanded Florence.

'I love this painting. Is it of somewhere local?'

'It's of Dartmoor, why?'

'I think… I think my aunt Iris had a photo in a frame in her flat just like this. It looks like the same place.'

Florence paused for a moment before gesturing at an armchair next to the stone-framed window. 'You're probably mistaken. You'd best take a seat, Miss Starcross. I don't have a lot of time.'

Lettie sank into the armchair, trying not to dwell on the painting and how similar it was to the photo she'd looked at countless times in Iris's flat. She and Florence were the only two people in the room, which smelled strongly of lavender, and a shiver of disappointment ran through her.

As though she could read the younger woman's mind, Florence sighed. 'My grandson thought me speaking to you was a good idea, though I'm not so sure myself. He tells me that speaking of painful things can be beneficial, though it's rather hypocritical of him when he won't speak about Grace's—'

She stopped talking abruptly and gave her head a slight shake.

'Is Corey at work?' asked Lettie, curious to know more about his ex-wife.

'He is.'

'He's not out on the lifeboat, then,' she said, trying to make conversation.

'Not this time. Makes a change with so many grockles around at the moment, thinking they can master the sea. Outsiders who don't belong round here,' said Florence pointedly. 'But at least you're on time so the tea's still warm.' Without asking, she poured Lettie a cup from the china pot beside her and handed it over. 'The sugar's still in the kitchen if you need any.'

Lettie assured her she didn't and took a sip.

'Have you lived in Heaven's Cove a long time, Mrs Allford?' she asked, trying to thaw the frosty atmosphere.

'I was born in this house almost ninety years ago and have lived here ever since.'

The soft burr of the old woman's accent rolled over Lettie and was soothing, in spite of the distrust in her eyes.

'The village seems to have hardly changed in that time. It's like a living museum.'

'And that's a bad thing, is it?'

'No, not at all. It's wonderful. I'd love to hear your stories of how life used to be here, when you were growing up.'

'It was hard, Miss Starcross, and not quite the romantic picture that you and other outsiders tend to have of it.'

Lettie groaned inside. Her plan to initiate a general – hopefully pleasant – chat before gently asking about Cornelius's relationship with Iris wasn't going too well.

'I'm sure it was very hard,' she replied levelly. 'I'm very interested in social history and how the past has affected the present.'

'Is that right?' said Florence, brushing a strand of snow-white hair from her wrinkled forehead.

'I've always been interested in—'

'So what do you know about my brother, Miss Starcross?' Florence cut across her, slowly stirring her tea.

'Please call me Lettie.'

'Hmm.' Florence sipped her drink, her pale eyes never leaving Lettie's face.

'I know very little but I think he and my aunt Iris might have been... good friends a long time ago.' Florence continued to stare at Lettie until she felt her cheeks flaring red.

'And what makes you think that?'

'I found a photo in Claude's archives of the two of them together.'

Florence blinked rapidly. 'Did Claude let you into his cottage?'

'He did, after a little persuasion.'

'You seem to be rather good at persuading people, Miss Starcross, including my grandson.' She held out her hand. 'Let me see.'

Lettie gave her the photo and Florence stared at it for a moment before handing it back.

'That's the two of them together, yes. Is that all you have to show me? My grandson was rather enigmatic.'

'I wondered if Cornelius and Iris went out together?'

'Out together?'

'I mean, were they sweethearts, back then?'

Florence sighed. 'Why do you want to know this? Why on earth does it matter to you?'

Lettie took a deep breath. It was time to tell the whole truth and hope that Florence could shed some light on the mystery. 'Because of the last thing Iris said to me before she died.'

When Florence carefully set down her cup on the small table next to her, her hand was shaking slightly.

'When exactly did your great-aunt die?'

'About six weeks ago. She'd been ill for some time.'

However many times she said it, her voice always caught in her throat. A spark of sympathy flared in Florence's eyes. 'She must have been approaching a hundred years old.'

'She was ninety-nine.'

'Then she was fortunate to have had so long,' muttered Florence, her eyes hardening. Lettie bit down hard on her lower lip to stop the tears that were threatening to fall. 'So what did she say to you before she died?'

Lettie shivered, thinking back to those final few moments when Iris bridged the gap between life and death.

'She said "Find out for me, darling girl."'

Florence frowned. 'That makes no sense. Find out what exactly?'

'Find out more about this, I think.'

Lettie undid the clasp of the necklace that was beneath her sundress and passed it without a word to Florence, who studied the small filigree key nestling in her palm.

'Is this what Corey meant when he said you had something to show me? Where did you get this?'

'Iris wore it every day.' The chain dangled through Florence's fingers, catching beams of sunlight streaming through the window. 'And I found this in her handbag after she… she passed away.'

Lettie pulled the envelope from her handbag and, taking out the paper inside, handed it to Florence, who read the words before putting her hand to her mouth. To Lettie's horror, her face suddenly crumpled and a tear ran down her wrinkled cheek. Lettie fished in her bag for a clean tissue which she handed over.

'I'm so sorry, Mrs Allford. I hate upsetting you, but is that your brother's writing?'

Florence nodded, dabbing at her eyes with the tissue. 'It is.' She read it aloud. '*Sit where I sat, darling girl, with the key to my heart and all will become clear.* All these years I've wondered what he said.'

The words were uttered so quietly, Lettie had to lean forward to catch them. 'Did you know about the key and this letter already?'

Florence crumpled the tissue into a ball and drew back her frail shoulders.

'I delivered that envelope from my brother to your great-aunt on the day that he went off to war. The last day that I ever saw him.' She stared at her hands for a moment. 'I peeped inside. I wasn't supposed to but I was curious. What was my brother sending to Iris Starcross? I saw the necklace but I never read the letter. I already felt guilty enough for peeking.'

She picked up the letter again, her mouth moving slightly as she re-read the words.

'Do you know what it means?' asked Lettie gently.

Florence shrugged. 'A declaration of love, I presume.'

'And the key? Do you know what it opens?'

Disappointment flooded through Lettie when the elderly woman shook her head. 'I have no idea. Perhaps it opens nothing and you're here, raking up the past, for nothing.'

'Perhaps.'

She should leave it. Lettie knew she should stop asking questions now she'd ascertained that Florence was as much in the dark as her. But having a chance to find out more about Iris as a young woman and the man who'd seemingly loved her was too tempting. 'I'm so sorry that your brother never had the chance to live a long life. What sort of a man was he?'

'A good one.' Florence gave a long sigh that seemed to hang in the air. 'He was annoying at times, as all older brothers are, and always playing jokes on me. Things were never quite what they seemed with Cornelius. But he was kind and gentle and artistic. He was training to be a carpenter, and he was a poet. He'd sit for hours up at Cora Head or at his desk upstairs when the weather turned, writing his poetry. He made the desk himself. He had real talent.'

'Did he write poems for Iris?' asked Lettie gently.

'Probably.'

Florence steepled her fingers in her lap and closed her eyes for a moment, breathing in and out so heavily, Lettie began to get worried. Was revisiting the past too much for her?

But then she opened her eyes and there was the hint of a smile.

'Cornelius was my big brother and the apple of my eye. Do you have an older sibling, Miss Starcross?'

'I have an older brother and sister.'

'And are you close?'

Lettie shrugged. 'Fairly close, I suppose.'

'Cornelius and I were very close, even though he was a lot older than me. My mother was always busy working so Cornelius helped to bring me up. He'd take me swimming and walking across the headland, pointing out the wild flowers and the seals swimming in the bay. I adored him.'

'You must have been devastated when he died.'

'It was a difficult time for many reasons.'

Florence's mouth pulled into a thin line as she handed the letter and necklace back to Lettie.

'I think perhaps you need to leave now, Miss Starcross. I've seen what you have to show me and I've told you I delivered these items to your great-aunt, even though my parents would have been furious if they'd known. But I don't know what they mean. The past stays in the past and I'm afraid I can't help you.'

When she pushed herself to her feet, Lettie took her cue and stood up. She looped her bag over her body and walked to the door. But she looked back before stepping into the narrow hallway.

'Thank you for your time, Mrs Allford. Can I ask you one more question? Why would your parents have been angry with you for delivering this envelope to Iris?'

'They wanted us to have nothing to do with your great-aunt after Cornelius went to war.'

'But why? I'm sorry. I know it's hard for you to talk about this but I just don't understand why your parents were so against Iris.'

Florence met Lettie's gaze. 'Because it was all her fault, of course.'

'What was her fault?' asked Lettie slowly.

'Everything. Iris was responsible for Cornelius dying, and for all that followed.'

A clock ticking on the mantelpiece fractured the silence as Lettie reeled from Florence's words.

'But your brother died in the war.'

'He shouldn't have gone to war at all, Miss Starcross. That's the whole point.' Florence almost spat out the words. 'He had a problem with his lungs that should have kept him out of the forces and we were pleased that he was safe. We were hearing such terrible news from the front. Two young men in the village had already been killed. Their poor, poor families were destroyed, and Cornelius said he would stay with us. He stood with me on the headland and told me not to worry because he'd never leave me.' She brushed a hand across her face as though to steady herself. 'But then Iris changed everything.'

'I still don't understand.'

'Your great-aunt was a wicked woman. She encouraged my brother to go to war.'

'She'd never have done that,' said Lettie quietly, finding it hard to breathe. '*Why* would she have done that?'

'She didn't like having a sweetheart who wasn't bravely fighting. That's what my parents said. She was embarrassed that her boyfriend was still here in Heaven's Cove when other men were in uniform, fighting for our freedom. So he fudged his papers and lied about his health and joined up. Your great-aunt wore his key around her neck for the rest of her long life not because she loved him but because she felt guilty.'

Florence's expression suddenly softened and she sank back down into her chair. 'I'm sorry, Miss Starcross. I know you loved your great-aunt but that's the long and the short of it. My brother loved Iris to the end. He wanted to leave her the desk he'd spent hours making but my parents would have none of it. They ignored the instructions he'd left them and the Starcrosses were never spoken of again.'

'Is that why they left Heaven's Cove?'

'They weren't popular in the village after Cornelius died.'

It suddenly all made sense. This was the scandal her mother had talked about, and the reason Iris had rarely talked about her youth, or the beautiful place where she grew up.

'So they were hounded out.'

'It was their decision to up sticks and go.'

Lettie took in a deep breath, her mind still reeling.

'I believe that Iris was truly heartbroken by your brother's death.'

Florence shook her head and stared out of the window at puffs of white cloud. 'At first, maybe. Until someone else came along.'

'Mrs Allford, I don't think anyone else ever came along. My great-aunt lived alone to the very end.'

'So she never married or had children?'

'No. I don't remember her ever being in a relationship.'

'But she obviously never mentioned my brother to you.'

'No, she didn't. But she wore that key around her neck every day and I found that letter stuffed into the lining of her handbag after she died. As though it was precious and she couldn't bear to be parted from it.'

Florence stared at her for a moment before giving a sad smile.

'It's all in the past now, Miss Starcross. It's all long gone and we'd best move on. You too. Go back to London and remember Iris as she was in your eyes. Thank you for showing me those mementos of my brother. Now, I daresay you can see yourself out.'

Lettie wandered slowly through the village. For the first time, she hardly noticed the pretty winding lanes and historic cottages with tiny front gardens filled with flowers.

Florence's revelations had hit her for six. She couldn't believe that kind, gentle Iris had encouraged anyone to go to war, let alone the man that she loved. If Iris *had* done that, the guilt of his death would have haunted her.

Florence was wrong that the past stayed in the past. Whatever had truly happened eighty years ago was spilling over, like an unstoppable wave about to engulf the present. Lettie shivered, even though the sun was warm today, and quickened her pace towards Driftwood House – the house that had been Iris's home until she and her family were more or less run out of the village, by the sound of it.

As she walked, Lettie took Iris's key from her pocket and fastened it back around her neck. Far from putting her off from finding out any more, Florence's tale had galvanised Lettie to discover the real truth, whatever it might be.

Chapter Seventeen

Lettie rolled over and groaned. Her bed here at the top of Driftwood House was comfy enough but sleep was eluding her.

She'd been woken by gulls screeching as a pale dawn spread across the sky, chasing away the shadows in her bedroom, and immediately her head was filled with worries and concerns: why did she feel guilty for taking a few days away from family responsibilities; why was she procrastinating when it came to looking for a new job; and, most pressing of all, did Iris, the great-aunt she loved and missed so much, really encourage a man she cared about to go to war when he didn't need to?

There was something else Florence had said that was running on a loop through Lettie's mind. Cornelius had wanted to leave the desk he made to Iris in the event of his death – the desk where he'd sat for hours writing poetry. *Sit where I sat, darling girl, and all will become clear.* Maybe the mysterious key fitted a lock in the desk, but how would she ever get to see it?

Lettie groaned again before swinging her legs out of bed and stretching her arms above her head. Rather than lying here, stewing in the thoughts going round her head, she would take an early walk into the village. There was something she wanted to do.

Lettie slipped quietly out of the house, her hair still damp from the shower. The grass was wet with dew and wisps of navy cloud were drifting across the sky. It was glorious out here, with the sun rising above the horizon and splashing the sky with a palette of pink and gold. The air was warm already and carried a tang of salt and sea.

Walking to the cliff edge, Lettie began to pick some of the bright wildflowers littering the grass. And, when she had a good bunch, she made her way down the cliff path, marvelling at the views across the rolling ocean.

Heaven's Cove was empty of tourists, its narrow winding streets free of bustle and shops still closed, except for the newsagent's. The newsagent waved at Lettie as she walked past and she waved back, feeling a flush of pleasure as if she belonged in this historic village.

Making her way along Weaver's Row, Lettie saw the war memorial in the middle of the green, its stone glowing in the early morning sunshine. Delving into her bag, she found a pen, and an elastic hair tie which she used to secure the flowers together in a tidy bunch. Then, she pulled a piece of paper from the tiny notebook she always carried.

In loving memory of Cornelius Allford, a brave man who was and is loved, she wrote, before pushing the note through the hair tie and placing the flowers on the memorial plinth. They were a splash of colour against the pale stone.

Lettie bowed her head for a moment, thinking of the young man who had loved her great-aunt; the young man whose life was cut cruelly short. And she thought of the grief Iris and his family must have felt. A grief compounded for her great-aunt by being blamed for his death.

It was such a sad story, and one that felt unfinished. Both Iris and Cornelius were now gone, but the consequences of decisions made by them and in their name were still rippling down the decades, causing anger and pain.

'It's surely time to lay things to rest,' said Lettie out loud, before looking around to make sure that no one had heard the weird outsider talking to herself. She was still alone, so she traced her finger across Cornelius's name, etched into the stone. Quite how she was going to lay things to rest wasn't yet certain but, the more she thought about it, the more she wondered if his old desk was important.

Lettie didn't feel like going back to Driftwood House so she walked through the village, pausing at the quayside to watch fishermen unloading their catches, as gulls wheeled overhead. The acrid tang of fish followed her as she went past the castle ruins and Liam's farm, until she reached the cove. The sun was now a brilliant globe, chasing away the night and painting broad strokes of gold and orange across the heavens.

It was really warm already and Lettie sat on the deserted sand, watching small waves break on the shore before rushing back to the huge body of water. She closed her eyes for a moment and listened to the cry of seagulls overhead and the soft whoosh of waves. She felt close to Iris here and could imagine her sitting beside her on the soft sand.

She would give Lettie a hug, followed, no doubt, by advice on her job dilemma. Her family would encourage her to apply for any sort of customer service work that might be available. Lettie could hear her mum's voice in her head: *You've got bills to pay so you can't be picky.* But Iris would say… What would she say? *Follow your heart, Lettie. Be brave and do what you truly want to do.*

Iris had known what Lettie truly wanted to do: study history while doing a job that took her into the world of the past. But that had never happened and now she was twenty-nine years old with too many responsibilities to veer from the path she was on. Unless she was brave. Was she brave?

Lettie opened her eyes and stared at the sea which had turned silver-blue as the sun nudged its way fully over the horizon.

Before she had time to change her mind, she pulled off her sandals and marched down to the waterline. The sea was calm and couldn't harm her. Suddenly a wave burst onto the sand and a curve of bubbling water rushed towards her toes.

She stepped back, her heart hammering. This was pathetic. Of course she wasn't brave enough to change the direction of her life when she didn't even have the courage to step into the sea.

She stood, hands on her hips, looking out at the water, for ages, so lost in thought, she didn't hear heavy breathing until it was almost next to her.

Startled, she turned around to see Corey standing, panting, bent over with his hands on his thighs.

'I thought that was you. What are you doing here so early in the morning?' he puffed. He was wearing black shorts and a pale blue T-shirt with blue trainers.

Lettie felt disorientated at seeing him suddenly appear.

'I couldn't sleep.'

'Too much on your mind?'

'You could say that.' She hesitated. 'I need to thank you for encouraging your gran to have a word with me.'

'Hmm.' Corey looked down and shuffled his feet into the sand. 'From what I hear, that didn't go too well. I hope she wasn't too... unwelcoming.'

'She made her feelings towards my great-aunt quite clear, but losing her brother when she was young must have been awful.'

'It was.'

Corey looked at her for a moment, as though he was going to say something more about his grandmother, but then he looked down at her toes, curling into the wet sand.

'So are you going for a paddle?'

'No, I don't think so.'

'Why not? It's late summer and not so cold.'

He must be joking, thought Lettie, as the dying edge of a wave washed over her toes. It was absolutely freezing.

'I don't feel like it.'

'So why are you standing here with bare feet?'

What was Corey Allford, the water police? 'If you must know, I was trying to summon up the courage to paddle.'

She waited for him to laugh but he tilted his head to one side and looked at her. 'Why would it take courage?'

Lettie swallowed and blinked to shake off the image of cold water closing over her head. 'Because I'm fed up with being frightened of the sea. Fear of deep water is one of my…' She paused, trying to find the right word to convey the terror that gripped her. 'It's one of my demons, I suppose. But I wanted to prove that I could do it.' She pulled her shoulders back, keen to move on from the subject. 'So what are you doing on the beach at this time of the morning?'

'Running.' He pointed at his shorts and trainers. 'I often run at this time, before the streets and the beach are full of people. It's a good way of clearing my head of *my* demons.' He stopped speaking and stared straight at her. 'So are you going to paddle then, or just talk about it?'

'I'm… not sure.'

'I can help you if you'd like.'

'Why would you do that?'

'Because it's a shame to let fear rule your life.'

'Fear of the sea hardly rules my life. London doesn't have a lot of coastline.'

When Corey shrugged and turned away, Lettie had second thoughts. 'Although…'

'Although?'

She took a deep breath. 'I do want to paddle. I'm just not sure I can. Pathetic, huh?'

'Come on,' said Corey gruffly, bending to pull off his trainers and socks. He threw them across the sand, farther away from the tide, and strode into the waves until they were over his ankles. Then he held out his hand.

Lettie hesitated. What was the point of this? She could go back to London and never set foot near the sea again, if she chose.

'Are you a scaredy cat?' Corey's face creased into a smile as he waggled his fingers at her, his arm still outstretched.

'Definitely not.' She shook her head. 'Possibly.'

'Don't worry, scaredy cat.' He grinned. 'I promise that I won't let you drown. That wouldn't do my reputation on the lifeboat much good. So what do you reckon?'

Before she could chicken out, Lettie grasped his hand and stepped into the water. Jeez, it was even colder than she'd thought. An incoming wave broke around her feet and swirled freezing water around her calves. She could feel her chest tightening and her throat constricting. She took in short, shallow breaths and tried to resist the urge to run back to the safety of dry sand.

It's ridiculous, she told herself, *the sea is calm and it's not even reached your knees. Young children do this all the time.* But images of cold, dark water crashing over her head began to swirl through her mind. She couldn't breathe.

'You're all right,' said a low, calm voice beside her and she felt Corey's hand tighten around hers. 'The sea is really calm today. Do you want to go farther out or back to the beach?'

'A bit farther out,' she gasped, desperate to be brave, like Iris would have encouraged her to be.

'Come on then, step by step. And remember, if you ever lose your footing in the sea and you can't get up, try to float on your back.'

Slowly, they shuffled farther out from the beach and the water got higher, until it was past her knees and halfway up her thighs. Water splashed, leaving dark marks on her pale blue shorts.

She could feel her heart hammering in her chest and suddenly it all became too much – the swell of the water and the memories of falling and not being able to push her way back to the air. Memories of not being able to breathe.

'I'm sorry,' she gasped. 'It's so stupid.' Tears were running down her cheeks and she was so agitated, the pull of a wave destabilised her and she wobbled and almost fell. But suddenly she felt arms around her, grounding her, and when she opened her eyes, her face was against Corey's chest.

He held her tightly for a moment before sweeping her into his arms and carrying her out of the waves and back onto the sand.

'There.'

When he put her feet back on solid ground, she stood for a moment, enjoying the sensation of her head on his chest, before he dropped his arms. She stepped backwards, feeling foolish. Here was a man who put himself in danger to rescue people from mountainous seas, and she'd had a panic attack while paddling.

'Sorry,' she muttered, using the heels of her hands to rub her eyes.

'No, I'm sorry. I shouldn't have urged you to come into the water. I didn't realise quite how scared you are.'

'It's not your fault. I was just trying to be brave, and failing horribly.'

Lettie bent to put her sandals on but Corey sat on the sand and pulled her down next to him.

'Sit down for a minute and tell me what happened to make you so afraid.'

And he looked so concerned, his face so close to hers, Lettie decided to tell him.

'I almost drowned when I was eight years old and on a family trip to the Essex coast. The rest of my family didn't notice when I went under for the third time, but Iris did and she waded in, dress tucked into her knickers, to rescue me. It scared me so much I've hated the water ever since.'

Corey's mouth twitched in the corner. 'Your great-aunt sounds like quite a woman.'

'She was. She reminds me of your gran. She was fierce and resilient, and stubborn at times.'

'That does indeed sound like Gran,' murmured Corey.

'Did your gran tell you that she and her parents thought Iris was responsible for her brother's death?'

'She told me last night.'

Lettie looked at the waves, breaking gently on the shore, that terrified her so much.

'I can't believe my great-aunt would encourage the man she loved to go to war. I knew her so well.'

'Maybe you're right, but she was younger then, and even the people you know the best and trust the most can surprise you.'

Lettie glanced at Corey, who was staring out to sea too. From the bitter tone in his voice, she wasn't sure he was talking about Iris any more.

He suddenly shook his head and gave her a smile that didn't quite reach his eyes. 'So did talking to Gran help at all?'

'Kind of. It explained why Iris rarely spoke of her life in Devon and never wanted to come back to Heaven's Cove. But it doesn't solve the mystery of this.' Lettie felt for the key around her neck and ran it along the chain. 'Although…'

'Although?'

Lettie shifted round in the sand until she was facing him. 'Your gran mentioned in passing that your great-uncle left instructions for his parents – if he died, I suppose – that his writing desk should go to Iris.'

Corey nodded. 'Gran opened up about the whole thing last night and showed me the letter he left for his parents to open if he died.'

Lettie winced, imagining how that letter must have taunted Cornelius's mum and dad, waiting anxiously for news of their son as the war raged on. They must have hoped against hope that they would never ever have to open it. But one day the worst had happened and the letter had been read.

'What did it say?'

'It was strange reading it after all this time – like words from beyond the grave.' Corey swallowed and rubbed his hand across his eyes. 'It said he was sorry for causing his parents such upset and he left most of his meagre belongings to Gran. He also said not to blame Iris and that he'd like her to have his writing desk to remember him by.'

'But his parents did still blame Iris, and they never gave her the desk.'

'They never even told her about the desk, according to Gran.'

'It's just that I've been wondering if maybe my key fits that desk. *Sit where I sat, darling girl...* That's what the letter to Iris said. And your gran said Cornelius used to sit there for hours. Do you still have it?'

Corey frowned. 'Yes, it's still upstairs. But I don't think any of the drawers have a lock.'

'Are you sure?'

'Pretty sure. And none of the drawers are actually locked, even if they do have keyholes.'

Lettie sighed with disappointment, noticing that damp from the sand was seeping through the backside of her shorts. She'd started to feel so certain that the desk held all the answers, but maybe that was only because it felt like her last chance – her last chance to solve the mystery of the key for Iris and perhaps even to clear her name. Some detective she'd turned out to be!

'Never mind,' she told Corey. 'It was a long shot anyway. I hope your gran wasn't too upset by me bringing up the past.'

Corey shrugged. 'She seemed fine last night and more able to talk about the things that have bothered her for years. And they seem to have bothered her more over the last few months, since she became more unwell.'

'I didn't realise she was ill.'

'She has a lung condition. That's why I've moved in, to keep an eye on her. But the doctors say she'll go on for a while yet.'

'You're a good grandson.'

Corey shrugged again. 'Gran was good to me when I was growing up and it's only right that I repay her.'

'I am sorry for bothering her though.'

'Don't worry about it. These things can't stay hidden forever. Letting things fester only leads to heartache and pain.'

Again, Lettie got the feeling he'd strayed off topic and was talking about something else entirely. She remembered Rosie's words, that Corey's marriage had ended acrimoniously and she itched to ask about it. But she'd already poked her nose enough into the Allfords' affairs.

She got to her feet and shook off sand.

'Thank you for getting your gran to speak to me, and… for that.' She wrinkled her nose and nodded towards the waves which were retreating, leaving in their wake curved lines of foam that fizzed into nothing.

Corey got to his feet too, being careful, Lettie noticed, not to shake sand over her.

'I suppose I'd better finish my run.'

'And I'll head back to Driftwood House for breakfast. Rosie will wonder where I've gone. So thanks for the paddle and the chat. It can get a bit lonely actually, being on holiday on your own.'

Corey finished lacing up his trainers and stood up straight. 'What are you doing for the rest of the day?'

Lettie thought for a moment. 'I think I'll see if I can explore Dartmoor. Iris hardly ever mentioned Heaven's Cove, but she had a framed photograph of a Dartmoor waterfall on the wall of her flat. I think it was the same place as the painting on your gran's wall.'

'Really?' Corey pushed his hands into the pockets of his shorts while Lettie tried not to stare at his tanned, muscled legs. 'Getting to Dartmoor by bus is a bit of a pain but I'm free later and could take you. I can borrow Gran's car.'

'You and me?' asked Lettie, thrown by the invitation.

'That's right.' He gave her a small smile. 'No worries if you don't fancy it.'

'No, I mean yes, I do fancy it, if you've got the time. Though I'm not sure your gran will approve of you borrowing her car in order to spend time with a Starcross.'

Corey grinned. 'I think she's starting to regret being abrupt with you yesterday. Perhaps she's starting to realise that, as you're not Iris, you're not culpable for her sins.'

'Sins is a strong word,' said Lettie with a frown.

'Sins is entirely the wrong word. Sorry.' He gave her a bigger smile this time. 'It's early in the morning and I haven't yet had the necessary caffeine intake to enable me to fire on all cylinders. If you're up for a trip to Dartmoor, I'll be free at midday. Could you meet me at the cottage and we can go straight from there? I'm not sure Gran's old banger will make it to the top of the cliff road.'

'Yes, that's fine. Though I'm not sure your gran will be delighted to see me.'

'She'll be out, visiting her friend Maude. They have lunch together.'

'OK. I'll see you later, then.'

He ran off across the beach, every step puffing up a small cloud of sand. Lettie wasn't sure if the butterflies in her stomach meant she was happy, or nervous, or a mixture of both. Why on earth had she said yes to a trip that wasn't going to be at all relaxing?

You know why, said a little voice in her head that sounded rather like Iris.

'Hey, hold on a minute!'

Lettie's heart sank when she spotted Simon heading towards her, weaving between the tourists who'd started arriving in the village.

'Hi, Simon. Are you still here?'

'Of course.' He smoothed down his immaculate blond hair and gave her a very obvious once-over. 'I don't give up easily and there's still more to be done here. What have you been up to?'

'What do you mean?' asked Lettie, her heart suddenly hammering as she remembered resting her head on Corey's chest.

'You're covered in sand.'

'Oh, I went to the beach and sat on the sand for a while. It's a beautiful cove.'

'Yeah, not bad,' said Simon, as Lettie brushed at her gritty legs. 'Where are you going now?'

'I'm heading back to Driftwood House. I haven't had breakfast yet.'

'I'll walk with you for a while.' Lettie's heart sank even further when he fell into step beside her, his polished shoes squeaking slightly with every pace. 'So what have you been doing round here?' he asked again.

'Oh, you know. What people always do on holiday – seeing the sights, relaxing, eating my weight in ice cream.'

'Ha, yeah. The local ice cream isn't bad.' He gave her a sideways glance as they walked. 'I haven't seen you in the pub.'

'I haven't been in there for a couple of days.'

He stopped walking abruptly. 'I was wondering… if you fancied having a drink one evening? Perhaps tomorrow, if you're not busy?'

Lettie appreciated being asked out on two dates within the space of ten minutes. It had never happened before and Kelly, knee-deep in Tilly's nappies, would be mega impressed. But she winced inside at the thought of spending an evening with Simon. That didn't sound like fun, but how could she be busy when she was on holiday on her own?

'I'm not sure what I'm doing tomorrow so I can't commit to anything.'

'Well, I'll be there at seven if you fancy a date *avec moi*.' He winked. 'Anyways, have you found out any more about that woman you were interested in?'

'Do you mean my great-aunt?'

'That's the one.'

'Not really.'

'And what about Cora Head? Did you go up there?'

'I had a walk there a couple of days ago.'

'What did you think?'

'It's a wonderful place. The views are magnificent.'

'Absolutely, which is why it's such a prime spot for building.'

They walked a few paces in silence before Simon suddenly blurted out: 'I know you've seen Mrs Allford.'

'Really? How do you know that?'

'I saw you going into her cottage yesterday.'

'Are you following me, Simon?' asked Lettie, suddenly feeling stalked. Was this why he wanted to go for a drink? To quiz her about Florence?

'Ha, of course not. This is a very small village and I just happened to be—'

'Staking out Florence's home.'

Simon gave a mirthless laugh. 'You're very funny, Lettie. I just wondered if the subject of the headland had come up during your conversation?'

'I'm afraid it didn't.'

'Not at all?'

'Not once.'

When he shook his head, a spicy aroma of aftershave wafted towards her. 'That's a shame. It really would be for the best if Mrs Allford – Florence – sold the land to me.'

'The best for you.'

'Good for me, obviously, but good for her too because just think what she could do with the money. She could move somewhere far more luxurious.'

'I don't think she wants to move.'

'She just doesn't realise what other options are available to her.'

'You really shouldn't be…' Lettie stopped walking so suddenly, the man walking behind ran into her. 'Sorry!' She winced as the man stalked off, complaining bitterly.

'Are you all right?' asked Simon, doubling back.

'I'm fine, but you need to leave Florence alone,' said Lettie passionately, surprised at how protective she felt towards the elderly woman. 'She's given you your answer and I'm sorry it's not what you want to hear, but that's that.'

'And that is where you're entirely wrong. You wouldn't believe how many people have said no to me.'

'I really would,' muttered Lettie, desperately looking around for an escape.

'But after a little persuasion and persistence on my part, they change their minds. Just like that.'

'Well, you need to leave Florence alone. She's not particularly well and doesn't need any extra stress.'

'Is that right? I didn't know—'

'Oh, is that Claude?' said Lettie, waving wildly towards the quay and determining to give the pub a wide berth tomorrow evening. 'Sorry, Simon, but I said I'd call in to see him. Maybe catch you later.'

With that, she hurried off as fast as she could, vaguely registering that she might have just escaped from the frying pan into the fire because Claude, sitting outside his cottage smoking a pipe, was looking rather alarmed by her wave.

Chapter Eighteen

Claude

So she was coming back. Claude, feeling nervous, tapped out his pipe on the ground and stood up from his doorstep. He sat here most mornings, enjoying the gentle slap of the sea against the quay before the place was overrun with yelling tourists. At least the holidaymakers next door were having a lie-in today and all was blessedly quiet.

He smoothed down his best old jumper, the one he'd put on in case she returned. He'd even tidied up inside, put on a clean pair of jeans and washed his hair. It probably wouldn't matter really, but he'd decided to ask for help and that wasn't something he was used to doing. And for some reason, presenting himself and his home in their best light while seeking Lettie's assistance seemed important.

What was the girl doing? She'd waved and started walking purposefully towards him but now had slowed down, almost as though she'd changed her mind.

Buster suddenly hurtled past him, out of the cottage and up to the girl, who bent to pat him as he leapt up and down. The daft dog really had taken to her.

She said some words into the animal's ear before leading him into the garden.

'Are you talking to my dog?' asked Claude, brushing a trace of breakfast egg from his beard.

'Not really. Well, maybe. Sorry if that's a bit weird.'

Claude stared at her, unsmiling, then he shrugged. 'I talk to Buster all the time. But then I am the local eccentric.'

She didn't know how to take that remark so he smiled, and then she smiled back. She looked pretty, with her long hair pulled back into a ponytail and wearing shorts and a sweatshirt.

'My family thinks I'm slightly eccentric too.'

'Why?'

'Because I'm not like them.'

'Are you more like your great-aunt Iris?'

'Yes, I guess so.'

'She sounds like a good woman. What were you doing with that property man?'

'Trying to escape him, mostly.'

'That sounds very wise. I don't like him much. Shifty eyes.' Claude stepped back and pushed his front door wide open. 'You'd best come in then.'

She knew that he'd tidied up. He could see it in her eyes as she took in that the table was free of dishes, the dog hairs were gone from the sofa, and the layer of dust on the dresser had disappeared. The old dark wood was glowing in a beam of light coming through the small window, and the silver-framed photo that Lettie had taken an interest in the last time she was here had been moved from the back of the dresser to the front.

Was now a good time to ask her? It was probably best not to bombard her the moment she walked through the door, and he needed to build himself up to it.

'Sit down and I'll get the cuttings I found. I went through some of them, looking for wartime information,' he told her. Then he added brusquely, because it was what people usually asked, 'Do you want tea or anything?'

'No, thank you. It's good of you to see me. I almost didn't come back because I thought you might be busy.'

'I said for you to call in, didn't I?'

'You did.'

'Well, then. I'll get the cuttings.'

He went down to the cellar, Buster at his heels, and picked up the small pile of additional cuttings and wartime photos he'd found. He wasn't sure there was anything useful in them but that was for the girl to decide.

By the time he returned, Lettie was standing by the window. The light was shining on her auburn hair, making it glow a rich dark red.

'I was imagining all the people who've lived here over the centuries,' she said. 'They must have all looked out of this window and watched the sea.'

'They respected the sea. It gave them their living. It gave them life and sometimes it took those lives away.'

Claude noticed Lettie shudder before she walked to the sofa and sat down. He passed her the cuttings and she began to leaf through them.

'Have you found out any more about your relative?'

'A little.'

Was now the right time? Before he could think too much about it, Claude moved to the dresser and picked up the photo. The colours had faded almost to sepia, but a middle-aged woman in a boat, with long dark hair, was smiling at the photographer. She was smiling at him.

'I want to ask you something,' he blurted out.

'Of course.' Lettie looked at him expectantly.

Silence stretched between them as a child outside ran by screaming at a seagull.

'It's to do with this photo. The woman in this photo.' Claude closed his eyes for a moment before opening them and staring at Lettie. It had been so long since he'd even mentioned her name out loud. 'I don't like to ask for help. Never have.' He paused, and swallowed. 'But I wondered if you could help me find out what happened to her?'

She looked at him curiously. 'Who is she?'

'She's a woman I used to know.'

'How long ago?'

Claude hesitated, hardly able to believe the answer he was about to give. 'It's been almost forty years since I last saw her.'

'That's a very long time.'

'It is. Yes.'

Claude's mind reeled back over the last four decades. Even though much had happened since then, he felt as though he'd been in limbo all the while. As though real life had stopped the day she left and all that had remained was a façade of what life could be.

'Why are you asking me about her?' asked Lettie, with a gentle tone to her voice that he appreciated. 'Can't your friends in the village help with finding this lady?'

Claude shook his head. 'Belinda has eyes and ears everywhere, and I don't want to be the subject of village gossip. I've always kept myself to myself and that's how I want it to remain.'

He almost said *for as long as I have left*. But that would give the game away, which wouldn't do. If Lettie was sympathetic about his impending demise, as he felt sure she would be, he might break.

'I'm not sure how I can help you, Claude.'

'Can't you try to find her on your computer? I thought you could find everybody on the internet these days, and you seem interested in chasing down people from long ago.'

'I can look online, if you give me her details, but couldn't you do that yourself?'

Claude huffed. 'I've never had a computer and don't know anything about all this new technology. It does nothing but cause problems from what I read about the social stuff.'

'Social media can be challenging at times.'

'All those people shouting into a void.' Claude shuddered. 'And the outsiders in Heaven's Cove, most of them are too busy looking at their phones to truly notice the colour of the sea and the passing seasons making their mark on the countryside. I don't want anything to do with that. But I would like to know what happened to Esther. If you don't mind, that is.' There, he'd said her name out loud.

He studied his hands in his lap. It had cost him a great deal to ask for help, and maybe an outsider wasn't the best person to ask. She'd come to Heaven's Cove to find out about her great-aunt, not to get embroiled in a pathetic old romance that had petered out because Esther hadn't loved him enough.

Lettie stared at him for a moment before giving him a smile. 'You'd better tell me about her and exactly what you'd like me to do.'

Claude's shoulders relaxed and he felt a prickling in his eyes that he studiously ignored.

'Will what I tell you stay between us?'

'Of course. I can keep a secret.'

She was a stranger and Claude shouldn't trust her. He didn't trust many people these days, but there was something about her that reminded him of the woman he'd lost. And sometimes in life you had to take risks.

He picked up the photo and passed it to Lettie.

'I met Esther when I was in my early thirties, at a large restaurant business that we used to sell our fish to, along the coast. There was a man there who worked in the office, a man with no sense of humour and a cruel mouth. I didn't trust him but I liked his wife when I bumped into her a couple of times. That was my Esther.'

He folded his large hands on his lap. 'I thought nothing much of it but then I saw her sitting at Cora Head one day, looking so sad. I said hello and we chatted, about nothing really – the weather, the state of the world, and I made her laugh.' He stared into the distance for a moment, the ghost of a smile on his lips. 'We started meeting there more regularly, just to talk, and, well… she became very dear to me.'

He lapsed into silence.

'Did anyone else know?' asked Lettie, after a few moments.

Claude shook his head. He hadn't told anyone this story, not really, but now it was all spilling out.

'There was nothing much to know. It was all very chaste. You youngsters today would laugh at us. She was a woman of honour and didn't want to cheat on her husband. But we kept on meeting. We were very discreet and kept out of Heaven's Cove completely.'

'And you came to really care about her?'

'She was the love of my life.' Claude stared at Lettie defiantly, daring her to mock him. But he saw nothing but sadness in her big hazel eyes.

'What happened?' she asked softly.

'I think her husband must have found out, or suspected at the very least. He suddenly got a new job miles away and told her they were moving. Just like that. No discussion, no chance of compromise. She wasn't going to go with him at first. She was going to tell him the marriage was over and stay with me. She told me she loved me.'

A silence stretched between them broken only by the steady ticking of the clock on the mantelpiece.

'But?' prompted Lettie gently, after a while.

'But she changed her mind and moved away with him, up country, and that was that.'

'Do you know why she changed her mind?'

He was getting to the heart of the story now and suddenly stumbled over his words. 'She... she found out she was pregnant. I told her... I said I'd take on the child as mine but she couldn't do it, not to the child, nor to her husband. She must have still loved him, I suppose.'

'Did she keep in touch with you?'

'No. She said it was best to have a clean break. And she was right. There was no future in it so what was the point in prolonging things? It was better for her and better for the child. She was a religious woman with a strong moral code and she didn't find our... friendship easy.'

Claude stared disconsolately out of the window, as Buster laid his head in his lap. He pushed his fingers through the dog's thick fur. There was no point in telling Lettie the rest of it... that she'd sent a note telling him that their relationship – such as it was – was over. That he'd had a premonition of that the last time he'd seen her and had deliberately not watched her walk away because it was too painful.

'I'm so sorry, Claude. But that was a long time ago. Why do you want to contact her now?'

'I'm seventy-five years old, Miss Starcross, and my health's not what it was.' The doctor's face when he'd given him the news flashed through Claude's mind but he pushed the memory away. Now wasn't the time to get maudlin over something he couldn't change. 'I won't go on for ever and I need to know what happened to Esther before I go.'

'You're not going anywhere soon though, are you?' asked Lettie, as though it really mattered.

'Soon enough. But if I'm asking too much, it doesn't matter. I don't expect you to care about someone like me.'

But Lettie brushed her hand across her cheek, as though it was wet, and smiled.

'Of course I'll help you. I'll do my best but I can't guarantee that I can find her.'

'I'm only asking you to try.' He gave Lettie a small smile. 'I appreciate your kindness.'

Lettie left, ten minutes later, with the old newspaper cuttings, and a piece of paper with Esther's details written down in his heavy capitals.

She'd done a quick check on her phone before leaving, but couldn't find an Esther Kenvale of the right sort of age.

Perhaps she's passed away. Claude could hardly bear to think of that and couldn't say the words, but Lettie had guessed what he was thinking. She'd reassured him that there would probably have been some mention of it, an obituary or the like, in the cloud thing that the youngsters all talked about.

Claude picked up Esther's photo and spoke to the woman smiling back at him, as he'd often done over the long, lonely years.

'I'm coming to find you, my love. But do you want to be found?'

Chapter Nineteen

Lettie

'Bye, Lettie. Have a great time,' shouted Rosie, waving from the doorway of Driftwood House. 'Enjoy the sandwiches.'

Lettie waved back, wishing she'd kept quiet about Corey driving her to Dartmoor. She'd only mentioned it because Rosie was trying to press a bus timetable on her, and she'd been surprised by the enthusiasm with which Rosie had greeted the news.

'That's wonderful,' she'd exclaimed, smiling broadly. 'Corey deserves some fun after what happened with his wife. His life is all about work and helping other people at the moment.'

Her comments – as well as making Lettie desperate to find out exactly what *had* happened with his wife – had made Lettie feel, rather absurdly, that she had to ensure the outing went especially well. So she'd spent longer than usual choosing what to wear, from her limited stock of clothes, and she'd brushed her hair into some semblance of order and had even put on a little make-up. She wore it all the time in London but here, under the summer sun in Heaven's Cove, sunblock and a slick of lip gloss had seemed sufficient.

The good weather had brought out hordes of meandering tourists today who blocked her way as she walked as briskly as she could through the lanes towards the Allfords' house.

She glanced at Claude's cottage as she went past the quay but he was nowhere to be seen. Did he regret telling her his story? she wondered. Lettie hoped not because she felt honoured, as well as surprised, that he'd shared it with her. And even though she now had an extra mystery to try and solve, at least this one involved people who were both – hopefully – still alive.

The sun was hot on her back as she climbed the hill towards Florence's cottage, looking forward to exploring Dartmoor but feeling anxious all the same. And the flutters in her stomach only got worse with every step until she felt a bundle of nerves by the time she knocked on the door.

She smoothed down her hair and plastered on a smile when she heard footsteps in the hallway, but her smile froze when the door was pulled open by Florence.

'Oh!' Lettie involuntarily took a step backwards. 'I thought you'd be out. Corey mentioned that you'd be seeing a friend. He and I are…'

Lettie petered off, wondering if Florence was about to put the kybosh on their afternoon trip. She'd hardly approve of her beloved grandson fraternising with a Starcross. But the elderly woman pulled the door fully open and stepped to the side.

'You'd best come in for a minute. He's out the back, fixing my washing line.'

'Are you sure?' asked Lettie, hovering on the doorstep.

'I wouldn't have said so, otherwise. You can wait in the kitchen.'

Lettie followed her into the small room that overlooked the garden. Outside, she could see Corey hard at work securing a line to the back wall.

'The damn thing fell down this morning and brought my clean clothes with it.' Florence nodded at one of the kitchen chairs. 'Sit down, will you? You're making the place look untidy.'

Lettie sat as directed and looked around her. The Shaker kitchen units were painted cream and pots marked *coffee*, *tea* and *sugar* were lined up on the wooden worktop. The teapot was sporting a striped woollen tea cosy and half a dozen yellow egg cups were sitting on a shelf.

Lettie drummed her feet against the chair, feeling acutely uncomfortable. It was awkward being alone with Florence after the way they'd last parted, and it was going to be rather awkward being alone with Corey for the afternoon. She sighed quietly, wishing she'd caught the bus instead. What on earth had made her agree to this?

'Was it you who left flowers at the war memorial?' asked Florence, bending to take a golden-brown cake from the oven. 'The ones I saw this morning.'

'Uh-huh, that was me,' said Lettie, wondering if she was about to be berated for it.

Florence carefully turned out the cake onto a wire tray before asking: 'Why did you do that?'

'I wanted to pay my respects.'

'Even though you didn't know him?'

Lettie thought for a moment as a delicious aroma of cooked currants and sugar filled the kitchen. 'I might not have known your brother but Iris did and I know that she never forgot him. Whatever you might think of her, I was with Iris when she died and I'm pretty sure Cornelius was on her mind right until the very end.'

'Hmm.'

'And I'm so sorry that you lost him when he and you were so young. I can't imagine how awful it must have been.'

Florence dropped the cake pan into the sink without looking at Lettie and turned on the tap.

'My grandson says it's not polite or kind of me to take out what happened in the past on you.'

'Did he?' Lettie couldn't imagine saying anything like that to her. Florence might be a lovely kind old lady beneath her spiky façade, but she still scared Lettie a little. 'It's all right, honestly. I understand that you still feel very deeply about it. Who wouldn't?'

'Indeed. Though it's not your fault, is it. Have you found out any more about what my brother's letter might mean?' She glanced at the back door as it swung open. 'Ah, here's Corey. Is the line fixed?'

'Yep, it shouldn't drag all your washing through the dirt again. Oh!' When he spotted Lettie, a smile spread across his face. Then he glanced at his watch. 'I didn't realise how time was getting on. I'm sorry to have kept you waiting, Lettie. Is everything all right in here?'

He looked nervously between the two women, who both nodded.

'I was just asking Miss Starcross if she'd made any headway with unravelling Cornelius's letter. He was never straightforward.'

'Not really.' Lettie paused, wary of upsetting the fragile peace that now seemed to exist between them, but unable to resist trying one more time to find out what the key might open. Corey had said he thought the desk didn't have any locks… but what if he'd been wrong? She took a deep breath. 'Although I did wonder if your brother might have been referring to the desk that he made when he told Iris to "sit where I sat". The desk that he wanted to leave to my great-aunt.'

'I know the desk you mean,' said Florence tartly.

'But there are no locks,' said Corey, stepping forward. 'I checked after what you said at the beach, and the drawers don't lock. They never have. I'm sorry, Lettie.'

So that was that, then. Lettie tried to smile, to show she was grateful to Corey for checking, but made a pretty bad job of it. She hadn't realised quite how much she wanted the desk to hold all the answers.

Florence was watching Lettie, and her face softened. 'The desk is priceless to me but it's nothing out of the ordinary.' She looked at Corey, who gave a slight nod, before asking: 'Would you like to see it?'

There wasn't much point any more, but this was an olive branch indeed. So Lettie smiled and nodded.

'That would be wonderful, if you wouldn't mind.'

'You'd better follow me upstairs then.'

The stairs were narrow and led to a small landing with four doors leading off. Two were open – one to a bathroom with a white enamel basin and bath, and the other to what Lettie assumed must be Corey's bedroom. A thick grey jumper was thrown over the back of a chair and a large pair of blue trainers lay on the floor where they'd been kicked off. The duvet was pulled back on the bed and a pair of cotton pyjama bottoms were half-hidden beneath the cover. Lettie had a sudden mental image of Corey lying spread-eagled and half-naked across the mattress, his dark hair fanning out across the pillow. It was so unexpected she felt her cheeks flush and she was grateful that he hadn't yet followed them upstairs.

'Come along then,' urged Florence, opening one of the closed doors. 'Corey's waiting for you and it'll do him good to get out for the afternoon. He works too hard.'

She was still standing in the doorway when Lettie reached her.

'This was Cornelius's room, Miss Starcross. It's our guest bedroom though it's hardly ever used. It's much as my brother left it.'

Lettie gasped. The room was a social historian's delight. The walls were a pale blue and plain brown curtains hung from a metal rail above the window. The single bed had a metal frame with no headboard and was draped in an apricot satin-valanced cover. To the side of the bed, a small rug covered the bare floorboards and there was the model of an aircraft on the bedside table. A small wardrobe stood in the corner of the room, and a dark-wood writing desk was against the wall, opposite the window.

'Is it all right if I go inside?' asked Lettie.

When Florence nodded, she stepped over the threshold, feeling as though she was entering a museum or sacred space.

Cornelius's books were still stacked on top of the desk which was a solid piece of furniture, functional rather than attractive but obviously made with care. Two large drawers were topped by a flat writing area, above which stood wooden cubbyholes filled with stationery.

'Take a look at the desk if you'd like, Miss Starcross,' said Florence, who'd followed Lettie into the room. 'Cornelius spent hours making it and he was very proud of his handiwork. As my grandson said, it has no locks.'

Lettie stepped closer to the desk and ran her fingers across its smooth surface. She suddenly had a sharp mental image of Cornelius, the man her great-aunt had lost her heart to, sitting here writing the letter to Iris. Before he went to war. Before he never came back.

But Corey and Florence were right. There were definitely no keyholes here. His letter to Iris must have been a simple declaration of love. That was all it could be and Lettie really was chasing ghosts. She suddenly had an overwhelming urge to cry and dug her nails into her palms to stop herself.

'Have you seen enough?' Florence stepped aside for Lettie to leave her brother's room.

'I have. Thank you.' She took a deep breath before blurting out: 'What happened to your brother is so sad and I'm so sorry, Mrs Allford. I'm sorry it ever happened and I'm sorry for bringing it all back up again. I know you loved Cornelius. It's just that I loved Iris too.'

Lettie sniffed as a tear dropped onto Cornelius's desk and rolled along the grain of the wood.

Florence stepped forward and brushed it away.

'Love can be painful, child, but it's far more painful to have never loved at all.' She moved to the door and waited for Lettie to leave the room.

Downstairs, Corey was pacing the small hallway, his body almost filling the narrow space.

'Is everything OK?' he asked, his forehead creased with concern.

'She's seen the desk,' said Florence, carefully minding her step as she came down the stairs. 'And now I need to leave for Maude's or I'll be late. Where exactly are you taking Miss Starcross?'

'To Granite Tor and then I thought perhaps to Kellen Woods. We'll see.'

A look passed between Florence and Corey that Lettie couldn't read. Then the old woman nodded.

'Whatever you think is best.'

Chapter Twenty

Florence's old car had a peculiar fishy smell and, after a while, as they drove through country lanes, Lettie wound down her window and let the warm breeze blow through her hair. The sky was the same vivid blue she'd only seen before in the South of France and the puffs of cloud looked like scoops of vanilla ice cream.

She stared at the vapour trail left by an airplane high above before stealing a glance at Corey. He was sitting up straight, gripping the steering wheel, his eyes fixed on the road ahead which appeared to be getting narrower. The landscape had changed, from picturesque villages surrounded by greenery to more barren land, scattered with huge rocks. She could see for miles.

'Where are we going?' asked Lettie, glancing at the phone in her lap which had just beeped with a text.

Hi. Have got chance of long weekend in France with Laura at end of the month. Am thinking you'll have the kids? Mum won't do it and Jase is hopeless. Daisy x

Daisy's texts always ended with a kiss when she wanted something.

Corey glanced across at her from the road ahead. 'I want to show you a bit of Dartmoor that means a lot to me. If that's all right?'

'That sounds great. I really appreciate you showing me such an amazing place.'

'It's my favourite place in the whole world.'

Lettie's phone beeped again.

Also, parents need someone to clear out their guttering. You're good at finding people so said you'd sort it when you're back. Don't forget they need radiator in kitchen fixed too x

Lettie closed her eyes for a moment.

'Is everything OK?' asked Corey, slowing down and waiting for a brown horse with a white patch on its head to cross the road.

'Yeah, fine. It's just my sister organising my life.'

She laughed so as not to sound too bitter, before typing: *Have you tried asking Ed and Fran to have kids? x* and pressing 'send'.

Daisy's reply was almost immediate: *No point. They're always too busy. But you'll be back by then, won't you? X*

Lettie's fingered hovered over the keys for a moment before she replied: *Not sure, I'm afraid. Might still be in Devon x*

What about Ella's birthday cake and your job? Those glue complaints won't fix themselves came back immediately – with no kiss this time, Lettie noted.

She looked at Corey beside her. He did a job he loved. It wasn't the job for her, clearly – it was far too… watery – but he seemed to find being a fisherman fulfilling. Whereas 'fulfilling' was not the f-word she'd ever used when describing her role with a 'customer dream team'.

Quickly, before she could change her mind, she texted Daisy back: *No longer have a job to rush back for so might stay a bit longer. Will let*

*you know. Think they sell rainbow birthday cakes in Sainsbury's. Phone
signal patchy cos am on Dartmoor x*

That would put the cat among the pigeons. Lettie, feeling bizarrely
brave, switched her phone off and slipped it into her handbag. Now
she could concentrate on the amazing landscape all around her and,
for just a little while, forget about demanding families and lost lovers
and secrets that didn't want to be revealed.

Just when Lettie thought the road was becoming so narrow it was
impassable, Corey swung off and parked on a patch of rough ground.
He switched off the ignition and turned to look at her.

'We're here.'

'Where's here?'

'In the middle of the moor and we can walk to the top of that tor
over there.' He nodded through the windscreen at a high rocky outcrop
that rose above the landscape. 'Are you up for it?'

'Absolutely.'

A fresh breeze ruffled Lettie's hair when she got out of the car, and
whipped at the cotton of her wide grey trousers. She grabbed her green
cardigan from the back of the seat and looped it around her shoulders.

Corey pushed the car keys into his pocket and set off at a cracking
pace, with Lettie trying to keep up. After a few minutes, she stopped
and put her hands on her hips.

'Can you slow down a bit?'

Corey stopped and turned around. 'Sorry. I'm used to being out
here on my own.'

He waited for her to catch up before carrying on at a more manage-
able speed.

'Do you come out here often?'

'Quite a lot, to get away from the crowds in the village and have some thinking time. I can't bear it when it gets too busy and the streets are packed. It reminds me of living in London.'

'When did *you* live in London? I thought you were Devon through and through.'

'I lived in Hammersmith for three years before moving back to Devon two years ago. Grace had the chance to work for an advertising business in the capital. It was quite a promotion and I didn't want to hold her back, so we went together.'

Lettie hesitated, noting that this was the first time Corey had ever mentioned his wife.

'If you don't like the tourists here, how on earth did you cope with all the crowds there?' she asked, picturing him marooned in a milling throng of people. The entire population of Heaven's Cove plus tourists would hardly make a dent on Oxford Street on a Saturday afternoon.

'It was fine for a while. I was younger and more carefree.' His face twisted into a sardonic grin and he brushed away a fly that was buzzing around his head.

'I don't suppose there's much call for sea fishing in London.'

'You suppose right, which is why I ended up working at a bar in the city, serving braying businessmen like Simon.'

'Is that another reason why you don't like him?'

'Probably.'

Corey's face clouded over and Lettie kicked herself for asking the question.

'Now you're back, do you think you'll stay in Heaven's Cove forever?' she said quickly, keen to put Simon behind them.

'Forever is a long time.' He shrugged. 'Who knows?'

'Well, I don't know how you could even think about leaving such a wonderful village.'

'It is pretty special. Maybe you should move in.'

'A Starcross back in Heaven's Cove? I'm not sure it would be allowed,' said Lettie, raising an eyebrow.

He smiled at that and they walked on, chatting about London and Devon, climbing all the time. He was quite easy to talk to out here, realised Lettie, as though the sun had lifted the cloud that seemed to hover over him.

Shaggy brown sheep with white faces watched dispassionately as they went past, the land turning from green to yellow to brown as they neared a huge mound of bare granite blocks that rose out of the ground – the stone layered as though a giant had made cuts into it with a sword.

Corey began to climb up the tumble of rocks, grasping Lettie's hand and helping her to navigate the steeper sections. At the top was a flat section where Corey flopped down and took off his black backpack. Lettie stood for a moment enjoying the panoramic view, the wind whipping at her hair. There was no one for miles. Just tree-less land in all directions, dotted with granite tors. They were so high up here, the clouds could almost be in touching distance. Lettie stretched out her hand before withdrawing it, feeling foolish.

'This place is awesome,' she said, sitting down beside Corey. 'Thank you for bringing me up here.'

'It's wonderful, isn't it? I come up here whenever I can.' He started pulling food from his backpack.

'What's this?'

'A picnic. I thought you might enjoy having lunch up here, though it's nothing special – just the spoils of Gran's food cupboard plus a quick trip to the grocery shop.'

Lettie looked at the home-made ham sandwiches he was unwrapping, the cherry tomatoes and packets of crisps.

'Snap!' She laughed and unpacked ham sandwiches from her bag. 'Rosie made these for us. She insisted that I bring food, so we're definitely not going to starve.'

She sank her teeth into a doorstep chunk of fresh bread and savoured the taste of thick ham and hot mustard.

The two of them ate for several minutes in silence punctuated only by the rush of the wind and the mournful cry of a bird of prey circling overhead.

'What happened upstairs with Gran this morning?' asked Corey after a while, wiping crumbs from his chin.

'It was fine. She's quite a formidable woman, your grandmother, and she's very proud of the Allford family.'

'She certainly is. So much so that she insisted her husband take on the Allford name.'

Lettie laughed. 'So I heard.'

'The name was set to die out with Cornelius but she wasn't going to let that happen. I also don't think she fancied becoming a Smith, which was what would have happened otherwise.' He grinned. 'She was very happily married for over fifty years to John, who was a lovely man. We both still miss him.' He stared across the landscape for a moment. 'I almost came upstairs with you and Gran but thought it was probably best to leave you to it.'

Lettie thought back to the writing desk that she'd hoped might help to unravel old secrets.

'We got on OK. I apologised to your gran for upsetting her and I had a look at the desk. But you're right, there are no locks.'

'So nowhere for this key to fit.'

When Corey reached across and picked up the key that was hanging around her neck, Lettie realised she'd stopped breathing. He was so close, she could see the individual prickles of stubble on his chin and the faint white lines around his eyes where he squinted in the sun.

'You look a lot like Cornelius,' she managed, imagining how it must feel to see a man like Corey go off to war and never come back.

'That's what Gran says.' He dropped hold of the key and leaned back, his cheeks flushed. 'There's somewhere I'd like to take you once we've finished lunch; somewhere I think you might like to see.'

One picnic and a half hour drive later and Lettie was in very different surroundings. Corey had driven them into a deep, green valley on the fringe of Dartmoor and parked at the edge of a dense wood that lined the banks of a shallow, rushing river. The tor had been breathtakingly beautiful in its barrenness, whereas this place was full of life – from the birds tweeting in the trees and the rustle of leaves in the breeze to the barking of dogs splashing in the water.

Together, they walked along the bank of the river which twisted and turned among the trees. A small child ran along the opposite bank, followed by a young couple walking hand in hand.

'Where are we?' asked Lettie, to the sound of water tumbling over stones.

'The locals call it Kellen Woods, but my sister and I called it the Secret Wood when we were growing up. Mum and Dad used to bring us here all the time. It's my family's favourite spot, other than Cora Head, obviously.'

'Then I feel honoured that you've brought me here. Is your sister older or younger than you?

'Evie's two years younger.'

'Rosie told me you have a nephew too?'

'That's right. Mum has moved to live near her so she can help with George.'

'And you're here helping your gran.'

Lettie saw the shrug of his shoulders, even though the path had narrowed and he was ahead of her. 'I don't mind. She needs the help around the house, and the company. There isn't really anyone else.'

It was a little like her helping out her parents and sister all the time, thought Lettie. Though, in her case, there were others who *could* help out – if they would only decide to.

Corey walked on a few more steps before stopping again and turning round.

'So here I am, a single divorcé who's living with his elderly grandmother. It's not quite how I imagined my life would be in my mid-thirties.'

'Me neither. Life doesn't always turn out the way it should, which is pretty outrageous really.'

She'd wanted to make Corey smile so she was delighted when he laughed.

'It's totally out of order.' His face became serious again. 'So tell me about your life, Lettie Starcross. What hasn't turned out for you the way it should?'

Where to start, wondered Lettie.

'Well, I live alone in a bedsit on a busy road with a neighbour who fancies himself the next Eric Clapton and practises electric guitar in the early hours, my family thinks I'm their PA, my mum constantly sets me up on blind dates, and I've just been fired from my job.'

'Gosh.' Corey's face creased into a beaming smile. 'I don't mean to be lacking in empathy but you've just made me feel a whole lot better about my life.'

'Charming!'

Lettie slipped on the mud when she stepped forward and he steadied her when she shot out an arm.

'Careful, or you'll have a broken leg to add to your woes. If you don't mind me asking, why were you fired?'

'I strongly advised a customer to go and get a life.'

It felt good to say it out loud. She hadn't told anyone, except Kelly, exactly what she'd done in a moment of madness.

Corey burst out laughing, startling birds in the trees nearby who rose as one into the air. 'Why did you do that?'

'I worked on the customer care team for a company making adhesives, and this man rang in to complain, very pompously and at great length, that our product was too sticky.'

'Oh dear.' Corey was properly laughing now, great belly laughs that made Lettie's heart feel glad.

'It wouldn't have been so bad but Iris had just died and I wasn't sleeping and he just went on and on until I thought I might scream. So I said what I thought and put the phone down on him.'

Lettie had been mortified at the time. But Corey's laughter took the sting out of the memory.

'Well,' he said, still grinning widely. 'I think your advice was spot on.'

'My manager didn't think so when the bloke rang back to complain about me. I was out on my ear.'

Corey frowned. 'Can they do that these days?'

'I don't know. I hadn't been there that long so I was kind of still on probation, but I don't care anyway because I hated the job. I want to…'

Lettie stopped, aware that she was burbling. But Corey stared at her, his dark eyes almost black under the shade of the trees.

'What do you want?'

'Don't laugh but I'd like to change career direction and do something historical – work in a museum or something similar.' She stopped and smiled. 'And I'd like to study history too.'

Lettie had known for a while that working in a museum would be her dream job, but the urge to study history properly had only intensified recently – since she'd started immersing herself in the past of Heaven's Cove.

Corey tilted his head to one side. 'Why would I laugh at that?'

'People do.' She sighed. 'My family do.'

'Why?'

'Who knows? Because they don't think wanting to change your life is practical. Because they like me being free to help them out. Because it's not what Starcrosses do.' Though Daisy had done it, thought Lettie rebelliously. She'd suddenly decided to train as a life coach and no one had batted an eyelid at that. 'Iris kept encouraging me to do my own thing and now she's gone it seems even more important, suddenly.' She breathed out slowly. 'Sorry. I'm wittering on about myself when you've got a broken marriage to contend with.'

Corey shook his head. 'It happened a while ago now. I was pretty cut up at the time.'

'I'm so sorry.'

'It's OK. Life doesn't always work out as you think it will.'

Pain flickered across his strong features and he suddenly took a step towards Lettie. He was so close, she could smell his citrusy aftershave.

'You should live the life you want, Lettie. Even if it takes courage to break away from how things are right now.'

'I'm not sure I'm brave enough. I can't even paddle in the sea, as you well know.'

'But you got into the water even though you were frightened. That's what I call courage.'

A lock of dark hair flopped across Corey's forehead and Lettie wanted so much to brush it away. She reached out her hand, but pulled it back when a tsunami of splashing punctured the moment. A Labrador out on a walk had bounded into the stream and, by the time Lettie had looked away from the dog, Corey had stepped back again.

'Come on,' he said gruffly, moving aside to allow the dog's owner to overtake him on the path. 'We're almost there.'

They walked on in silence, as the path got narrower and trees pressed in around them. Lettie felt shaken, not by the revelations from Corey or how easy it had felt to tell him what her life was really like, but by the rush of emotions she'd felt when he'd stepped towards her. It was as though a different life had suddenly revealed itself: a more fulfilling life away from family responsibilities.

Maybe a life here, in Heaven's Cove.

A roaring noise got louder as they walked on and, when they turned a corner, in front of them was a waterfall. A very familiar waterfall. White water streamed and gushed over moss-covered boulders into a whirling mass of black water below.

'Oh, my goodness! This is the same place as the photo on Iris's wall,' exclaimed Lettie. 'She told me it was Dartmoor but always changed the subject whenever I asked anything else about it.'

'And the same as the painting on Gran's wall too. I thought you might like to see the waterfall for real. It's a magical place.'

It really was magical. Lettie watched the water cascading and marvelled at the permanence of this wonder of nature. Whatever she decided about her job, about her life, the water would fall and smooth the rocks in its path. It gave her a feeling of peace and she closed her eyes.

When she opened them, Corey was looking at her. 'That's how I feel about this place too. I come here when life gets… overwhelming.'

'So Iris must have known about this waterfall.'

'Gran said that Cornelius would sometimes bring her here.'

'Wow. So it was a special place for both of them.'

Lettie could imagine young Iris clambering over the rocks and cooling her feet in the shallow river before it tumbled over the edge of the land. Then sitting with Cornelius, the man she loved, watching the never-ending stream of water. *Sit where I sat, darling girl.* But there was nothing here that could possibly link to the key that was hanging right now around her neck.

'Come and see,' said Corey, pointing at a small pile of stones at the bottom of the waterfall, to the side. 'It can be a bit slippery so be careful.'

Corey held out his hand and, when she placed her hand in his, his fingers closed around her palm. He held on tight, all the way over the water-slicked rocks, his skin warm and his grip firm.

At the bottom of the falls, he let go and walked to the stones which, she realised, were carefully arranged into a pyramid shape, with the largest stones forming a base.

One of the largest stones carried a plaque, corroded by water splashes, but the wording was still visible: *In loving memory of Cornelius Allford, a true son of Devon. Never forgotten. Always missed.*

'We don't know exactly where Cornelius is buried but Gran and her family made their own memorial,' said Corey. 'There's the general one in Weaver's Row in the village, but they wanted a personal one just for him. Here, in a place that he loved.'

Lettie ran her fingers across the plaque. Beneath it was a smaller brass plate. She brushed away the water splashes so she could make out the inscription: *And also Elizabeth Allford, for whom the loss of her beloved son was too much to bear in this life.*

So the gravestone on the edge of Heaven's Cove churchyard definitely *was* for Florence's mother.

'What happened to your great-grandmother after Cornelius died?' asked Lettie gently.

'She died soon afterwards.'

'But what exactly happened?'

'She drowned.'

'How?' whispered Lettie, dreading the answer but having to know.

Corey rubbed a hand across his eyes. 'She was a fragile woman who was overcome with grief.' He winced. 'She walked into the sea fully clothed.'

'In Heaven's Cove?'

Corey nodded as Lettie imagined the sea closing over her head and her lungs burning as they filled with salt water. How unutterably awful for Elizabeth, and for Florence, who was already reeling from tragedy.

Lettie couldn't bear to imagine losing her own mother as a child. However annoying her mum could be, with her constant matchmaking and moves to manage Lettie's life, she knew that she was loved. And Florence had lost that special person so soon after losing her brother.

'No wonder your gran has traumatic memories from that time, and it's understandable that she still hates Iris if she sees her as the source of all her heartbreak.'

Corey gently touched her arm but Lettie hardly noticed. 'It was ages ago,' he told her. 'It's in the past and long gone.'

'It's in the past but it's not gone, is it? Not so long as someone remembers.'

Corey sighed and looked up at the sky. The weather was turning.

'We'd better be heading back before we get caught in a downpour, and I'm on lifeboat duty this evening.'

Dark clouds had gathered above them and Lettie shivered. The woods, on their trek back to the car, seemed dark and threatening now the sun had gone. And though they talked most of the way back, the ghost of Elizabeth Allford seemed to hover between them, lowering the mood.

Back in Heaven's Cove, at the turn off for the cliff road, Corey pulled the car up onto a grass verge.

'Are you sure you don't want me to take you back to Driftwood House?'

'No, I can walk and you'd better save your gran's suspension. Thank you so much for a lovely afternoon.'

'You're welcome. I enjoyed myself too.'

He hesitated, as though he wanted to say more, but when he stayed silent, Lettie opened the door and stepped out into the lane.

She bent down into the car. 'Give my best regards to your gran, for what they're worth.'

Corey nodded. 'I will. I expect she's got more jobs for me to do on the cottage before I head over to the lifeboat station. The cottage is more than two hundred years old and falling down. It's quite a headache for her.' He twisted his mouth. 'And for me.'

He looked tired and sad, and Lettie's heart ached.

'It's a shame in a way because if your gran did sell the headland, she could afford to have the cottage completely repaired or even move somewhere else. Then you'd be more free.'

Lettie only meant to be sympathetic but Corey's posture stiffened. 'She doesn't want to move somewhere else.'

'No, I appreciate that.' She was putting her foot in it big time but it was too late to take the words back. 'I just meant the money might make her life, and yours, easier if it was all getting too much. But I know she doesn't want to sell, and why.'

'Gran's adamant about it. Contrary to what Simon says, I haven't been whispering in her ear, instructing her to turn down his offer.'

'I know you haven't been. I just meant that selling the land might have been a way for you to move on. That's all.' A sudden gust of wind rocked the car as Corey stared through the windscreen at the churning ocean in the distance.

Lettie sighed. 'Well, thanks again and I'd better let you get back to your grandmother.'

She closed the door and watched while the car pulled away towards the centre of Heaven's Cove.

'Nice one, Lettie,' she muttered to herself. How to spoil a perfectly good afternoon by bringing down the mood: first, ask about a poor, desperate woman who'd walked into the sea, and then sound like Simon's mouthpiece. Why did she bring up the blessed headland? Perhaps her family was right and she'd be better off back in London – rather than upsetting the locals in Heaven's Cove.

Fat raindrops had started to fall and Lettie hurried up the cliff path, berating herself all the way.

Chapter Twenty-One

Lettie sat on the floor of her room at Driftwood House, in a patch of sunlight that formed a bright rectangle on the grey carpet.

There was a small armchair in the corner and the bed to sit on, but she needed space. The cuttings and photos Claude had given her were spread across the floor – she'd preferred to immerse herself in the past today, rather than dwell on her last moments with Corey yesterday, which had turned such a lovely afternoon into an awkward mess.

She cast her eye again over the pictures and documents. The way they portrayed life in 1930s and 40s Heaven's Cove was fascinating, but there was nothing more here about Iris and Cornelius.

Her time would have been more profitably spent looking for a new job.

Lettie groaned and stretched. She'd been sitting in the same position ever since she returned from her morning walk over the cliffs, and her joints were aching. The arrival of an email suddenly pinged on her phone and her breathing quickened when she saw who it was from.

A woman called Esther Kenvale had lived in a small Cheshire village, according to a news snippet Lettie had finally managed to track down online. She was part of a fundraising group for a local hospice. In desperation, rather than hope, Lettie had emailed the group that

morning, and now someone had replied. She opened the email and
scanned it quickly.

Dear Miss Starcross,

*I'm afraid Esther is no longer a member of our group and, in fact,
no longer lives in the area. She's moved back to Devon, where
she's from originally, and I believe she now lives in sheltered
housing in Shelton Ford. She moved before I took over the group
and I don't have her address, but I do hope you're successful in
tracing your old friend. Please do give her our regards.*

Best wishes,
Lorraine Chamberlain

She's moved back to Devon, where she's from originally… It must be her.
Claude's long-lost love. Lettie lifted her face to the skylight and revelled
in the warmth of the sun streaming through it. Esther Kenvale had been
found – almost. And with so little effort compared to her seemingly hopeless quest when it came to finding out the truth about Iris and Cornelius.

Finding Esther was a quick win-win and that was why she'd taken
on the search, she told herself, before admitting it had more to do with
Claude's haunted face when he'd spoken of the woman he'd loved. Plus,
it had been another excuse to stay on in Heaven's Cove. The village
seemed to be getting under her skin.

When a quick search online revealed only one sheltered housing
complex in Shelton Ford, Lettie sent a quick email to the admin

address, asking if she could visit Mrs Kenvale. Shelton Ford was only twenty miles away – there must be a bus – and this wasn't the kind of conversation to be had with her on the phone.

She'd only just gone back to studying the archive cuttings when there was a tap on her door.

'Come in.'

Rosie poked her head into the room, a crease between her eyebrows, and glanced at all the papers spread across the floor. 'Sorry to disturb you but there's a lady here for you.'

'She's asked for me?'

'That's right. She's adamant that she needs to see you right away.'

'It's not Florence, is it?'

Rosie frowned. 'No, are you expecting her?'

'No, not at all. Sorry. Of course you'd know it was Florence if she turned up. I'll come right down.'

Lettie followed Rosie down the stairs and into the hall where a woman was standing with her back to them, next to a large brown and tan suitcase. As they got closer, she turned around.

'Lettie!' cried Daisy. 'There you are.'

Lettie's heart began to hammer. 'Why are you here? Are Mum and Dad all right?'

'Of course they are.'

'What about the kids? And Ed and his family?'

'Stop panicking. Everyone's fine.'

'Then why are you here?'

Daisy flung out her arms. 'I've come to keep you company, Letts. I'm here on a short break! Isn't that brilliant? I was hoping I could stay here?'

She glanced at Rosie, who nodded. 'Of course you can. We have a room available. Are you Lettie's…?'

'I'm her sister,' said Daisy, looping her denim jacket over the coat stand. 'I didn't inherit the same crazy hair but we have loads of other things in common, don't we, sis?'

'Um.' Lettie couldn't think of many but she was too dumbfounded to comment. Daisy never chose to spend time alone with her. Why on earth would she suddenly turn up at Driftwood House? And why was she referring to her as 'sis'?

'Are you quite sure you're not here with bad news?'

'Of course I'm not.' Daisy grinned at Rosie. 'Honestly, what is my sister like? I surprise her and she goes all doom and gloom on me. You kept telling me how wonderful Heaven's Cove was so I thought I'd come and have a look for myself.'

'I'll go and prepare the room for you,' said Rosie, taking hold of Daisy's knock-off Louis Vuitton suitcase that Lettie noticed was much larger than hers. Exactly how long was her sister planning on staying?

'Thank you so much, and in the meantime my sister can show me the fabulous view.' Daisy linked her arm through Lettie's and almost dragged her through the open front door and out onto the cliff top. Her small car was parked on the grass. 'Go on then. Show me the sights! I could do with a walk after bouncing up that cliff road. The potholes are shocking.'

A warm breeze ruffled their hair as Lettie led Daisy across the grass, towards the cliff edge.

'Very nice!' said Daisy, looking at the sea sparkling in the sunshine. 'Is that a castle over there?'

'It's the ruins of one, yes. So why exactly *are* you here, Daisy?'

'Honestly, anyone would think you weren't pleased to see me.' Daisy scowled.

'Of course I'm pleased to see you but I still don't understand why you've suddenly turned up.'

'I was envious that you were enjoying a few days away and I thought you might be lonely, so I've come to join you for a little while. Plus, you haven't been answering your phone.'

'The signal around here is pretty rubbish,' muttered Lettie, who'd enjoyed having her phone switched off. 'Is Jason all right with you being here?'

Daisy sat down on the grass and shielded her eyes against the sun. 'Of course. He said I could stay as long as I want.'

Lettie sat down as well, her heart sinking. She loved her sister, but Daisy appearing out of the blue like this was disconcerting. It was rather like being ambushed.

'What about the kids?'

'They're fine. I've booked them onto a summer camp, seeing as you're not around to help out and Mum's a nightmare with them.'

Lettie sighed. She'd wondered how long it would be before everything was her fault.

'What about your life coaching course? Won't you get behind?'

'We're on a break. More to the point, what about *your* job?'

'I decided it wasn't the right job for me.'

'Really?'

Daisy stared into Lettie's eyes while she tried to remain calm and unflustered. She wasn't about to launch into the truth while she was still unsure exactly why Daisy was here in the first place.

Daisy eyeballed her for a few more moments before breaking into a smile.

'Honestly, Lettie. Don't look so serious. You are pleased to see me, aren't you? I'll leave if you'd rather.'

'Of course I wouldn't rather you left,' replied Lettie, with a familiar sense of being boxed into a corner by her sister.

'Great. So! Tell me what you've found out about Iris.'

'Not much, really. Though I—'

'So the mystery of the letter remains,' interrupted Daisy. 'Mum told me about it.' She suddenly jumped to her feet and put her hands on her hips. 'God, the view from here really is amazing. Heaven's Cove is so picturesque and absolutely teeny tiny, like a toy town. It'll be great for some Insta posts. And look at all that water, and there's a beach too!' She moved closer to the edge of the cliff and looked over, making Lettie's stomach churn. 'It's so pretty. Have you been swimming?'

Lettie shook her head, resigned to her sibling's lack of knowledge about her, and the annoying habit she had of interrupting when something else caught her attention.

'You're not still phobic about water, are you? Isn't it about time you got over that? It's years since you fell over on our holiday and got water in your face.'

'I almost drowned, Daisy.'

'Yeah, if you say so.'

Lettie frowned, fed up with her family downplaying what had happened that day and how badly it had affected her. 'I do say so. Iris saved me.'

'Saint Iris, patron saint of drowning swimmers. Is that when you started hero-worshipping her?'

'I didn't hero-worship Iris. I just loved her.'

'You were always her favourite. She left everything to you.'

'Daisy, for goodness' sake!' They'd already been over this... many times. 'She hardly had anything to leave after the fire, and I said you could have anything you wanted.'

'I didn't really want anything.'

'Well, then. What's the problem?'

Daisy pouted and pushed her dark hair behind her ears. 'It was the principle of the thing, her leaving every single possession to you.'

'That's because I was the only one who ever paid her any attention.'

'Whatever.' Daisy shrugged. 'She was a bit different, like you. But chasing off to Heaven's Cove to try and resurrect her is… well, frankly it's very odd.'

'That's not what I'm doing. I'm merely trying to find out what her life was like here as a young woman.'

'But why?'

'Because I feel I have to.'

Lettie bit her lip, unable to describe to abrupt, practical Daisy the feeling that drew her to this place and the secrets it held.

'So what *have* you found out?'

'Not a lot. Iris was in love with a man called Cornelius Allford who died in the Second World War.'

'That's sad.' Daisy frowned. 'I didn't realise. Do you think that's why she never married?'

'Maybe.'

'I just thought she'd always been a loner. But that's a real shame. Poor old Iris.' She stared across the water for a few moments before grabbing Lettie's arm. 'Let's go and see if the guesthouse owner will make me a cup of tea. I'm parched and knackered after that long journey from London.'

It's strange that two sisters can be so different, thought Lettie, as she was pulled across the clifftop, towards Driftwood House. She'd been poleaxed by the thought of Iris losing the man she loved, whereas it seemed only of fleeting interest to Daisy, and far less important than the prospect of a cuppa. This unexpected family visit was shaping up to be challenging.

Rosie was in the kitchen, spooning cake mixture into two baking tins, when they came back into Driftwood House.

'Victoria sponge,' she said, by way of greeting. 'Liam's favourite. Liam's my boyfriend,' she explained to Daisy.

'Are you engaged?'

Lettie cringed at Daisy's forthright style but Rosie didn't seem to mind. 'Not yet, but who knows?' She glanced at the ring on Daisy's left hand. 'Can you recommend marriage?'

'Definitely. I've been married for over ten years—'

Here we go, thought Lettie.

'—and we share everything. I don't like to boast but our marriage is practically perfect. We're soulmates.'

'That's wonderful!' Lettie noticed Rosie's smile looked rather forced.

A blast of heat radiated through the kitchen when Rosie opened the Aga and popped the tins inside. She wiped her hands on her apron. 'Can I make you both a cup of tea?'

'I thought you'd never ask,' said Daisy, sinking onto a kitchen chair as though she'd been at Driftwood House for days.

Two cups of tea later and Daisy was revived. She'd talked non-stop about her perfect family and had started regaling Rosie with tales of her life coaching brilliance when Rosie glanced at the clock on the wall. It was fast approaching six thirty.

'Sorry to interrupt, Daisy, but I was just thinking that you both might like to head to The Smugglers Haunt for something to eat. If you get there before around seven-ish you'll get the pick of the best fish.'

'The Smugglers what?' asked Daisy, her teacup halfway to her mouth.

'Haunt,' said Lettie. 'It's a pub in the village, and that's a very good idea, Rosie. Do you need to change first, Daisy?'

'I suppose I could change my top.'

Rosie gave Lettie a grateful smile as they left the kitchen and headed for Daisy's bedroom.

Daisy's room was on the first floor. It was smaller than the attic room, but still warm and cosy, with walls painted cream, a double bed with a pale blue duvet, a small wardrobe in the corner and more paintings of Dartmoor on the walls.

Daisy looked around and nodded. 'It's rather nice up here. I thought Driftwood House would be a bit chintzy and naff, but it's been done up very nicely.' She turned to face Lettie. 'What kind of pub is The Smugglers Haunt?'

'It's a lovely old village pub. Very historic.'

'Right up your street then.' Daisy opened her suitcase – which was crammed, Lettie noticed – and pulled out a blue top with batwing sleeves. 'I daresay this'll do. I don't need anything too fancy for a village local.' She slipped off her T-shirt and into the cleaner top. 'Come on, then. Heaven's Cove, here I come!'

Chapter Twenty-Two

'It's hard to believe that Auntie Iris grew up here.' Daisy peered into the window of a gift shop at the cream tea hampers, local pottery, aprons bearing Devon flags and sweets. 'And it's even harder to believe that she was in love with a local guy with a weird name. What was it again?'

'Cornelius,' said Lettie quietly, her mind whirring. Exactly how long was Daisy planning on staying, and why was she here in the first place? Daisy had never shown any great desire to keep her company before.

'Cornelius,' repeated Daisy slowly. 'That sounds rather posh, but I don't suppose he was if he lived round here. Has he still got family in the village?'

'His sister lives at the top of the hill over there.'

'After all these years? She must be ancient. Have you met her?'

'Briefly,' said Lettie, not in the mood to explain any further.

'It's so sad, that she was in love with someone who died in the war.' Daisy flicked back her hair and checked out her lipstick in the shop window reflection. 'I'm surprised she never told us about it. Well, surprised she never told you. She hardly ever spoke to us.'

'That's because you lot hardly ever spoke to her and, when you did, you treated her like she was a bit gaga.'

'I did not, and anyway, she was a bit strange. Like you.'

'She was just lonely in London.'

'Hello, Simon. This is Daisy, my sister.'

'Oh.' Simon's eyes opened wide. 'You've brought your sister along with you?' He recovered his composure almost instantly. 'How lovely. You look like peas in a pod.'

Lettie doubted that – Daisy was petite with dark hair, whereas she was, according to her brother Ed, 'a lanky redhead'.

'I didn't realise your sister was in Heaven's Cove.'

'I only arrived this afternoon,' trilled Daisy, sounding very unlike her usual self. 'I thought I'd come and spend a day or two with Lettie. I didn't realise she already had a friend to keep her company.'

Was she fluttering her eyelashes at Simon? Daisy never flirted with anyone. She was rock solid with Jason, the perfect husband.

'Can I get you ladies a drink?' Simon got to his feet.

'A vodka and lime, please,' said Daisy.

'What about you, Lettie?'

'A gin and tonic, please.'

'One G&T and vodka and lime coming up.'

'Who the hell is that?' hissed Daisy, as Simon made his way through the busy pub to the bar. 'Here's me thinking you were moping about in Heaven's Cove, feeling miserable. He's not the fisherman you mentioned, is he?'

'That's Simon, who is *not* a fisherman. He's a property entrepreneur.'

'A what?'

Lettie shrugged. 'I'm not exactly sure but he buys up land for development.'

'Does he live around here?'

'No, he's based in London.'

'Well, that's handy.'

'Hmm.' Lettie and Daisy walked on, past the quay and in narrow lane near the tiny grocery store, before Daisy suddenly to a halt. 'Are *you* lonely in London?' she asked.

'Sometimes.'

Concern flickered in Daisy's eyes before she pursed her lips. '1 you need to settle down and stop faffing about and being too picky your own good. What you need is a man like Jason.' She looked u| the pub sign swinging in the breeze. 'Is this it, then?'

'Yep, this is The Smugglers Haunt.'

'Nice. I like the flower baskets. Very pretty.'

She ran her fingers across the petals of a particularly bright displ before pushing open the pub door and stepping inside, with Lett following.

The first person Lettie clocked eyes on was Simon. He was sitting by the stone fireplace, looking like a clean-cut film star in a dark browr suede jacket and brown trousers. His fair hair was slicked to one side and his sunglasses were perched, incongruously, on his head.

'Hey, Lettie,' he called, waving across the busy pub. 'You found me irresistible after all, then.'

'Oh God,' muttered Lettie. With Daisy's arrival, her plan to avoid the pub and Simon's 'date' this evening had totally slipped her mind. He probably only wanted to pick her brains for information about Florence.

'Someone you know?' asked Daisy, opening her eyes wide.

'Yes, it is, and please behave yourself,' murmured Lettie, leading the way over to him.

'I'm so glad you took up my offer.' Simon stood up and kissed Lettie on the cheek. 'And may I say that you're looking particularly gorgeous this evening.' He glanced at Daisy curiously.

When Daisy winked, Lettie felt sick. Spending the evening on a 'date' with Simon with her suggestive sister in tow was going to be challenging. Especially if he did start grilling her about the Allfords.

'Simon's just a friend. Well, he's not even that, really.'

'That's probably not what he thinks.' Daisy leaned across the table. 'Stop being so damn picky, Lettie. He's good-looking and you say he lives in London so you could see him when you're back home. Whereabouts does he live?'

'Kensington.'

'Fancy.' Daisy folded her arms, looking impressed. 'By the way, did I tell you that Elsa got top marks in the judo test she did last week?'

Lettie settled back in her chair to hear all about her young niece's prowess at martial arts. She didn't mind. She loved her niece and her nephew, and at least the conversation had moved on from her love life.

Daisy was still in full flow by the time Simon returned with their drinks, and he listened attentively, sipping at his beer. He caught Lettie's eye at one point and winked before rubbing his foot along her calf. She moved her leg, feeling confused. Did he really fancy her or was this all a ploy to gather information on the Allfords? If so, he was going to be severely disappointed because it was information she didn't have.

Fortunately, Daisy kept the conversation flowing and Lettie was miles away, thinking about her trip to Dartmoor with Corey, when Simon interrupted her thoughts.

'Oh, good grief.' His eyes were on the door to the pub. 'Here comes trouble.'

Lettie twisted round in her seat to see people parting to make way for Corey himself, who scanned the pub before marching over to them.

'I thought you might be in here,' he said to Simon, barely registering Lettie's presence. His cheeks were flushed against his dark stubble.

'Not many other places to go in this place, old chap,' said Simon smoothly, giving Corey a smile that didn't reach his eyes. 'What can I do for you?'

'You can keep away from my grandmother!' ordered Corey, his jaw tightening.

'I beg your pardon?'

'You accosted her again this afternoon.'

'Accosted? That's rather a loaded word. Quite honestly, I don't know what you're getting in such a state about. I simply saw your grandmother in the post office and had a quick word with her.'

'You badgered her again about selling Cora Head, and you told her that, as she was ill, selling now would be a good idea.'

Corey shot Lettie a hostile glare and she shrank back in her seat. She'd told Simon that Florence was unwell in the hope of warding off any other approaches. But it seemed to have had the opposite effect.

'Calm down, mate,' said Simon levelly. 'I'm sure your old gran could do with the money.'

'My grandmother doesn't want to sell the land. She's told you that several times. And I most definitely am not your mate.'

'*She* doesn't want to sell, or *you* don't?'

Corey's voice rose. 'What exactly are you implying?'

'Nothing.' Simon raised his hands in supplication. 'I'm just enjoying a nice drink with Lettie and her sister and I don't much appreciate being accosted in the pub.'

'Just as my grandmother doesn't appreciate being accosted in the village where she's lived her whole life. So leave her alone.'

'Whatever you say,' said Simon, with a grin, which Lettie didn't consider very wise in the circumstances.

With a final scowl, Corey swept out of the pub and the locals glared at Simon, Lettie and Daisy.

'Who the hell was that?' muttered Daisy out of the side of her mouth, while Simon took another sip of his lager, seemingly unflustered by the whole commotion.

'That's Corey, a local fisherman whose grandmother owns some land.'

'Is that the fisherman you mentioned on the phone when… Gosh. It's very *Poldark* around here, isn't it?'

She gulped down her third vodka and lime in one go, as Simon sat back and smoothed down his pristine shirt.

'I'm so sorry you had to see that, ladies. I think Mr Allford is rather concerned about his inheritance and has plans of his own for the land.'

'Or perhaps he doesn't like his grandmother being hassled when she's already given you an answer,' Lettie shot back at him.

Simon's gaze was cold for a moment, then he smiled. 'I see it all the time. People take a while to think about my proposal before they understand it's the best way forward for them. They change their minds.'

'I told you she wasn't well in confidence.'

'Sorry, Lettie.' He leaned forward and started stroking the back of Lettie's hand, before she yanked it away. 'Don't be cross with me. I didn't mean to get you into trouble with the dour fisherman.' He turned to Daisy. 'What do you think? I've offered an old lady shedloads of cash for a piece of land she never uses.'

Daisy shot Lettie a nervous glance. 'I'm not sure of the ins and outs of it all, but it sounds reasonable.'

'Exactly. More than reasonable. But Mr Allford is proving an immovable object.' Simon sighed. 'Anyway, enough about my business deals. Let's forget Corey Allford's tantrums and continue with our very pleasant evening. I don't know about you but I'm having a lovely time.'

Chapter Twenty-Three

'You're a dark horse,' said Daisy, as they walked back to Driftwood House before ten o'clock. She'd had far too much to drink and was wobbling slightly as she negotiated the cobbles.

Lamps were glowing in cottage windows but there was still some residual brightness in the sky to light their way. Garden walls and trees were casting shadows across the cobbled lanes.

'What do you mean, a dark horse?'

'Having two men on the go, when I thought you were a boring Goody Two-Shoes.'

'What are you talking about?' demanded Lettie, who had a headache and wanted her bed.

'Sexy Simon and the *very* brooding, angry fisherman.'

'Corey Allford definitely isn't interested in me.'

That might not have been true during their Dartmoor trip. He'd seemed to like her well enough then. But now, after she'd blabbed to Simon about his grandmother being ill, it was certainly true.

'Ha,' said Daisy, stumbling on a loose stone after several vodkas and lime. 'Are you saying Simon *is* interested? Though he certainly seems to be, to be fair. But did you clock the fisherman's face when he first came into the pub?'

'Yes, he looked furious when he saw Simon.'

'He did. Really furious. I thought he was going to reach across us with his muscly arms at one point and drag Simon across the table.' Daisy didn't look wholly unhappy at this prospect. 'But he spotted you first, before he started scowling at Simon, and his face changed. He looked…' Daisy thought for a moment as the dull boom of waves hitting rock sounded through the night air. '… thrown. As though he wasn't expecting you to be there with Simon. Disappointed, in fact.'

Lettie shook her head. 'You're imagining things.'

'I know what I saw! So, how well do you know this Corey bloke, who would look bloody marvellous in britches and a tricorn hat. Nice arse, too.'

Daisy was *so* drunk. Lettie pushed her arm through her sister's to make sure she stayed upright. 'I've spoken to his grandmother, Florence, who's the sister of Cornelius, who Iris was in love with almost eighty years ago.'

'Say that again?'

'I've already told you all this.'

'Tell me again.'

So Lettie did, very slowly, and Daisy thought for a moment before shaking her head. 'Nah, I still don't get it.'

'Never mind.'

'Does he just do his fishing thing?'

'I don't know what else he does, apart from being a lifeboat volunteer.'

Daisy stopped walking and threw her arms wide. 'Oh my God. He's a hero too. A hero who wears those sexy yellow rubber uniform thingies. Way to go, sis. Though I hope you haven't been leading him on, not when you'll be back in London soon. Simon is by far the more sensible choice.'

Lettie sighed. Her sister really didn't know her at all. 'I don't lead people on. That's not what I do. And I don't think I'm Corey's favourite person at the moment anyway, not now he thinks I've been talking to Simon about his gran.'

'Talking to who about what?'

Daisy went to sit down on the cobbles but Lettie grabbed her and started marching her towards the cliff path. 'Never mind. I need to get you to bed.'

'You will be coming back to London soon, won't you, Letts?'

When Lettie didn't answer, Daisy sniffed. They'd reached the bottom of the cliff path and her voice was wobbly when she added: 'You're so much luckier than me.'

'What on earth are you talking about?'

'I'm talking about you, being a lucky cow.'

How drunk was she? Lettie grabbed Daisy's arm more securely and began to half-pull her up the steep path.

'I'm not luckier, so pack it in.'

'You are. You really, honestly, truly are. Two men! Huh.'

'You have Jason.'

'I know. Lovely dependable Jason. Mum says he's just like Dad.'

Daisy stopped sniffing and started to sob, loudly.

'Come on,' said Lettie, patting her sister's shoulder awkwardly. 'Come on… sis. You've just had too much to drink after a tiring day.'

'I'm thinking of leaving him,' said Daisy, stopping so suddenly, Lettie almost slipped and fell.

'Leaving who?'

'Jason, of course.'

Jason, Superman Jason, 'the best husband in the world' Jason? Lettie could hardly believe what she was hearing.

'Why would you be thinking of leaving him? Is he playing away?'

Daisy stopped crying and stared at Lettie. 'An affair? Are you mad? Why would Jason find someone else? Do you think he has? Is he cheating on me?'

'No, of course not. He wouldn't. I just thought… you said you were thinking of leaving him.'

'I am.'

'Why?'

'Because my life is rubbish.'

'Your perfect life?' Lettie began to laugh but stopped when she saw Daisy's scowling face. 'You're joking, right? You're always telling me how wonderful and perfect your marriage is.'

'I'm lying,' said Daisy bluntly. 'It's no fun at all. In fact, it's boring. I'm either working or doing housework or looking after the kids.'

'You have a lovely house,' said Lettie desperately.

'It's only lovely because I work my fingers to the bone on it.'

'You are quite…' Lettie winced. 'House-proud. Maybe you do more housework than you need?'

Daisy stared at her sister as though she'd taken leave of her senses. 'House-proud? I have standards, Lettie. That's all. Standards. But do you know what my loving husband surprised me with for my birthday last month?' She barrelled on without giving Lettie a chance to reply. 'A steam mop.'

'You said he'd bought you a night in a spa.'

'I… was economical with the truth. I got it myself off the internet when it was on special offer.'

'A mop isn't the most romantic of presents, but Jason's quite a practical man, I suppose. That's what you love about him.'

'He's boring,' wailed Daisy.

'But you've always told me that boring is just the way life can be and there's no point in wanting more.'

'Are you quite sure I said that? I thought solid and dependable was what I wanted, but now I'm not so sure. I want to have two men on the go, like you.'

Daisy blew her nose loudly into a tissue while Lettie wondered what on earth to do. She'd never seen her sister like this before.

'And then,' gulped Daisy, 'you don't help by waltzing off into the sunset and sabotaging my evenings out.'

'Can't you get Mum to babysit?'

'She helps out a bit but doesn't seem that keen, to be honest. I don't think she likes me much.'

'Oh, now you're being ridiculous. You're the perfect daughter, the chosen one.'

'Hardly.' She pouted, pushing her hands through her hair. 'If I were the perfect one, which I'm not saying I am, which one are you?'

'The weird, unplanned one.'

'Mmmm.' Daisy nodded. 'You are weird. But I'm still envious of your life.'

Now Lettie did laugh. 'You're envious of me? Are you kidding?'

'No. You have your own place, lots of free time, and you don't have a job that involves listening to people blather on endlessly about their problems.'

Not for the first time, Lettie wondered if Daisy really was cut out for life coaching.

'A steam mop, Lettie.' Daisy grasped hold of her shoulders and held on tight. 'A freaking steam mop. That's the sort of present Dad would get Mum and she's, like, proper old and she's let herself go. I'm turning into my mother.'

She started snivelling again as Lettie put her hand under her sister's arm and propelled her up the path. The sky was fading from grey to black. Soon it would be too dark to see where they were walking, and the boom of the waves was getting louder.

Lettie let herself into Driftwood House, using the key Rosie had given her. She called out a quick hello to Rosie, who was sitting watching TV, and almost pushed Daisy up the stairs and into her bedroom. An art deco lamp on the bedside table had already been turned on and was casting an amber glow around the room.

'Think I'm drunk, Letts,' slurred Daisy, collapsing face first onto the bed.

'I know,' said Lettie, pulling off Daisy's shoes before wrapping the duvet around her. 'You're absolutely hammered.'

'I love you, Letts. Lots.' Daisy lifted her head before slamming it back down onto the bed. 'Jeez, the room is going round and round.'

'You'd better get some sleep, Daisy, and we can talk in the morning.'

Lettie poured a glass of water from the carafe on the bedside table and left it within reach before softly closing the bedroom door behind her. She made her way up to the attic where she got ready for bed and slipped beneath the covers. The window was open and she could hear the soporific sound of the waves.

What an evening! A disastrous 'date' with Simon and a drunken Daisy spouting all kinds of nonsense. Or perhaps being sozzled had unleashed the truth and her life wasn't quite as perfect as she always made out.

Lettie was worried about her sister, but her thoughts kept straying to Corey and what he must think of her for telling Simon about his grandmother's ill health. She'd only been trying to keep him away from Florence, but it would reignite Corey's suspicions that she and Simon were in cahoots – especially as he'd found the two of them together in the pub.

He'd been so furious, standing there with his fists balled and his dark hair flopping over his eyes. Furious and – Daisy was right – disappointed.

All coming to Heaven's Cove seemed to have done was make things worse. There was still no answer to the mystery of Iris's key, she'd upset Corey, and Daisy had turned up out of the blue and was acting quite unlike herself. At least she'd found Esther, but getting involved in Claude's search was probably no more than a subconscious distraction – so she could avoid finding a new job and getting her life sorted out.

Lettie screwed up her face to stop herself from crying but it was too late. Tears dribbled down her cheeks and into the pillow as she drifted off into sleep.

Chapter Twenty-Four

Daisy was sitting huddled over a cup of tea when Lettie went into the kitchen the next morning.

'Good morning. I didn't expect to see you up so early.'

'I'd have loved a lie-in but those big birds are so loud at the crack of freaking dawn and the light is so bright here. It's ridiculous.'

She put her head in her hands and inhaled the steam rising from her cup.

'Those big birds are seagulls. How's your head?'

'Perfectly fine, thank you. How's yours?'

'Fine, but I didn't drink as much as you last night.'

'I didn't have much,' mumbled Daisy, wincing when her phone rang on the table beside her. She glanced at it before rejecting the call.

'Who was that?'

'Jason. I'll speak to him later.'

Lettie made herself a cup of tea and sat at the big oak table, opposite Daisy. She'd woken early too and had lain in bed thinking about the goings-on of the night before.

'Have you seen Rosie this morning?' she ventured.

'Briefly. She was heading out to meet up with her boyfriend – Lucas, Leo, L-something.'

'Liam.'

'That's the one. He's a local farmer, apparently. She said to help ourselves to breakfast. There's all sorts in the fridge and that cupboard by the Aga. She offered to cook us a full English but…' She paused and swallowed. 'I didn't fancy it, to be honest. So I told her we'd sort ourselves out and she could go out. She's very trusting, leaving us here on our own.'

'I suppose you have to be when you're letting strangers into your home. Plus, we don't much look like burglars, and she has my home address if anything goes missing.'

'Ha.' Daisy tried to laugh but closed her eyes and swallowed again instead. Her face was almost the same shade as the dove-grey cupboards.

'I think you might need to go and lie down again.'

'I will in a minute.'

Lettie watched her for a moment, sipping her tea, before saying: 'I'm glad you felt you could confide in me last night.'

'Confide in you? What do you mean?'

'What you said on the way from the pub back to Driftwood House.' Daisy stared at Lettie blearily over her un-drunk tea. 'While we were walking up the cliff path.'

'I don't know what you're talking about.'

'You told me a bit about your life and your marriage and your feelings.'

'Did I? That sounds very unlike me.'

'You were a bit drunk. Are you saying you can't remember any of it?'

'It's a total blank.'

Lettie eyeballed Daisy but her sister didn't blink.

'However you want to play it, Daisy, but I just want to say that it's OK not to have a perfect life. Nobody does. Everyone's life is a little bit shit.'

'That's true enough when it comes to you, though I was impressed with your two suitors last night.'

'Come on, Daisy! You're using insults and trying to throw me to deflect from yourself. I might not be training to be a life coach like you but even I can see that.'

'Hmm.' Daisy looked impressed for a moment before pushing herself slowly to her feet. 'I really do need to go and catch up on my sleep. What are your plans for today?'

Lettie had come to a decision while lying in bed that morning. There was no point in leaving a task half finished, not when it would mean so much to a lonely elderly man. 'I thought I might see if there's a bus to a local village called Shelton Ford.'

'Why? Is it good there?'

'I've no idea but someone lives there who I'd like to speak to about the past.'

Daisy gave a great juddering sigh. 'Not more sleuthing, Lettie! Iris is gone but she seems to be at the root of all your strange behaviour lately. Bereavement certainly changes people. And do you ever take that key necklace off?'

'Hardly ever.' Lettie pushed the key protectively beneath the neckline of her T-shirt. 'It's pretty and it makes me feel close to Iris.'

'Unhealthy attachment to the dead,' muttered Daisy.

'Anyway,' said Lettie, stung by Daisy's cod psychology. 'I'm not going to see someone about Iris. I'm doing a favour for a friend.'

'What friend?'

'A local man called Claude.'

'Another man? You're suddenly insatiable!' cried Daisy, before wincing at the noise she was making.

Lettie laughed at the thought of being some sort of femme fatale. 'Claude is in his seventies and has asked me to help him to find someone and I said I would.'

'You really do think you're Sherlock Holmes these days. When will you be back?'

'It depends on the buses. Lunchtime, hopefully.'

Daisy started swaying slightly. 'I would drive you there only…'

'…only you need to go back to bed. It's fine.'

'Take my car. It's a Sunday so who knows if the buses run around here.' She leaned forward and pushed her handbag across the table. 'The keys are in there and you're insured.'

That was true enough. Daisy and Jason had put her on their insurance so she could pick the children up from their after-school clubs and weekend activities.

'Thanks. It'll be quicker than waiting for buses.'

Daisy nodded and walked to the door. She suddenly stopped and, with her back to Lettie, said: 'I do love Jason, you know.'

'I know you do, and he loves you too, even if he isn't the most romantic of men.'

'Mmm.' Daisy closed the door very quietly behind her and Lettie heard her walking up the stairs.

Chapter Twenty-Five

Shelton Ford, a small inland village bisected by a busy main road, lacked the beauty of Heaven's Cove, but many of its tiny stone cottages had charm.

Sadly, any trace of charm was lacking in Carro Lodge sheltered housing complex. A modern, four-storey building, it was flanked on both sides by ordinary semi-detached houses and set back a little from the busy road. A scrubby lawn and two circular flower beds fronted the complex which had a shiny black door.

Lettie looked for *Kenvale* on the list of doorbells, rang the right one and waited. What would Claude think of her being here? She'd kept quiet about finding Esther so far, just in case this didn't go well.

'Yes?' said a robotic voice through the intercom. 'Can I help you?'

'Is that Mrs Kenvale? My name's Lettie Starcross. I received a message that you were happy to see me.'

'Oh, yes. Hold on a minute. First floor.'

The intercom crackled as it was clicked off, and there followed a loud buzzing sound. The front door swung open and Lettie stepped into an anodyne entrance hall. A wilting pot plant stood in the corner of the blue-carpeted space, next to a lift. The whole area looked unloved. Doors, presumably to flats, led off from the hallway, and there was one with a laminated card saying *Office* pinned to it.

Lettie took the stairs to the first floor. The place smelled of over-cooked cabbage overlaid with furniture polish.

Waiting for her in the open doorway to her flat was a slight woman with white hair pulled into a bun. She ran her fingers along the string of pearls at her neck. She was immaculately dressed, in a pink and grey tea dress, with a cream cardigan around her shoulders. There were pearls in her ears too, and it crossed Lettie's mind that Mrs Kenvale had dressed up in her honour.

'Hello. I'm Lettie Starcross.'

'I'm Esther Kenvale and I believe you wanted to see me.' She paused slightly, before turning slowly. 'Follow me.'

She made her way into her flat, using a Zimmer frame to support her.

'Dodgy hip,' she said over her shoulder, before showing Lettie into a small, sunny lounge. A cookery programme was blaring from the television. Esther reached into a pouch attached to the Zimmer and used the remote control to turn the TV volume down.

A glazed door leading to a tiny balcony was flung open and Lettie glimpsed a small communal garden, with gravel paths and large pots of plants. Wooden seats were dotted around, one of which was occupied by an elderly man who seemed to be asleep.

'That's Gordon,' said Esther, following Lettie's line of sight. 'He falls asleep at the drop of a hat. It can be quite alarming if you think he's died, but I daresay he'll outlive us all. Take a seat and you can explain properly why you're here. I was told it was something to do with... with Claude.' She hesitated. '*He's* not dead, is he?'

'No, absolutely not,' Lettie assured her, glad that Esther was keen to get right to the heart of the matter straight away. It was refreshing after Florence's initial reticence to talk to her. 'Claude is very much alive.'

'I see.' Esther stood for a moment, supported by the frame. Then she smiled. 'Where are my manners? Can I get you a cup of tea? I have biscuits.'

'That would be lovely, thank you.'

'Did you drive from Heaven's Cove?'

'I did.'

'Just as well. The buses aren't terribly regular. Please do sit while I get your tea.'

'Would you like a hand?'

'I can manage, thank you.'

After Esther had shuffled into the kitchen, Lettie looked around the room. It was cosy but cluttered, with far too much furniture for the available space. The walls, covered in a floral paper, were festooned with paintings of the sea, and every available surface was covered with either a photograph or an ornament. A large gilt cross had pride of place on the mantelpiece.

A framed photograph on the coffee table next to her showed a middle-aged couple with a young boy. The woman was obviously Esther – a slightly older version than the woman in Claude's picture. Beside it was a more modern photo of a different, middle-aged couple, with two young adults standing behind them.

A rolling sound came from the hall and Esther reappeared pushing a trolley with a teapot, two cups and a plate of chocolate digestives on top of it.

'Would you mind serving the tea?'

Esther settled herself into her chair and waited while Lettie poured out the tea, gave her a cup and took one for herself.

'Now what is this all about?' She carefully placed her cup and saucer on the small table by her side.

'I'm here on behalf of Claude. I do hope it was all right me coming to see you but he asked me to see if I could find you.'

Esther studied her hands in her lap and her fingers went to the wedding ring that shone brightly on her bony hand.

'Did he now? And why would he do that?'

'He's always wondered what happened after you left Devon and went to live up north. He didn't realise that you'd come back to the county.'

'That's because I didn't tell him.' She shook her head. 'Forgive me for being abrupt but I made my bed a long time ago. If he told you about our friendship, I assume you're close to him, Miss Starcross?'

'Please call me Lettie, and no, Claude and I aren't close at all. I only met him a short while ago but…' Lettie paused. How could she describe the way her heart had gone out to the grumpy, slightly strange man she'd only just met? 'He's got under my skin, I suppose.'

'He does that,' said Esther quietly. 'This is all rather awkward. I assumed that he'd forgotten all about me. Does he know that I'm here?'

'No. I haven't told him yet. I thought I'd better talk to you face-to-face first.'

'That was considerate of you.' Esther closed her eyes for a moment and let her head rest against the back of her armchair. Then she sat up straight. 'Did Claude tell you about the two of us?'

Lettie glanced at the cross prominently displayed above the fireplace. Claude had said Esther was religious and ashamed of their relationship, even though it all sounded very chaste. 'He hardly told me anything at all,' she told her, 'but I do know that he's never forgotten you.'

Esther shook her head slightly and gazed out of the window.

'Has he ever married? Does he have children?'

'No, he's never married and he has no children that I'm aware of. He still lives in Lobster Pot Cottage on the quayside in Heaven's Cove.'

'On his own?' When Lettie nodded, Esther murmured, 'Always on his own. Oh, Claude.'

She suddenly covered her eyes with her hands and Lettie began to regret coming today. What was she doing, getting involved in all of this? She was meddling in other people's lives, just as Daisy and her mum did all the time.

'I'm so sorry to upset you. Perhaps I shouldn't have come. I should leave you in peace.'

'No, please don't go. I'm glad you're here. I've often thought about Claude and wondered what happened to him. It's just a shock knowing that he's trying to find me.'

Lettie settled back into her chair. 'How long have you lived here?'

'Not very long. My husband, Terry, and I came back to Devon three years ago. Then he died, and our son lives in London, and, well, I needed to move into this place so I wasn't alone.' She gave a sad smile. 'I thought about moving to London to be near my son, but I've always been a Devon girl at heart and I'm glad to be back here. I like being closer to the sea.'

Esther sounded content with her decision, and Lettie could understand why. It had surprised her how much she'd loved being close to the sea over the last few days, even though she was too scared to go in it.

'Do you live in Heaven's Cove?' asked Esther, ignoring her cooling tea.

'No, I'm just visiting. I live in London and am in Devon on holiday.'

'Have you fallen in love with the village?'

Lettie smiled. 'I suppose I have a little bit.'

'It's a beautiful place, or it always was. I could have imagined myself living there all those years ago. If things had been different. I haven't been back there since I returned to Devon.'

'The village is still really beautiful and probably pretty unchanged from the last time you saw it.' Lettie put down her untouched tea and picked up the photo closest to her. 'Is this your son?'

'That's right, with his children. I don't see my grandchildren very often but they talk to me on the phone, sometimes.'

'That must be nice,' said Lettie, thinking how different Esther's life with a family had been from Claude's.

'It's lovely to speak to them but I must admit that sometimes I do get rather lonely. The other residents keep themselves to themselves, and though the woman who keeps an eye on us all has a cup of tea with me sometimes, she oversees other sheltered housing places as well, so rarely has the time.' Esther sighed quietly. 'Take no notice of me, Miss Starcross. I wasn't always so… worn down by life. When Claude knew me I was very different. But the life we have is the culmination of the choices we make and, with hindsight, I didn't always choose wisely. I chose duty over love, head over heart. But there you have it.' She turned her palms to the ceiling. 'It's far too late to change or to dwell in the past, and I have a son whom I love and marvellous grandchildren I wouldn't be without. Tell me, how did you come to know Claude?'

'I'm trying to find out more about my great-aunt Iris who grew up in Heaven's Cove, and Claude has been helping me.'

'Is your great-aunt still with us?'

'I'm afraid not. She died a few weeks ago.'

'I'm very sorry to hear that. Did she have children?'

'No, she never married.'

'Then I imagine you must have been like a daughter to her.'

'A granddaughter, maybe,' said Lettie, feeling comforted by the very idea.

'Have you managed to find out much about her early life?'

'Only sad things, unfortunately. She was in love with a local man who died in the Second World War.'

'That *is* sad. The end of a love affair is always devastating.' Esther took a deep breath. 'So what do you intend to do now you've tracked me down, Lettie? Would Claude like to see me?'

'I think so.'

Esther stared into the distance for a few moments, as music sounded faintly from the television and the programme went to adverts. Then she turned to Lettie.

'I appreciate your work in finding me and it's been pleasant to chat with you. I am glad to hear about Claude, but I'm not the person I was when Claude last knew me. I fear I would disappoint him all over again.'

'Claude has changed too,' insisted Lettie, though, on reflection, she wasn't sure of that at all. His old-fashioned cottage with its archive in the cellar made her suspect that Claude had hardly changed in decades.

But Esther nodded. 'I'm sure he has.' She paused a moment as though weighing up what to do next. 'However, I feel it's better to retain the status quo. What would be gained from the two of us rehashing old times?'

'Friendship, perhaps?'

Esther's blue eyes twinkled when she smiled. 'We *were* friends, at first. Good friends, but my marriage vows meant a lot to me. Terry, my husband, has gone now and I don't see that it would serve any purpose to meet with Claude. But I will pray for him.'

A wave of sadness washed over Lettie. It seemed that Claude would continue to be all alone. 'Can I say anything to persuade you to change your mind?'

'I'm afraid not. There's no point in rehashing the past at my age. I'm so sorry you've had a wasted journey. And I'd be grateful if you didn't tell Claude where I am. Tell him you found me by all means and say that I wish him well, but that's all.'

Lettie was tempted to plead Claude's case some more. But she barely knew him, let alone this woman, and it wasn't her job to persuade Esther to do something she clearly didn't want to do.

'Of course,' she told her. 'If that's what you want.'

'It is, and you seem the type of woman who will respect my wishes. Claude chose you well, and I know that Claude will respect my wishes too. He always was an honourable man.' Esther closed her eyes and leaned back, the sun streaming through the window showing up the wrinkles on her face. 'Forgive me but I'm feeling rather tired.'

'Then I'll leave you in peace, and thank you so much for seeing me.'

'It was lovely to meet you, Lettie Starcross.'

Lettie stood up, ready to go, but the thought of telling Claude that the woman he'd loved for so many years would remain a stranger made her hesitate. She fished in her bag and brought out a small notebook and pen. 'I'll write down my phone number and please call me if you should change your mind.'

Esther opened her eyes and watched while Lettie scribbled down her number and placed the piece of paper on the coffee table.

'I'll be in Heaven's Cove for a few more days.'

'Lettie,' Esther said, as Lettie reached the door. 'Try to do what makes you happy in life.'

'That sounds like very good advice.'

'It is, though, sadly, I didn't always take it. Give Claude my best and please tell him that I never forgot him either. He was often on my mind over the years.'

'I will tell him. I promise.'

Lettie blinked quickly to ward off her tears as she let herself out of Esther's flat.

Chapter Twenty-Six

Five minutes later, Lettie was sitting in Daisy's car, breathing in lemon fumes from the air freshener stuck to the dashboard. Shelton Ford was in her rear-view mirror and she was heading for the coast.

She wasn't looking forward to breaking the news to Claude but she felt inexplicably keen to get back to the village. There was something about the place that drew her to it – a peace and a quiet that she didn't experience in busy London, a city that had never quite suited her.

For a moment, she let herself imagine living in the village and pursuing her dream of studying history. The countryside would soothe her far more than an urban landscape ever could, and it was easy to imagine being happy in this picturesque part of Devon.

She pulled over for a moment and, knowing it was pointless, googled part-time history courses in the area. There were a few possibilities, but she'd still need money to pay for her studies and support herself. It was merely a pipe dream and yet... *Try to do what makes you happy in life.* Esther's words sounded in her head, like a clarion call as she put down her phone and drove off again. Esther, who had chosen duty over love, head over heart.

When she reached the very edge of Heaven's Cove, Lettie pulled over and walked until she reached a park, set back from the road.

Dahlias, pinks and hollyhocks were a profusion of colour in the beds that stretched through the park as far as Lettie could see. She could smell the sea here – it couldn't be far away – and butterflies flitted through the heavy summer air.

Everyone fell in love with their holiday location and dreamed of moving there full-time. Lettie knew she was a walking cliché for feeling the same way. Hadn't she wanted to up sticks and move immediately after visiting French chateaux, the Italian Alps, and Greek islands? They'd offered a vision of change, of total reinvention.

But Heaven's Cove was different. She could live here as herself and she had the family connection which made her feel, in some small part, as if she belonged already. Iris would probably haunt her for not finding out what Cornelius had meant in his letter, but Lettie instinctively felt she'd be happy for her great-niece to live in this village.

It was a lovely dream – but a dream nonetheless. Lettie might not have a job as yet, but she had family in London to get back to – a family who needed her. And some of the locals round here would be glad to see the back of her, anyway.

She pushed down the thought of Corey's disappointed face as she walked back to the car. And when she drove past the steep road that led to his cottage, she resisted the urge to call in and explain why she'd told Simon that Florence wasn't well. What was the point when she'd soon be far away from here?

And what was the point in breaking Claude's heart all over again? That was her next task and one she was dreading. But it had to be done. He'd trusted her with the search for Esther and he would expect her to tell him the truth.

*

Lettie parked close to the quay and walked the rest of the way to Claude's cottage. Part of her hoped that he wouldn't be home, but the front door was pulled open a few seconds after she'd knocked.

'You're back!' Claude, in a grey T-shirt marked with what looked like ketchup stains, stood aside for Lettie to come inside. 'Do you have news?' he asked impatiently.

'I do,' said Lettie, her heart hurting when she saw hope flare in his eyes. 'I do, but it's not all good news, I'm afraid.'

'I see.' He bent and stroked Buster's head. 'Well, you'd best come in and tell me it anyway.'

Lettie followed him into the front room and took a seat on the sofa which was covered, once more, in dog hair. Claude sat opposite her, on the hardback chair by the window, with his hands in his lap.

'You said it's not *all* good news so there must be something positive to tell me.'

'The good news is that I found Esther.'

Claude bowed his head for a moment as though he was praying.

'She's widowed now and back living in Devon.'

'She's living back round here?' Claude's head shot up. 'Is she well?'

'She looks very well.'

'Did you see her?'

'I did,' said Lettie, feeling awful. She'd seen Esther, the woman he loved, but he never would again.

'That's wonderful,' said Claude, his grizzled face lighting up. 'And does she remember me?'

Lettie could have cried at the longing in his voice. 'Of course she remembers you. She said she's often thought about you over the years.'

'Is that right?' Claude looked at the photo of Esther, taken so long ago, and smiled. 'That's good to know.'

'But I'm afraid…' Lettie hesitated. How could she say this without breaking his heart all over again? 'Esther was so glad to hear that you're well and still in Heaven's Cove, but she thinks it's best if the two of you don't renew your friendship. I think she's worried that too much has changed over the years and she doesn't want to… disappoint you.'

'She could never disappoint me,' said Claude gruffly.

'That's what I told her, but she was quite adamant that things should stay as they are. She thinks it's best if you don't meet.'

'What about talking on the phone?'

'I'm afraid not. She doesn't want any contact right now. I think she's frightened of re-opening old wounds.'

'And there was no changing her mind?'

'No, I'm so sorry.'

Claude looked out of the window for a few moments, at the tourists walking by and the boats coming into harbour. Then he shook his head. 'What have you got to be sorry about? You found Esther for me and now I know she's all right. That's the main thing I wanted, and I'm very grateful to you.' He was trying to be so brave, it brought a lump to Lettie's throat. 'Well, I won't keep you,' he said, getting to his feet. 'I'm sure you've got lots to do.'

Lettie followed him into the narrow hallway but he paused with his hand on the door latch. 'How far away is Esther living?' he asked.

'She's about twenty miles or so from here.'

'That's not so far, is it?' said Claude, opening the door and stepping back so Lettie could get by him. 'So I shall know she's close by whenever I look at her picture.'

Lettie nodded, unable to speak. But she grasped Claude's hand and gave it a squeeze as she walked out into the afternoon. Once the door had closed behind her, Lettie cried all the way back to the car.

Chapter Twenty-Seven

'It's not bad here, is it?'

Daisy knocked back the last of the lemonade they'd bought from the village grocery store and waved her arm vaguely at the view. She and Lettie had walked a little way over the cliffs from Driftwood House before settling down for their lunchtime picnic.

Lettie stopped replying to Kelly's text and looked up from her phone. The pale blue sky was scudded with puffs of white cloud and the shining, shifting sea was sparkling as though it was scattered with diamonds. The view was absolutely breath-taking.

'I can see the benefit of growing up somewhere like this, rather than the middle of London like we did,' mused Daisy, opening a packet of crisps. 'Though I don't suppose they have many nightclubs around here. How would I have got through my late teens without Cinderella's and The Top Club?'

'I did. They'd gone before I reached clubbing age. One had been turned into a fitness centre and the other into a games store.'

'Sacrilege.' Daisy brushed crumbs from Rosie's borrowed picnic rug, onto the grass. 'I forget how much younger you are than me sometimes.'

'Seven years.'

'And almost ten years younger than Ed. Mum must have been blindsided when she found out she was expecting you in her forties.'

'She was probably terrified. I was an unlucky accident.'

'Not really. Not unlucky, anyway. You're quite annoying, but we'd miss you if you weren't there.'

Lettie blinked and shoved the last of the Battenberg into her mouth. Daisy saying she loved her when she was off her head on drink was one thing, but admitting, when she was stone cold sober, that she'd miss her was most unusual.

It hadn't been plain sailing since Daisy had arrived four days ago. Treating Lettie as an unofficial tour guide, she'd dragged her around all the sights Lettie had already seen. Then she'd insisted on going to the beach and had taken the mick mercilessly when Lettie wouldn't so much as put a toe in the water.

She'd also put Lettie's teeth on edge by rattling on about 'the sexy fisherman' and 'the perfect property guy', although neither had been seen since the pub showdown. Lettie found herself looking out for Corey when she walked through the village, but he was busy elsewhere – or perhaps he was avoiding her. Either way, Daisy's rehashing of the last time they'd met didn't help to ease the disappointment she felt.

'Is the flapjack good?' Daisy prodded it with her finger and broke off a piece when Lettie nodded. 'Ooh, it's sticky! Do you remember when Mum made toffee and it was so sticky it pulled Dad's false teeth out?'

'I do. That's an image that's hard to forget.'

'And it set so hard, he almost had to chip his teeth out with a chisel.'

When they both laughed, Lettie realised that, minor irritations aside, it had been nice to spend proper time with her sister. Daisy was back to claiming that her marriage was practically perfect. But they'd shared their concerns about their parents getting older and had bonded over how pompous Ed could be when he thought he had the moral high ground.

But they still hadn't discussed Lettie's job – or rather, lack of it – properly. Lettie always changed the subject when it was raised, but it would have to come out some time. And better here, one on one, than in the midst of a family gathering.

Lettie savoured the last crumbs of her cake before twisting on the rug to face her sister.

'So do you want to know the real reason I no longer have a job?'

'Whatever.' Daisy shrugged as though she couldn't care less, though the glint in her eye rather gave her away.

'I was "let go" for being rude to someone who made a complaint.'

Daisy paused, a salt and vinegar crisp halfway to her mouth. 'You were sacked?'

'You say sacked. I say let go.'

'You were sacked for being rude? Wow, it's worse than I thought.'

'Why, what did you think?'

'Initially, when you went haring off to Heaven's Cove and acting all peculiar I thought you might be pregnant.'

'Pregnant?' spluttered Lettie. 'What on earth made you think that?'

Daisy gave Lettie's stomach a searching look.

'You've put on a bit of weight recently and you've been very secretive since Iris died. Then you mentioned on the phone that you no longer had a job, but you were knocking back the gins in the pub the other day with your two boyfriends so that blew holes in my theory.'

Lettie drew in a deep breath. 'One, I'm not pregnant, and two, as I've told you countless times already, I don't have two boyfriends. If I've put on any weight, which I dispute, it's on account of comfort eating while I was with Iris for the last couple of weeks, and after her death.'

Talking of Iris sent a sharp stab of guilt through Lettie, and her hand automatically felt for the key around her neck. She'd been so busy with Daisy, she hadn't given much thought to unravelling the mystery, and the next steps she could take – if there were any.

'Were you unemployed the last time I saw you at Mum and Dad's?' asked Daisy, interrupting her thoughts.

Lettie nodded.

'So why didn't you tell us?'

'I don't know. I had to get my head round the news myself, and Mum would be all over it like a rash.'

'Yeah, that's true. So what are you going to do? Shouldn't you be job-hunting in London rather than gallivanting around the South-West, trying to unearth stuff about our great-aunt, who's dead, and someone called Esther who you won't tell me much about?'

'I told you. I was helping out a friend.'

'You're being mysterious and you're not a mysterious person. Or at least you never used to be. It worries me.'

'Why?'

'It just does.' She ducked to avoid a drowsy wasp that was buzzing around the food. 'So what about getting a new job?'

'I can job-search online just as well from here.'

'And are you?'

Lettie hesitated. She'd been so busy chasing up information about Iris and trying to track down Esther and just generally unwinding and clearing her head, she'd done very little since arriving in Heaven's Cove.

'I wonder if losing my job is maybe a good thing and a chance to do something different with my life.'

'Like what?'

'I'm not sure. I've always wanted to have a job that involves the past, or to study history.'

'I've always wanted to travel the world but I'm not about to turn into Michael Palin.'

'Meaning?'

'Aren't you a bit old to become a student, and how on earth would you afford it anyway?'

'That's the problem, I don't think I could. I definitely couldn't afford it in London, even if I worked part-time. My rent is ridiculous.'

'You're not thinking of staying here and studying, are you? That *would* be ridiculous.'

Daisy sounded angry. A pink flush was spreading across her cheeks and she shoved her hand into the crisp packet so hard, it split at the bottom and potato chips scattered across the grass.

'What I mean' – Daisy's face softened and she shifted across the rug until she was closer to Lettie – 'is that it's time to get back to the real world.'

'What if I've decided I'm not that keen on the real world?'

'If you were a life coach client, I'd say that switching direction can be a good idea, especially if change is being forced upon you. But you also have to be realistic.' Her eyes suddenly lit up. 'Would you like to be one of my clients? I'm supposed to take on clients as part of my training.'

'That's really kind of you but...' *The thought of you meddling in my life makes me feel panicky.* '... I'm sure you'll have lots of other clients who need your skills far more than me.'

'Hmm.' Daisy narrowed her eyes. 'If you're sure. Heaven knows you could do with a bit of coaching. If you want my advice, I think you should come home, pursue a relationship with Simon and find a steady job.'

'I don't much like Simon.'

Daisy raised her eyebrows to the sky. 'There you go again, being picky. Ooh, these seagulls are a total menace.' She shooed away a gull who had swooped down for the scattered crisps. 'I'm going home first thing tomorrow morning to start the preparations for Elsa's party and you can come back with me. There, it's sorted!'

Daisy's smug smile and assumption that she *would* go home the next day made Lettie squirm.

'Maybe. I've still got my return train ticket.'

'Wouldn't the car be easier?'

It would be easier, thought Lettie, taking a bite of the remaining flapjack. It would be easier all round to go back to her life in London and to get another customer care job and to go back to looking after Daisy's kids and her parents. Far easier than moping after some amorphous new career and new kind of life with new people. Corey's face swam into her mind and she shook her head to try and dislodge his disappointed expression that seemed to haunt her thoughts these days.

'Can I let you know in the morning?'

'I suppose so but there isn't much to think about. You *have* to come home.'

Daisy sounded so panicky all of a sudden, Lettie grabbed her hand.

'Why are you so desperate for me to come back to London?'

'I'm not,' said Daisy, snatching her hand away.

'You're so desperate you came all the way to Devon to persuade me.'

'I needed a break,' said Daisy, sounding like a sulky teenager. 'And I came to keep you company.'

'I didn't need your company.'

'That's nice! I drive four hours to see you and you throw my good deed in my face.'

Lettie took a deep breath. This was all getting out of hand.

'I just want to understand what's going on with you, Daisy,' she said, as calmly as she could.

'What's going on with me? What's going on with you, more like.' Daisy got to her feet and started pacing across the grass, with the sea behind her. 'You've been different ever since Iris died. You run away from home and go all Sherlock Holmes over Iris's past. Then you switch off your phone – I'm not an idiot – and you tell me that you don't have a job any more and now you don't want to come back with me tomorrow.'

'You're concerned about me, which is lovely, but there's more to it than that. I can tell.'

Daisy stopped pacing. 'I'm frightened you're going to move away from us. There! Are you happy now?'

Lettie got to her feet, scattering crumbs across the grass.

'Why does that frighten you?'

'Because we need you at home.'

Your family take advantage. That's what Iris had told her – and it was true. Lettie pulled herself up taller.

'Sure. You need me to pick up your kids from school and babysit and take them to their weekend activities. Mum needs me to sort out her supermarket trips and help cook Sunday lunch and arrange any work that needs doing in their house.'

'But you have the time to do all that.'

'I have the time?' Lettie could feel her composure starting to slip. 'I have the time because I don't have a life, Daisy. And one big reason why I don't have a life is because I'm always so busy sorting out the Starcross family.'

'I thought you loved your family.'

'Of course I do. I love spending time with Elsa and Danny, and you and Mum and Dad. But sometimes it feels that all my life consists of, apart from jobs that I don't enjoy, is running round after you lot. You lot who think you know what's right for me.'

'That's a bit harsh,' protested Daisy, with a frown.

'It's a bit harsh but true. Unlike you, I don't have a perfect life.'

'That's why we try to set you up with suitable men who—'

'—who aren't right for me. Men like Simon.'

'But Simon's ideal. He lives in London and is charming and—' Daisy stopped talking and bit down hard on her lower lip. 'OK, maybe the matchmaking is a bit over the top. But my life isn't so perfect either.'

'You're always telling me and everyone else that it is, and it seems pretty damn good. So Jason bought you a steam mop for your birthday, so what? He loves you and you love him. And you have two gorgeous children and a beautiful home and you're forging a new career, and you always look immaculate. Look at me!'

When Lettie ran her hands down her body, over her hair being whipped into her eyes by the wind, her old T-shirt and holey jeans, the corner of Daisy's mouth lifted.

'Jason can occasionally be *very* annoying, though I'll deny it if you tell anyone else.' She sighed, and the fight seemed to go right out of her. 'To be honest, my life is only practically perfect because you're picking up the slack. I'm not sure I could do everything without your help with the kids. And I can't take on Mum and Dad too. Ed's hopeless and Fran is too involved with her own family to take on ours. We need you, Lettie. I need you.'

That was quite an admission! Lettie grabbed Daisy's hands and held on tight when she tried to snatch them away.

'You could get some proper childcare and Mum could take up the offers of lifts and outings from friends that she always turns down.'

'Proper childcare would cost a fortune. I'd have to give up my course.'

'No you wouldn't. You'd all manage perfectly well without me because you'd have to.'

'Good grief, you *are* thinking of staying here.'

When Daisy managed to pull her hands free, Lettie turned to face the sea. It was all very well having a minor rebellion, but she had to be practical.

'No, I'm not,' she told her sister. 'Not really. I know staying in Heaven's Cove is just a daft dream and I wouldn't be particularly welcome here. Rather like Iris.'

Daisy stepped in front of her and narrowed her eyes. 'Why wasn't Iris welcome here?'

Damn. Lettie shrugged. 'What I meant was that Iris didn't want to come back to the village after she left so perhaps she didn't find the place particularly welcoming.' Daisy looked wholly unconvinced so Lettie ploughed on. 'I just need some time on my own to figure a few things out.'

'And you've had almost two weeks here so you've had a break and you've realised there's no great mystery over the letter to Iris so it's time to come home to sort out your employment situation and to fit back into the family. That's the right thing to do, Lettie, and you know it.'

The squeals of children far below on the curve of golden sand caught Lettie's attention and she glanced towards the village which was buzzing with tourists on such a gorgeous summer's day. She was tired of arguing when she was surrounded by such beauty.

'Let's finish our picnic and enjoy our walk, especially if you're heading back to London tomorrow,' she said, using the conciliatory tone she often used when Elsa and Danny were squabbling. 'We can sort everything else out later.'

'But you are coming back, aren't you?'

Lettie sighed. 'Yes, of course I am.'

Suitably placated, Daisy sat back on the picnic rug and started unwrapping a punnet of strawberries. But Lettie stayed standing, staring out over the sea.

Lettie slept fitfully that night. A storm in the early hours kept her awake, wondering if Corey and his crew were in danger out at sea. And when she did eventually slip into sleep, she was assailed by dreams of Iris and a golden key which unlocked a door that led nowhere.

She woke at dawn, feeling exhausted, and padded from her bed to the window. Great streaks of gold and pink were scoring the sky near the horizon but dark clouds were massing overhead. Dark clouds that matched her mood.

She glanced at her suitcase on the floor, which she'd half-filled last night, and touched the key that was nestled against her pyjamas. If only she could speak to Iris about all of this. What would she think of it – of Daisy pleading for her to come home, of talking about the past with Florence, of seeing the memorial to Cornelius by the waterfall, of meeting Corey?

Find out for me, darling girl, seemed to whisper in the wind that was blowing around the eaves of Driftwood House.

Lettie stepped away from the window, put on her dressing gown against the chill of the morning, and started to unpack her case. She'd found out who'd written the letter, and what had happened to Cornelius and Iris all those years ago. But there was more. The mystery of the key remained and she was the only person who cared enough to solve it.

*

Two hours later, Daisy had gone and Lettie was standing on the grass outside Driftwood House.

More guests were arriving in a couple of days' time, according to Rosie, so Daisy's vacated room wouldn't stay empty for long. It seemed right that Iris's childhood home would soon be filled with people once more. Lettie felt her great-aunt would approve.

And tonight, Lettie would have the house completely to herself. Daisy, it seemed, had rather presumptuously informed Rosie that they would both be leaving. So Rosie, thinking the house would be empty, had arranged to stay in a local spa hotel overnight with Liam and his parents.

It was an impromptu treat to celebrate his parents' thirty-fifth wedding anniversary, she told Lettie, who'd overheard her trying to change her booking. But the hotel wouldn't budge and she'd been grateful when Lettie had offered to stay at Driftwood House overnight on her own.

For her part, Lettie felt honoured that Rosie trusted her to look after the house, and she'd especially loved it when Rosie said: 'I feel that you care about the house because of your family connection to it.'

She did care about the house, thought Lettie, admiring its white-washed walls and sparkling windows that overlooked the sea. It was a link to Iris and her life.

Lettie walked to the edge of the cliff and looked to the horizon, where dark clouds were clustered.

Daisy would probably be past Exeter by now, on her way back to London and raiding Sainsbury's on the way for the rainbow cake her daughter had requested. Lettie had suggested she might make the cake herself but Daisy's horrified expression had put paid to that idea.

Her sister had been miffed, to say the least, when Lettie appeared at breakfast without her suitcase and had only been placated when Lettie assured her she was only staying for a couple more days. She would have to work fast if she was going to achieve Iris's dying wish. The problem was she wasn't quite sure where to start.

Chapter Twenty-Eight

Claude

Last night's storm had passed over within an hour or two, but there would be another one today. Claude looked up at the morning sky which had changed in the last half hour from gunmetal grey to navy. The sun was obscured by a thick bank of cloud and tourists on the quayside were shivering in their shorts. Didn't they ever look at the forecast and dress appropriately for the weather?

Claude rubbed his eyes and swallowed a yawn. He was so tired and his bed was calling, but how could he sleep in the circumstances? He sat on the low garden wall of his cottage and put his head in his hands. He would have to ask for help. Again.

'Is everything all right, Claude?'

There was a light brush on his shoulder and, when he looked up, Belinda was standing over him, her metal-rimmed glasses on the end of her nose.

Usually, Claude avoided Belinda whenever possible, but her incessant curiosity might be useful for once.

'You don't look well,' continued Belinda, narrowing her eyes. 'Are you ill or has something awful happened?'

Both, thought Claude. He closed his eyes for a moment, and when he steadied himself and opened them, Belinda was sitting beside him on the wall. She brushed small stones from her skirt and turned to face him.

'Talk to me, Claude.'

If Claude hadn't been so desperate, he'd have made some excuse and hurried back into his cottage. But Belinda had something he needed – a complete inability to keep anything to herself.

'Tell me, Claude, whatever it is,' she urged. 'Rest assured that I am the height of discretion.'

The sheer hypocrisy of the woman!

Claude gritted his teeth and said gruffly, 'I need help.'

'Really?' said Belinda, sounding excited. 'What exactly is the problem?'

'Buster's gone.'

Belinda blinked behind her glasses. 'Gone? What do you mean by gone?'

'Some lads were setting off fireworks last night near the castle.'

'I heard. I rang the police to complain but I don't know if anything much was done. I don't know what Heaven's Cove is coming to. I used to think it was tourists causing problems but now I'm not so sure. Only the other day, a young lad who lives near…'

She looked at Claude's face and tailed off. 'Anyway, Claude. Tell me what's happened.'

'I took Buster for his late-night walk and one of the fireworks exploded almost in his face and he took fright and ran off.'

'That's dreadful. Where did he go?'

'I don't know. It was dark and he was very scared, and then the storm blew up and Buster hates thunder. I've been looking for him all night but he's nowhere to be seen.'

Claude swallowed hard. He thought he might cry through worry and exhaustion and that wouldn't do in front of Belinda. His reputation as a tough, emotionless loner would be severely dented. He began to shiver with cold.

'You poor man,' fussed Belinda, getting to her feet. 'You need to get some rest and leave it with me. I'll organise search parties to comb the village and the cliffs nearby.' She looked around and waved at the nearest passer-by. 'Hey, Simon!'

It was that property developer who'd been hanging around Heaven's Cove, upsetting people. 'Come here, will you?' she called.

'Me?' Simon looked around to see who Belinda was talking to before realising it was him and wandering over. He was immaculately dressed in grey trousers and a pale blue shirt, and Claude was pretty sure he wrinkled his nose when he spotted him in his tracksuit and trainers and snagged black jumper. Typical outsider!

'Are you busy today, Simon? Only we've got a village crisis on our hands and you might be able to help.'

'What sort of crisis? Only I've got a couple of meetings this morning.'

'Who with?' asked Belinda, before giving her head a shake. 'Never mind. Perhaps you can help afterwards.'

'With what?'

'The search for Buster, who's gone missing.'

'Is Buster a child? I'm not sure I—'

'He's a dog,' interrupted Claude.

'A dog,' repeated Simon, raising an eyebrow.

'Yeah, my dog, and he's run off.'

'I'm not sure I've got time to look for lost dogs.' He gave a brief laugh that carried across the quay.

'That's a shame. I'll be asking lots of locals to lend a hand, and a few outsiders, including Lettie Starcross if she's around,' said Belinda, giving Simon a sideways glance.

'Well, I could maybe help out once my meetings are over,' said Simon, loosening his collar which was fully buttoned up, even though he wasn't wearing a tie.

Fashion, thought Claude, trying desperately not to think of Buster, alone somewhere and terrified.

He stumbled to his feet. 'Thanks for any help you can give.'

Belinda started fussing again. 'You look exhausted. Go on in and have a cup of tea and a rest. We'll start the search. I know what poor Buster looks like.'

He was too tired and downhearted to disobey.

'Poor man,' he heard Belinda say as he walked to his front door. 'Such a sad and lonely character. He lives for that dog.'

Stepping into his cottage and shutting the door behind him, Claude stood for a moment before sinking to the floor. He sat with his back to the door, staring at Buster's water bowl on the flagstones in the passageway. Everything in the cottage was so quiet, he could hear the steady tick of his mother's clock on the mantelpiece, close to Esther's photograph.

Esther wanted nothing to do with him. Claude's chin dropped to his chest. Lettie had been kind when she'd told him, and he could understand why Esther had come to that decision. She'd moved on with her life and didn't want to rake up the past. It made sense, even though it hurt. But at least he knew that she was well and back living somewhere in Devon. And he still had her photo to talk to.

Was this how it would be from now on, if Buster was never found? Just him and his memories until the end? Pushing his fist against his mouth, to muffle the noise, Claude began to cry.

Chapter Twenty-Nine

Lettie

Lettie shivered as she stood on the beach, looking across the cove. The steel-grey sea was the same colour as the sky, and there were no tourists on the sand. They'd all been frightened away by the great British summer weather. The storm last night had been fierce but short-lived, but today's looked set in. At least the rain had eased for a while as she and the rest of Heaven's Cove, it seemed, searched for Claude's missing dog.

She'd planned to catch the bus to Exeter, to visit the library and museum and search for information about Heaven's Cove's past. But she'd been waylaid by Belinda at the bus stop and had put her plans on hold as soon as she'd heard the news. Poor Claude. He'd just lost the love of his life all over again and now his dog was gone too. It was so sad.

'Look at that sky! I think we'd better give our walk a miss and head for the pub,' urged Simon, who'd joined her in looking for Buster, though he kept suggesting going for a drink instead.

'I'd like to look for a little longer. It's going to get dark earlier than usual today with that sky and I hate to think of Buster out there on his own for a second night.'

'He's a dog, Lettie. He'll be all right.'

'I hope so. Claude will be lost without him.'

'The dog's probably home already, laughing at us suckers who are still out in this filthy weather looking for him.'

'I get the feeling you're not much of a dog person.'

'I love all animals,' protested Simon. 'Even daft dogs who run off and cause a lot of trouble.'

'He was frightened by fireworks.'

What did Simon say under his breath? It sounded like 'wimp'. Lettie looked across the heaving ocean and shuddered. How many skeletons of boats were lying beneath the waves, how many bones of people who'd drowned, gasping for air as their lungs burned?

'Do you want my coat if you're cold?' asked Simon, though he made no move to take off his jacket.

'No, you're all right. Thanks, though.'

'So are we going to the pub for a quick one and then maybe…?' Simon brushed Lettie's cheek with the side of his finger. 'What do you reckon? Don't worry. The dog'll turn up.'

So Simon *was* interested in her, rather than just seeing her as an information source. Daisy would be delighted at the hint of a relationship, but Lettie wasn't keen and, anyway, she was too cold and miserable to care. All she could think about was Claude desperately searching for the dog he loved.

'I'll look for a while longer. I might try the village again.'

She was just turning away from the wind-whipped beach when her attention was caught by a dark smudge at the base of the cliffs that edged one side of the cove. The foot of the cliffs were exposed when the water level dropped but were covered at high tide.

'What's that?' she asked, shielding her face against the spits of rain that were starting to fall.

'I can't see anything.' Simon pulled at her hand but she dug her feet into the sand.

'Over there. Just a little way out from the shore. Where the tide is coming in. Oh my God.'

Suddenly she knew exactly what she could see. Huddled on the rocks, with waves sweeping towards him, was an animal.

'It's Buster,' she shouted, above the wind which was whipping up the water and blowing gritty sand into her face.

The dog's terrified yelps suddenly carried across the cove.

'How did the stupid dog get over there?' shouted Simon, pulling up the hood of his jacket.

'He must have been at the bottom of the cliff before the tide came in, and now he's trapped.' Lettie looked desperately up and down the beach but there was no one around. Liam's farm was just up the road, but the tide was rising and the dog would drown before they got there and back with help. Liam and his parents would have left for the hotel already, anyway. 'We have to do something, Simon.'

'What can we do? It's really sad but, at the end of the day, it's just a dog.'

'It's Buster, Claude's dog. His companion.'

'He can get another one. Dogs don't last for ever.'

'Look at him, he's terrified.'

Without thinking it through, Lettie unbuckled her sandals and stepped onto the cool sand.

'What are you doing?'

'If we wade around the side of the cove, we can get to him before the tide comes fully in.'

Simon snorted. 'There's no way I'm getting wet for a stupid dog.'

'Well, I can't just watch him drown.'

Lettie ran towards the grey waves but stopped when she reached the waterline which was bubbling and white with foam. She couldn't go in. She couldn't.

A sudden whimper from the dog reached her. He was marooned with water all around him and too terrified to think of climbing higher up the cliff.

'Lettie, come back!' shouted Simon as she started wading into the water. Jeez, it was cold and the force of the waves was already catching at her legs and trying to lift them from the sand beneath her feet. When a wave splashed into her face, she tasted salt and childhood memories began to surface. She couldn't breathe. Fear and panic bubbled over, threatening to overwhelm her as the water swirled and eddied around her.

Buster had seen her and was barking loudly now. He rushed to the edge of the rocks, so close to the water, Lettie was worried he'd be washed away. Panic was still clutching at her throat and making her knees weak, but she couldn't abandon Claude's dog. Not when she was so close. But the water was getting deeper so quickly.

She pushed on as the water swirled around her waist and waves threatened to knock her off her feet. Was Simon with her? She looked around her but there was nothing but churning sea and grey sky. Where the two of them had been standing was now covered by water and Simon was standing farther back, his mouth a perfect 'o' of horror.

But at least she'd almost reached Buster. He yapped as she got closer and growled with fear.

'Calm down, Buster. I'm going to take you home to Claude,' she shouted, scrabbling up the rocks and grabbing the dog by his collar. She started pulling him with her. It was going to be all right. They could climb up the cliff to safety.

But when Lettie looked up at the cliff face above her, she felt like crying. It was almost sheer, with no hand holds. There was no way she could climb that on her own, let alone with a terrified animal.

'What are we going to do, Buster?' She patted his damp fur, trying to keep the panic from her voice. The dog was frightened enough. 'I need to get you home to Claude. He'd be lost without you.'

Lettie didn't see the wave behind her but she felt the force of it as it crashed into her back and knocked her off her feet.

It was happening again. The sky and land had disappeared. All she knew was water, cold water, swirling around her and over her, and she couldn't breathe. She mustn't breathe or her lungs would fill with water. Instinctively, she held her breath, still hanging on to Buster's collar as the water pushed and pulled her.

At last her head broke through the wave and into blessed air. She gulped in a huge lungful and pulled Buster towards her. She was disorientated and couldn't work out where she was. What was it that Corey had told her? *If you're ever in trouble, float on your back.*

Lettie flipped herself over and floated on her back for a moment, gazing up at the dark grey clouds above her as the waves kept on coming. And gradually her panicked, shallow breathing settled as an unexpected calm spread throughout her cold body.

I'm going to die because of a dog, she thought, picturing her family's incomprehension. *But Lettie hates the water, and she's never shown a great liking for animals. What on earth was she thinking?* Daisy would probably reckon she'd done it on purpose to get out of picking up the children.

Then she thought of Corey. He'd probably blame himself for encouraging her into the water when they'd met on the shoreline. Was that only a week ago? She pictured herself standing next to him in a calm sea, with his hand around her waist. He'd seemed so solid and sure that nothing bad would happen.

Lettie relaxed, still floating in the water, and let the waves push her and Buster, who was still paddling. Was this it, then? She'd be pulled out to sea and her bones and Iris's key would rest for ever on sand, fathoms down. And time would pass and her death would become just another piece of Heaven's Cove history. Like Elizabeth Allford. Like Cornelius.

A spark of indignation stirred in Lettie. This couldn't be it. She still had so much living to do.

Suddenly she caught sight of rocks that had tumbled from the cliff and now rested at its base. They were poking above the waves like tiny islands, and she was being pushed towards them by the swelling tide. She and Buster would be dashed against them, unless… Dragging Buster with her, she began to swim for the flattest rock. The cliff face behind it was steep but there was a ledge at head height that she might be able to get to with Buster.

At last, she felt rock scrape her legs and with a huge effort she dragged herself and Buster out of the water. But they weren't yet safe. Waves swirled over the rock, trying to pull them back into the water, and if they went back in, that was that. *Violet Starcross: 1990–2019.*

'Come on, Buster,' said Lettie, pushing the dog farther away from the rising tide. Scrambling over the rock, with Buster by her side, she climbed higher up the slippery rock face until they reached the ledge she'd seen from the water. They were above the water line here – for the moment, at least. Did the tide come up this far? Lettie looked up at the sheer rock face above them. There was nothing else she could do. Her mobile phone was still in the handbag she'd left on the sand, and it would have been ruined by now anyway if it had been in her pocket.

'Bugger,' said Lettie, sitting down, Buster by her side, with her elbows on her knees. 'I'm all out of ideas.' She scoured the beach for Simon but the seas were too high and she could no longer see the sand. She put her arm around the shivering animal and he pushed into her side, his head on her shoulder.

'It's OK, boy. We're going to get out of this,' she told him, trying not to look at the sea which swirled beneath the two of them and now almost covered the rock they'd clambered over. The sky was turning dark grey and soon the light would be gone. All that would be left was darkness and the roar of the sea.

Lettie rested her head back against the cliff and closed her eyes. What would Iris say right now if she were here? *I can't believe you were daft enough to risk your life for a dog.* Maybe. *I'm proud of you for pushing through your fear and going into the water.* Possibly, though there wasn't much point in conquering her fear of water if she subsequently drowned. The irony of the situation would have made her laugh if she wasn't quite so despondent. She clasped the key around her neck, relieved that the waves hadn't snatched it from her.

Salt spray splashed into her face and she opened her eyes. The water was getting higher and there were strands of seaweed on the ledge next to her, which didn't bode well for the high tide level.

'Sorry, Buster,' she told the dog, almost in tears. 'I've really cocked this one up.'

Suddenly, a flash of orange caught Lettie's eye. A boat was surging through the waves. She started waving her arms before realising, dejectedly, that there was no way the large boat could get close to the rocks without being dashed against them. Then she realised it was the lifeboat. Simon must have made an emergency call.

A sense of hope swirled through her. Maybe she and Buster would be OK.

The boat approached but didn't come in near to the rocks. Then a smaller orange lifeboat appeared. It was tossed in the seas and the water surged as it got closer, drenching her legs again. Two men, dressed in yellow and wearing red life jackets, were in the smaller craft and as they got near she saw that one of them was Corey.

He jumped out of the boat as it reached the rocks and almost slipped on the wet stone but righted himself.

'Are you all right?' he asked, clambering up to her. His words were almost drowned out by the roar of the sea behind him.

When Lettie nodded, too cold and terrified to speak, Corey put his arm around her shoulders and Lettie leaned into him. He seemed so big and reassuring in the midst of a crazy, scary world. Surely everything would be OK now he was here?

A sudden rush of water covered the ledge where she and Buster were sitting, soaking them both.

'Come on,' said Corey in her ear, pushing a lifejacket over her head and fastening it. 'We have to go because the tide's still rising and this ledge will soon be totally gone. Hold on to Buster and I'll hold on to you.'

She clung on to the dog, who whimpered against her chest as Corey put his arms around her and walked her towards the raging sea.

'You'll be fine,' he murmured in her ear when she hesitated.

She was in the swirling water again but this time she wasn't alone. Corey half dragged, half carried her to the waiting boat which was being pushed backwards and forwards by the momentum of the waves. She couldn't get into the boat. She didn't have the energy, but Corey pushed until the other man was able to drag her and Buster into the craft, and Corey followed.

She was safe! The embarrassment she'd normally feel at causing such a fuss was overwhelmed by the sheer relief of knowing that today was not her day to die.

Lettie closed her eyes for a moment and pulled the blanket she'd been given tighter around her. She was starting to warm up but the buffeting of the boat as it powered through the waves made her feel sick.

'What were you thinking?' asked Corey, patting Buster, who was covered in a blanket and lying at Lettie's feet. 'One minute you're terrified of the sea and the next you're choosing to go into the water. On a day like today, that's madness.'

Lettie's eyes filled with tears at Corey's harsh tone. 'I couldn't let him drown,' she told him, gently rubbing Buster's head with her foot and thinking of Esther in her flat, twenty miles away. 'He's all that Claude's got.'

Corey looked at her silently for a moment before covering her hand with his. 'That must have taken courage.'

'I didn't really have time to think about it. Simon had more sense and wouldn't come in with me.'

'For once, he did the right thing and called us. But then, after making a call for help, he watched while you got swept away.'

'You've already said I was foolish to get in the water. Would you have come in to save me?'

'Without hesitation.' Corey's eyes bored into Lettie's and she suddenly knew for sure that yes, even though it was beyond foolish, he would have waded into the churning sea for her. Lettie's heart fluttered and she smiled at him before closing her eyes again.

Chapter Thirty

An ambulance was waiting for the lifeboat at the quayside, with its blue lights flashing, and Lettie's insouciance about causing a fuss began to fade.

'I really don't want to go to hospital,' she insisted, but she let herself be checked over in the back of the ambulance by a nice paramedic called Shaz, who told her she was 'absolutely bonkers' to risk her life for a dog and asked, 'What would your mother think?' Lettie shuddered, hoping against hope that her mother would never find out, or she'd never hear the last of it.

Shaz and her crew mate wanted to 'pop' Lettie to the local hospital for a check-up but Lettie refused. The weather was filthy and the ambulance, she was sure, would be needed elsewhere tonight. And most of all she wanted to go to bed, to sink into a soft mattress and try to forget the sensation of churning water all around her.

Anyway, she was feeling so much better now. A woman who lived nearby, someone she'd never even met, had brought some spare clothes to the ambulance in a heartening display of community spirit. So she was in a dry jumper, and jeans held up with a belt because they were too big, and she was feeling much warmer. A hospital trip just wasn't necessary, she decided.

As Lettie stepped out of the ambulance, Claude came running along the quay, his hair flying in the wind. Buster spotted him and, leaving Lettie's side, started racing towards him. Claude got onto his knees and the dog leapt into his arms, his tail wagging nineteen to the dozen. 'Buster, you came back,' said Claude, burying his head into the dog's fur.

Lettie watched for a moment, tears in her eyes, before turning to go. It seemed too raw a moment to intrude upon. But Claude called out her name.

'Lettie Starcross.' When Lettie turned, he stood and walked towards her. 'I heard what you did to save Buster. Are you all right?'

'I'm fine, Claude. There's no need to worry.'

'You're lucky that the sea is so warm at the moment. What you did was brave, and foolish.'

Lettie raised an eyebrow. 'Don't worry, Claude. I've already been told off by Corey.'

Claude stood looking at her, his mouth trembling as though he wanted to say more but couldn't. Then he suddenly grabbed her and pulled her into a huge bear hug. He smelled of fish and damp. 'Thanks,' he said gruffly into her ear. 'I'll never forget what you did. Never.'

Lettie could see Corey standing behind Claude, watching as Claude released her. With a nod of thanks to Corey, Claude went back to his cottage with Buster trotting at his heels.

'You've made a friend for life, there,' said Corey, moving to stand beside her. 'And once Claude accepts you, you're a part of Heaven's Cove.' He looked down and smiled. 'Let's get you into the warm. I still think you should have gone to hospital for a check-up.'

'I'm fine, honestly. I don't think I swallowed any water. Someone very wise once told me to float on my back, so I did.'

Corey nodded, the lines around his eyes crinkling as he smiled. 'Excellent advice, but you need someone to keep an eye on you tonight and I heard that Rosie's away.' He paused, before continuing. 'You can stay with me and Gran.'

'No, I'll be fine. I don't want to cause even more of a fuss.'

'Do you really want to be alone tonight at Driftwood House, up there on the cliff, after what happened?'

Lettie really didn't, but staying with the Allfords could be awkward.

'I'm sure Gran will be fine with it when she hears the whole story. So what do you say?'

As Corey looked into her eyes, the gusting of the wind and the waves crashing against the quayside faded away. He leaned closer and for a moment Lettie thought he was going to kiss her. She wasn't sure how she'd react if he did. But he stepped back as a car screeched to a halt nearby and Simon jumped out.

'Bloody hell, Lettie.' To her surprise, he flung his arms around her and pulled her tightly against his chest. 'Are you all right? Oh, you smell of seaweed. I can't believe you went into the water to save a stupid dog.'

'I'm fine,' said Lettie, disentangling herself. 'I'm sorry I worried you and thank you so much for raising the alarm. I know it was a daft thing to do.'

'Your sister would have killed me if you'd drowned.'

'She really would have, but I'm OK, honestly. Just a bit cold.'

'I've got your handbag. You left it on the beach.' He handed it over before glancing at Corey. 'Were you on the lifeboat?'

Corey nodded.

'Corey came onto the rocks and rescued me,' said Lettie, shivering again at the thought of being stranded with darkness descending and the raging ocean all around her.

'Did he? That was very heroic of you, Corey,' said Simon, his nostrils flaring.

'It's my job,' said Corey gruffly.

'Are you going back to Driftwood House now?' asked Simon, turning his attention back to Lettie. 'You shouldn't be on your own tonight, especially in such foul weather. You won't sleep a wink up there on the cliff with the wind howling and the rain lashing. I'm sure you can stay at the upmarket B&B where I am and I can keep a close eye on you.'

It was kind of him to offer – perhaps he felt unwarranted guilt for not running into the water with her. But there was something about the way he said, 'I can keep a close eye on you' that sounded sleazy, and Lettie felt Corey bristle beside her. Was he expecting her to go with Simon?

'That's really thoughtful of you,' she heard herself say, 'but I've already accepted an offer to stay at Mrs Allford's house.'

'Are you sure about that?' asked Simon, shooting Corey a filthy look.

'Quite sure,' said Lettie, though she wasn't sure at all. Florence wouldn't be happy to see her, but the thought of being on her own at Driftwood House with nothing but her thoughts for company suddenly seemed overwhelming.

'Well, I'll call you at your guesthouse tomorrow to make sure everything is all right,' said Simon sulkily, before turning and walking back to his car.

'Are you taking up my offer, then?' asked Corey.

'I am, if your offer still stands.'

'Of course it does. I just wasn't sure you'd accept.'

'You're right. I don't want to be alone tonight.'

Corey's eyes searched Lettie's face and he opened his mouth as though he was going to say something but then snapped it shut. 'Come on then. Let's get you back to Gran's.'

*

An hour later, Lettie was wrapped up in a blanket in front of a roaring fire with a hot chocolate in her hands. She was wearing an old pair of Corey's pyjamas and her sodden clothes were already in the washing machine.

Florence, initially hostile and suspicious at Lettie's sudden arrival, had thawed considerably after hearing of Buster's rescue.

'That was a ridiculous thing to do, my girl, walking into a stormy sea like that,' she berated Lettie, bending to wrap the blanket tighter around her legs. 'My mother… my mother…'

When she couldn't continue, Lettie put her hand on top of Florence's and squeezed. 'I know about your mother, and I'm so sorry.'

Florence squeezed Lettie's hand in return before straightening up and going into the kitchen to find a hot water bottle. And it was Florence who was first to suggest that Lettie should stay overnight, before Corey had a chance to do so.

'You can stay in Cornelius's room.'

'I'm not sure I should,' said Lettie, feeling awkward, but Florence waved her concerns away.

'It's been used a few times over the years and I can't have you going back out tonight after what happened. Cornelius wouldn't want that, I don't want that and my grandson certainly doesn't.'

When she gave Corey a glance, he got to his feet from the chair where he'd been sitting with his fingers steepled beneath his chin.

'Then I'll go and make sure the room's ready. Thanks, Gran.'

'He's a good boy,' said Florence when it was just her and Lettie left, sitting in front of the crackling fire which was casting shadows around the room. 'He was terribly hurt by Grace and I would hate him to be hurt again.' She gave Lettie the same sideways glance she'd just given her grandson. 'He deserves to be happy.'

'That's one thing we definitely agree on.'

'Hmm.'

Florence stared into the fire as Lettie pulled the blanket tighter around her and watched shadows dancing on the thick stone hearth.

Chapter Thirty-One

Lettie snuggled under the covers and tried to get back to sleep. She'd fallen into an exhausted slumber the minute her head had hit the pillow in Florence's spare room. But now it was – she glanced at the luminous hands of the small alarm clock on the bedside table – half past three in the morning and she felt wide awake.

She closed her eyes again but was transported back to the rocks with salt spray hitting her face, and the thunder outside sounded like water booming as it smashed into the cliffs.

'Oh, for goodness' sake,' said Lettie as a streak of lightning lit up the small room. She swung her legs out of the narrow bed and her toes sank into the soft rug on the floorboards. This cottage was hundreds of years old and she wondered how many people had slept in this bedroom before her. People now long dead. Like Cornelius.

He was gone but an old coat that had most likely belonged to him was still hanging on the back of the door. And Lettie wouldn't be surprised if the metal-framed bed with its lumpy mattress had been his, too. Had Iris ever visited this room before the man she loved went off to war?

Lettie shivered and tugged down her pyjama top. She'd been offered a long broderie anglaise nightgown by Florence but had chosen to stay in Corey's old pyjamas – they were made of soft blue cotton and smelled faintly of amber and spice. She pulled her tumbling hair away from the collar and switched on the bedside lamp. A pale glow lit the room as another loud crash of thunder shook the cottage to its foundations.

Though she was a few streets back from the quay, Lettie could hear the sea roaring as it battered the stone walls. The force of it frightened and amazed her, and she hoped against hope that Corey wouldn't be called out again tonight. Even lifeboats sometimes went down in fierce storms. Iris had told her about one in Cornwall that had sunk many years ago as the brave men on it tried to save others. Just as Corey had saved her. She thought back to the relief of feeling his strong arm around her shoulders and realising that she wasn't going to die.

Padding around the room, Lettie peered at the framed photos on the walls. She recognised a young Cornelius in one of them, standing with his arm around a young girl who looked like Florence, and behind the both of them was a woman with kind eyes, presumably their mother. The three of them looked so happy, all blissfully unaware of the heartache to come. Just as Iris hadn't realised that sorrow was going to carve a path through her life.

Thinking about Iris made Lettie's eyes fill with tears. What would she have made of her great-niece in Cornelius's home? In his bedroom in the middle of the night?

Another flash of lightning heralded a crash of thunder and Lettie shivered in this spooky old room. She wouldn't be getting back to sleep any time soon. She looked around for a bookcase. Maybe she could lose herself in a story until exhaustion dragged her back into sleep. There were a few books on top of Cornelius's desk and Lettie picked one up. It was an Agatha Christie novel, *Murder on the Orient Express*. On the dark green cover, two men stood shovelling coal into the glowing belly of a steam train.

Inside the cover was written in thick black pen: *This book is the property of Cornelius Jeremiah Allford. Do not touch!* The small curling letters were the same as on the letter in Iris's belongings: *Sit where I sat, darling girl, with the key to my heart and all will become clear.*

A shiver went through Lettie as thunder grumbled around the cliffs of Heaven's Cove. Cornelius was a man from the past; a faded photo on a wall; a name on a war memorial. But seeing his writing here in this book somehow made him more real, as though he was in the room with her. She traced her finger across the ink and imagined him writing those words, all those years ago, not that long before his life was cut short. He was brave to sign up, when he didn't need to, and to leave behind everything he had here… a home, family, Iris.

And Heaven's Cove itself must have been hard to leave – for Cornelius and for Iris, too, after she'd lost the man she loved.

Life's just hard, thought Lettie, carefully placing the book back where it had been and sitting at the desk. She ran her fingers across the wood as another flash of lightning lit up the room.

Florence said her brother had made this piece of furniture himself. It was solid, made of dark wood which had developed a sheeny patina over the years. It was useful too, with its deep, sadly lock-less, drawers.

The desk would have looked out of place in Iris's tiny flat but she would have treasured it, if she'd ever received it as Cornelius had wanted.

Lettie pushed her fingers into the tiny open drawers that sat in cubby holes above the inlaid leather blotter. They released a smell of dust and ink that tickled her nose. Cornelius must have sat here for hours, writing his poetry. And this was probably exactly where he sat to pen the letter that he had entrusted Florence to deliver to Iris when he went to war. Cornelius, who loved playing jokes on his little sister. *Nothing was quite as it seemed with Cornelius.*

As she admired the grain of the wood, Lettie was reminded of a writing bureau she'd seen in a museum some years ago. Made of polished walnut, it was much fancier than Cornelius's desk, with ivory inlay and carved legs. It seemingly had nine drawers – three large drawers below the writing ledge and six smaller ones in the cubby holes above. Only that was an illusion because there were more drawers hidden at the back of the cubby holes. Lettie had spent ages imagining what treasures they'd once hidden away from prying eyes.

There was another flash of lightning, a thunder crash that shook the cottage, and the lamp suddenly went out. Lettie gasped. The sudden plunge into blackness was unnerving in this old room with its ghosts of people long gone.

She felt her way back to the bed and her mobile phone and switched on the phone's torch app. Her mobile only had a small amount of charge left, but there was a candle on the bedside table in a thin silver candlestick. She opened the top drawer of the table and, next to a small copy of the Bible bound in battered leather, was a box of matches.

When she lit the candle, the flame leaped up, casting shadows on the walls. She carried it across the small room, her feet chilly on the smooth floorboards, and placed it on top of the desk. Then, feeling a little guilty for prying, she eased open the large drawers beneath the writing ledge. They were lined with old newspapers that it was too dark to read and held just a few relics from Cornelius's life: some sheets of paper, a hairbrush and comb, a shoe horn and a few odd buttons.

Lettie ran her hands to the back of the drawers but there was nothing there. After closing them quietly, she pulled out the open drawers in the cubby holes above the writing ledge. They were mostly empty too, apart from more blank sheets of paper and a glass bottle that might have once held ink.

She pushed her hands to the back of the now drawer-less cubby holes but felt only wood. Secret hiding places indeed! Her imagination was running away with her in this spooky old room.

It was only as she was sliding the drawers back into place that she noticed the two at the centre of the cubby holes were less deep than the others. A partition of wood separated the spaces for the two drawers and when Lettie pulled this piece of wood, it came towards her, bringing with it a shallow rectangular box. At the front of the hidden box was a small ornate brass lock.

As the storm raged outside, Lettie stared at the box in the flickering candlelight.

Hardly breathing, she tried to lift the lid. When it wouldn't move, she carefully undid the chain around her neck and pushed the key into the lock. It fitted perfectly and turned easily. Lifting the lid, Lettie saw a small bundle of papers, tied with dark ribbon. She pulled them out, closed the box and pushed it back into its hiding space.

She was sitting with the papers in her hand, feeling rather stunned, when a shaft of light beneath her door sent her scampering across the room with the candle. She placed it on the bedside table before diving under the covers. The bundle of papers pressed into her side as the door creaked open.

Lettie's heart was hammering. She didn't really believe in ghosts but this house in the midst of this storm was enough to strike fear into anyone's heart. And hadn't she just found papers that were clearly not meant for her? Papers that had been in this room, under their noses, all along.

The door was wide open now and Lettie sighed with relief when she saw Corey standing on the landing. The beam from his torch lit up corners of her dark room.

'Are you all right?' he asked. 'The power has gone off.'

'Yes, thanks. I found some candles and a couple of matches.'

'That's very retro of you but I've got a torch you can have.'

He stepped into the room, his face and body still in shadow but Lettie could see he was in a short dressing gown and his legs were bare. He walked to the bed, his form suddenly outlined by a flash of lightning.

'It's quite a storm,' he said, as Lettie pulled the bedclothes up to her chin, feeling self-conscious. 'How are you feeling after today's drama?' He winced when thunder rumbled around the village.

'I'm remarkably well, thanks to you.'

'You were so foolish to go into the sea to save Buster.'

'I know. You've already told me, as has Claude, and Simon. And my mother will kill me if she ever finds out.'

'You were brave, too. I know how scared you are of the sea. How scared you *were* of the sea.'

'Oh, no. I'm still scared. It turns out that behaving like an idiot and almost drowning for a second time doesn't miraculously cure you of your fear of water.'

'Who knew?' He grinned, his strong features unearthly in the torchlight.

'Is your gran all right?'

'She's sleeping like a baby. She hasn't got her hearing aids in so she's oblivious to the storm.'

'Wow, she must be pretty deaf without them.'

'As a post.'

Corey was being so nice to her, even though he thought she'd been blabbing about his grandmother. The words Lettie had wanted to say to him for days tumbled out at top speed.

'I only told Simon that your gran wasn't in the best of health because I thought it would stop him from hassling her.'

Corey tilted his head, and stared at Lettie. 'OK.'

'It didn't work.'

'No.'

'But that was why I did it. I wouldn't normally pass on personal information. I just wanted you to know.'

'OK,' he said again, and added 'thank you,' before handing over the spare torch. It was huge and looked rusty but it worked when Lettie pressed its rubber button. 'It's ancient but it'll give you some light until the electricity comes back on.'

'Do you often get power cuts round here?' asked Lettie, relieved that she'd told him what had happened, and that the conversation had moved on so quickly from Simon.

'Almost never, but this storm is pretty fierce. The worst one we've had for ages. You're not getting too spooked by it, are you?'

'What, spooked by being in the pitch-black bedroom of an ancient cottage while a storm rages outside?' She laughed. 'I'm totally relaxed.'

'That's good to know.' He grinned again and glanced at the thin curtains, which were billowing in a draught blowing through the ill-fitting window frame.

'Are you warm enough in here?'

'I'm fine. Just grateful to be indoors and not out there in this weather. You're not likely to get a lifeboat call-out tonight, are you?'

He shrugged. 'Probably not. Most people knew this was coming and will have headed for harbour. I hope so. Rescues in weather like this can be pretty hairy and people can get hurt.'

'But you'd still go out in this weather if you were needed?'

'Yeah. It's what I've signed up for.'

When he shrugged again, his dressing gown opened slightly and the scar that trailed down his abdomen shone silver in the torchlight.

'Is that how you got your scar? Were you hurt during a rescue?'

Corey sat suddenly on the edge of the bed, his body heavy against her leg, crushing the papers beneath the covers.

'I was fishing from the rocks years ago, near the ones you were trapped on today, and I slipped and fell. My dad was with me and carried me to his car and took me to hospital. There was a lot of blood.'

'I can imagine.' Lettie hesitated. 'What happened to your dad? You've never mentioned him.'

'He died of a heart attack when I was twelve. He was a member of the lifeboat crew when I was growing up.'

'Is that why you joined up too?' asked Lettie, her heart breaking for young Corey. She thought of her own solid, dependable dad at home and suddenly missed her family. She'd give her mum a ring in the morning to check they were all OK, carefully omitting any mention of her Buster rescue mission.

'I guess so. I wanted to follow in his footsteps. What about your family? I heard that your sister had gone home.'

'She left yesterday morning.'

'But you didn't go with her?'

'No, not yet. I thought I'd have a bit more time on my own. My family are a bit in your face. Well, in my face. And quite controlling. And loud.' She laughed. 'I'm not painting a very good picture, am I? They're lovely, really. They're just…' She shrugged. 'You know.'

'Yeah, I know. Gran drives me nuts sometimes, but I wouldn't be without her and on my own.'

He suddenly looked so vulnerable, Lettie had an urge to throw back the covers, pull him into the bed and give him a huge hug. But, quite apart from being totally inappropriate, he would end up lying on the bundle of papers that were currently digging into her hip.

Guilt suddenly made her cheeks burn. He and Florence had been kind enough to give her a bed for the night. He'd literally saved her life only hours before. So how would it look if they found out she'd been rooting around Cornelius's writing desk in the small hours?

'I do appreciate you and your gran letting me stay here overnight,' said Lettie. 'And the whole rescuing me from certain death thing, too.'

Corey shifted in the gloom. 'You're welcome. I couldn't have let anything bad happen to you.'

Suddenly, he picked up a curl of her hair that was resting on the eiderdown, and ran it through his fingers. The action was so unexpected, so sensuous, Lettie caught her breath. What would happen next? What did she want to happen?

Without catching her eye, he dropped the curl and leaned forward. 'Good night, Lettie,' he said, quietly.

His lips brushed the corner of her mouth as he gave her a kiss on the cheek, before standing up.

'Good night,' squeaked Lettie, fighting the urge to ask him to stay.

Lettie watched Corey go, her breathing still ragged. Would she have asked him to stay if the papers from the desk weren't still under the covers?

She pulled out the papers and placed them on the bedside table, before squeezing her eyes tightly shut. Part of her ached to read them. But what might she find out? That was not a decision to be taken in the middle of the night when she'd just had a near-death experience and a visit to her room from Corey.

She was so close to solving the mystery that Iris had bequeathed her. But the closer she got to answers, the more complicated life seemed to become.

The storm was fading into the distance. Lettie could still hear the sea roaring but the lightning flashes were farther apart now, and the thunder was grumbling in the distance. She would go to sleep and sort everything out in the morning.

Chapter Thirty-Two

Lettie was woken soon after seven o'clock by gulls screeching outside. Sunlight was streaming through the thin curtains and pooling on the floorboards, and when she pulled the curtains back, Heaven's Cove was reborn.

The only trace of the storm was detritus strewn across the narrow, cobbled lane. Lettie spotted a lobster pot and fishing line tangled in a branch that the wind had ripped from a tree nearby. But the sky was a washed pale blue with no trace of cloud, and the sea was as calm as a millpond. The heavy heat of the last few days had dissipated, leaving a fresh early morning chill that made her shiver.

She jumped back into bed and looked at the papers on the bedside table. She should place them back in their hiding place, leave Heaven's Cove, go back to London and find a steady job in customer care. Daisy would welcome her with open arms and she could slip back into her routine of child care, Sunday lunches *en famille*, and fending off her mother's matchmaking efforts. It wouldn't be so bad really. Iris would have understood.

Lettie settled back down under the covers and closed her eyes, ready to slip back into sleep for another half hour.

Five minutes later, still wide awake, she sat up, grabbed the papers and began to untie the red satin ribbon that encircled them. She couldn't just pretend they'd never been found. Cornelius wanted Iris to have these, she told herself. That was why he bequeathed her his desk. And as Iris's great-niece, she surely had a right to read them. After all, Iris had left her the key and her dying wish had been for Lettie to 'find out'.

The bundle held a folded letter and a rolled-up piece of paper. Lettie carefully unfolded the letter first.

Iris, my best girl,

If you're reading this it means the worst has happened. I hope I was brave when death came calling and I didn't let you and my family down. I know for sure that you were on my mind as I drew my last breath. Don't cry, Iris. I don't regret being untruthful and going to war. It's the right thing to do when so many friends are facing danger for our future, and I have to do my bit. My only regrets are the tears you've shed trying to make me stay, and that our bright future will never be. You're a smashing girl, Iris, and you mean the world to me. But you will find another man who loves you. Take every chance to be happy, but throw a flower into the sea and think of me sometimes. I've left you this present. My family might jib against it so I'm making sure you receive it directly. Tell them it's what I want and they must respect my wishes or I shall return to haunt them! Tell them, too, that I love them, and make sure that darling Florrie behaves. I fear she will be lost without me.

Chin up, sweet Iris. We will meet again in the afterlife. I'm sure of it.

Your sweetheart,
Cornelius

*

Lettie wiped tears from her eyes and placed the letter on her pillow. Florence had believed all her life that when Cornelius had lied about his health to go to war, Iris had encouraged him. But this letter proved it was quite the contrary.

It was so sad that Iris had never received it, this outpouring of love from beyond the grave. All she had was a mystery that had remained unsolved. Perhaps she would have found another love in the years left to her if she'd thought she had Cornelius's permission? And what was the present for her that he talked about?

Lettie unrolled the second piece of paper. This seemed to be some sort of legal agreement. She scanned down it and noticed Cornelius's name scrawled at the end. The agreement spoke about a parcel of land, which Cornelius was leaving as a gift, *To Iris Eleanor Starcross and her descendants.*

Would Iris have stayed in Heaven's Cove if she'd received this? wondered Lettie. And how tragic that she never knew of Cornelius's generous gift. She shed more tears for the great-aunt she had loved, and the man she'd never met who had loved her too. There were sounds in the house – a door closing and the kettle whistling on the stove. Florence or Corey were up and about, which meant Lettie had to make a decision about what to do next. She really had opened a can of worms.

Lettie stood at the bedroom window, going back and forth over her choices. She could put the letter and legal paper back into their hiding place in the desk and pretend she'd never found them. That would save her confessing to Corey and his grandmother that she'd been snooping round the room in the middle of the night.

But Cornelius's words had been hidden for long enough, and they absolved Iris from the blame the Allfords had thrust upon her.

Cornelius had made up his own mind to go off to war and Iris had tried hard to stop him. They were also words from the grave that might give Florence some peace.

Lettie stood on tiptoes so she could glimpse the quayside. It looked a little battered after the storm. The waves must almost have reached Lobster Pot Cottage. She hoped that Claude had been all right overnight, and felt reassured that at least he'd had Buster for company.

'Yoo-hoo!'

Belinda was walking past in the street below and started waving madly, after glancing up at the window. Lettie waved back, aware that being in Florence's house first thing in the morning while wearing Corey's pyjamas was Gossip Gold.

'Are you all right after yesterday?' Belinda mouthed, her face contorting as she over-emphasised the words. News obviously travelled fast in Heaven's Cove. 'So brave!'

'Fine,' mouthed Lettie back, realising as she did so that her throat was sore from the salt water. But she smiled broadly anyway and Belinda nodded before trotting off at top speed, like a woman on a mission.

A rich smell of coffee and toast had started wafting upstairs and Lettie knew she couldn't stay in the bedroom much longer. She would have to make a decision and see it through.

When she opened the bedroom door, she found that a T-shirt and a pair of jeans she recognised as her own had been left outside in a neat pile on the landing, along with a faded bath towel. The handwritten note on top said: *Dropped off clothes first thing this morning. Hope you're OK. Rosie x* Rosie must have come home early and collected them from her room at Driftwood House. That was so kind of her.

But then Heaven's Cove was a kind sort of village, Lettie mused while she had a quick wash in the old-fashioned bathroom and slipped into her clothes. Neighbours here knew each other and seemed quick to lend a helping hand, whereas in London Lettie had never even spoken to some of the people who lived in her block of flats.

She was still thinking about her boxy flat with its view of the cemetery and its place under a noisy flightpath as she walked into the kitchen.

'You're up!' said Florence, lifting her head from the newspaper she was reading at the breakfast table. 'Corey wanted to check on you but I said you needed your sleep after all the drama yesterday.' She put the paper down and peered at Lettie over her half-moon glasses. 'Local people will be very impressed that you saved Claude's dog. That really was courageous and selfless of you.'

'It was rather stupid of me, to be honest. I don't know what I'd have done without your grandson coming to the rescue.'

'He is rather heroic, though don't tell him I said so. I don't want him getting a big head.'

'Who's got a big head?' asked Corey, coming into the kitchen. He was dressed for the day in jeans and a tight navy T-shirt. He nodded at Lettie.

'You'll have a big head if you get too many compliments.'

'No chance of that with you about, Gran.' Corey grinned, before taking a jar of marmalade from the carrier bag he was carrying, twisting off the lid and placing it on the table. 'That's the only type they had left in the shop.'

'It's got bits in,' said Florence sniffily.

'I'll put it in the cupboard, then.'

'No, no. You might as well leave it.' Florence sighed before dipping her knife into the jar. 'It'll do, I suppose.'

Corey and Lettie shared a smile over the elderly lady's head. There was so much about her that reminded Lettie of Iris. Ironically, the two of them would probably have got on like a house on fire if they'd stayed in touch.

'Did you manage to go back to sleep when the storm eased off?' asked Corey, putting two more slices of bread into the toaster on the worktop.

'Yes, thank you,' said Lettie, feeling her face flush when she remembered Corey's kiss goodnight. She glanced at him but he was busy making breakfast and didn't catch her eye. 'Thank you for letting me stay. I really appreciate it and Cornelius's old room is fascinating, a little like a time capsule.'

'Hmm. Time marches on but I don't want Cornelius to be forgotten,' said Florence, slathering her toast in bitty marmalade.

'Of course you don't. He sounds like a lovely man.'

'He was.' Florence looked up from her slathering. 'What is it? You look peaky. Are you feeling ill after yesterday's drama?'

'No, I'm fine.'

'What is it, then?' asked Florence. 'Tell me, child.'

Lettie swallowed. It would be so easy to just walk away. Iris was dead and gone and Florence would follow before too long. Did it matter what she thought of her great-aunt? But Lettie knew the answer before the thought was finished. It did matter and there had been too many secrets, for too long.

'I found something in Cornelius's room last night,' she blurted out, before she could change her mind.

'What do you mean you found something?' asked Florence sharply. She paused from buttering a second piece of toast, her knife in the air.

'I was looking at his desk and I found this.'

Corey glanced up as she took his great-uncle's letter from her jeans pocket.

Florence slowly put down her knife. 'What is that?'

'I don't want to upset you and I wasn't sure what to do with it,' babbled Lettie, nervously, 'but I thought you'd like to see it.'

She passed the letter to Florence, who glanced at it before handing it straight to Corey. 'This wasn't in the desk. My parents would have found it. They went through the drawers after he died.'

'It was hidden away. There was a drawer – a locked, secret box, really – that I came across by accident.'

'That's quite something to come across by accident.' Corey switched off the toaster as smoke started to curl towards the ceiling. 'What are you talking about?'

'It's probably best if I show you?'

Florence rose from the table without a word, holding on to her chair for stability, and she and Corey went upstairs, with Lettie leading the way. They clustered around the old desk.

'Show us, then,' demanded Florence, leaning on her grandson for support.

Lettie pulled out the two shallow drawers at the front of the cubby holes. 'These drawers are more shallow than the others and if you pull out this piece…'

She pulled the wooden partition and Florence gasped as the hidden box slid into view.

'How the hell did you come across this?' Corey picked up the box and studied the lock.

'I remembered an old writing bureau I'd seen in a museum that had hidden drawers, and I noticed that two of these cubby hole drawers were a different size from the rest.'

'Is the box locked?' asked Corey, after a moment's silence. He gave the lid a shake but it stayed put. It must have locked automatically when Lettie closed it in the early hours.

'How did you open it?' asked Florence.

'With the key that she wears around her neck,' answered Corey, his voice flat. 'Give it to me.'

Lettie undid the chain and handed over the key which Corey inserted into the lock. There was a click she hadn't heard before, in the midst of the storm, as the mechanism inside turned and the box sprang open.

'Oh, my.' Florence was staring inside the empty box in amazement. 'And the letter was inside, you say?'

'That's right.'

'Oh, my,' repeated Florence, fumbling behind her for the bed. 'Give me the letter, Corey.'

She sank heavily onto the covers and began to read, her hands shaking. Corey sat beside her and read Cornelius's words over her shoulder. Outside, last night's clouds had been chased away and the sun was shining in a clear blue sky. People were going about their business and Lettie could hear shouts from the quay and the clip of heels on the cobbles outside. But in here, in Cornelius's bedroom, time was spooling backwards as Florence read the words written by her brother almost eighty years earlier.

'I *was* lost without you, Cornelius,' she whispered, stroking the letter with her bony hand, criss-crossed with purple veins.

Corey put his arm around his grandmother's shoulder. 'It's a lot for my grandmother to take in,' he said to Lettie, his face set and his expression unreadable.

'Of course.'

'To think that his letter has been in this house for all these years, unread,' said Florence faintly. 'He meant it to go to Iris with the desk after he died. She'd have known there was more to it because of the key. She'd have found what he left behind.'

'His letter shows how much Cornelius thought of you all, and that Iris didn't encourage him to go to war,' said Lettie gently. 'In fact, the exact opposite. She tried to get him to stay. She wasn't responsible for his death after all.'

Florence bit her lip. 'It seems that my parents believed wrongly, as did I, and we have maligned Iris. We couldn't bear the thought that he'd wanted to leave us,' she whispered.

'He didn't want to go, Gran, but he felt it was his duty to fight,' said Corey. 'I can understand that. He saw his friends playing their part and didn't want to stay here, in a quiet backwater.'

Lettie suddenly imagined Corey in uniform, marching away from Heaven's Cove for good. The thought made her eyes water and she turned to look out of the window so no one would see. Iris must have been distraught, seeing the man she loved marching off to war. And then to be blamed by his family for his loss. No wonder she'd never wanted to return to the village.

'What is this gift that Cornelius is talking about?' asked Florence. 'He can't mean the desk. It means the world to me for obvious reasons but it can't have held great sentimental value to Cornelius.'

'I think he meant this. It was in the box with his letter.' Lettie pulled the deed from her pocket and handed it to Florence, who read through it quickly before passing it to Corey. He scanned through it, his face clouding over.

'Did you know about this?' he asked, a crease appearing between his eyebrows.

'No, of course not. I don't even know what land it's talking about.'

Corey tilted his head to one side and stared at Lettie. His gaze was hostile. 'The land this deed is talking about is Cora Head, the headland that Simon is so keen to get his hands on.'

Lettie began to feel wobbly and sank onto the chair behind her. 'How could Cornelius gift Iris a piece of land that belongs to your family?'

'It belonged to him,' said Florence, wiping a strand of white hair from her eyes. She stared at Lettie distrustfully. 'Did you know that already?'

'No, I honestly knew nothing about any of this.'

Florence stared again at the deed in Corey's hands. 'The land was no good for farming and no one was interested in developing it back then. But it was my brother's favourite spot – he would spend hours up there, looking over Heaven's Cove and watching the sea. He'd take me up there, to look for dolphins and seals and watch the boats coming into the quay after a night fish. So my father gave the land to him on his eighteenth birthday. Cornelius was planning to build a house there one day.' She blinked away tears. 'And he wanted it to go to Iris after his death, it seems. Iris, who tried to persuade him not to go to war, despite what my parents believed. *The key to my heart,* your letter said. It was Cornelius's final riddle.'

'I still don't properly understand.'

'The full name of the land is Corazon Head,' said Corey, still staring at the deed. 'And *corazón* in Spanish—'

'—means heart,' finished Lettie, as the final pieces of the puzzle fell into place.

'And now,' said Florence, 'according to this piece of paper, the land belongs to you.'

'No, it doesn't.' Lettie sprang to her feet.

'The land is left by my brother *to Iris and her descendants*. I under-stand that she left her belongings to you, Miss Starcross. Therefore, it makes sense that she would have also bequeathed you the land.'

'Gran, the deed may not be legally valid after all this time,' said Corey gently. 'Who knows if Cornelius made sure this was watertight, and your family might have disputed it at the time.'

'Oh, they would have. There's no doubt about that. They needed someone to blame. But it doesn't matter if the deed is valid or not, does it, Corey? Don't you understand? These are my brother's final words. This is what he wanted and his last wish has lain undone for far too long.'

'It's your land and—' began Lettie, but Florence cut her off with the wave of a hand.

'It seems that it's not been my land for almost eighty years, morally at least. And I'm tired of fighting over it. That young man who's in the village now is only the latest in a trickle of people who have tried to persuade me to sell over the last few years, and that trickle will become a stream before long. Times are changing, Miss Starcross, and I'm too old and tired to keep up. All I want to do is what my brother desired all those years ago. That at least is something I can do for him. So take the land and leave me in peace.'

'I don't want the land,' insisted Lettie but Florence had got to her feet, still unsteady but with a steeliness in her eyes that Lettie remembered from their first meeting in the castle ruins.

'You must have it, Miss Starcross. I want to carry out my brother's final wishes. Your great-aunt never received the land, but at least her descendant will do and my poor brother can rest in peace at last.'

'You can't just give the land away,' said Corey.

'Yes, I can. I am.'

'I really don't—' began Lettie, but Florence cut across her.

'I don't want to discuss it any further. Corey, will you please help me to my bedroom. I think I'll lie down for a while. Perhaps you'd leave us, Miss Starcross, and we can work out the details later.'

'Corey, it's not how it seems,' insisted Lettie, as he helped his grandmother from the room.

'Not now,' he said coldly.

After they'd gone from the bedroom, Lettie gathered up her belongings and left the house. She couldn't face Corey right now and she couldn't accept the land, even if it should have gone to Iris. The land belonged to Florence and, one day, it should pass to her grandson.

Chapter Thirty-Three

Lettie had reached the castle when she heard footsteps behind her and turned to see Corey running towards her.

'Did you know?' he demanded, puffing slightly. 'Did you know that Cornelius had left the land to your great-aunt?'

'Of course not. How would I know? Honestly, right now, I wish I'd never found the letter or the deed. I should have just put them back in their hiding place and kept quiet.'

But Corey, pacing up and down, hardly seemed to be listening. 'Maybe Cornelius told Iris that he planned to leave her the land before he went to war, but she didn't have proof when his desk wasn't passed on to her. But she told you all about it.'

'Really?' asked Lettie, hands on her hips. 'Do you really think I would come to Heaven's Cove to track down the deed and claim the land for myself?'

'Perhaps.'

Lettie laughed at the absurdity of it. 'Is that what you truly think of me? That I would tell a web of lies and deceive you to try and claim that land?'

'You said you wanted to change your life, to follow your dreams, and that takes money. And people lie and people cheat.'

'*Some* people lie and cheat but I certainly don't.'

Colour drained from Corey's face as he stopped pacing. 'Have you been working on this with Simon all along?'

'Oh, now it's a conspiracy, is it? This is ridiculous.' Lettie took a deep breath. 'Look, I shouldn't have been snooping around the desk. I've always been too curious for my own good. But I was only interested because Cornelius had wanted it to go to Iris. Before last night, I honestly didn't know anything about the hidden box or what was in it. Like I told you, I remembered an old writing bureau I saw in a museum once.'

Corey shook his head. 'You make it all sound so plausible, but then so did Grace, with all her lies and stories that made me think I was going crazy.'

'What's Grace got to do with it? And what… what did Grace do to you?'

Corey ignored her question. 'The worst thing about you is I started to think that we…' He stopped speaking and screwed up his face, his eyes tightly shut. Then he opened them and breathed out slowly. 'Congratulations. Cora Head is yours, it seems – my grandmother has never been one for changing her mind once it's made. I hope it will make you very happy.'

Then he turned on his heel and marched off, leaving Lettie blinking back tears. How could he think she had deliberately plotted all of this? Corey's bad opinion of her stung far more deeply than she would ever have imagined it could. Putting her head down, she trudged through the village and up the cliff, to Driftwood House.

Rosie was outside, painting a window frame and put down the brush as Lettie approached.

'Are you OK?' she called. 'We heard last night at the hotel what had happened. You're quite the local celebrity.'

'I'm all right,' said Lettie, trying not to cry. 'Thank you for dropping off the clothes. And I'm so sorry that I spoiled your evening out.'

'You didn't. I heard you were being looked after by the Allfords so I stayed overnight and just came back a bit earlier today. Liam needed to get back early anyway for the farm. I can't believe you saved Buster. Claude would be lost without him.' Rosie narrowed her eyes. 'Are you sure you're OK?'

'Yes, absolutely. I just need a lie-down.'

Lettie walked through the open front door and had reached the stairs when Rosie called to her again. She'd followed her into the hall and was wiping her brush on her painty apron.

'You're obviously not all right. My mum always swore by chamomile tea and I've got some in the cupboard. I'll put the kettle on. Come with me.'

She took hold of Lettie's arm, led her into the kitchen and sat her down at the large oak table. Then, she put the kettle on and found teabags in the back of a cupboard. She said nothing until the tea was made and she'd placed two steaming mugs on the table. Sitting opposite Lettie, she cradled one of the mugs in her hands.

'Are you feeling ill after what happened yesterday?' she asked gently.

'No, I feel all right about that. Corey and the lifeboat came out and rescued me and Buster.'

'So I heard. What you did was really brave.'

Lettie brushed her words aside. 'It's what happened after that…'

'You stayed at Florence's with her and Corey.'

'Mmm.' Lettie nodded, too choked to speak.

'Oh.' Rosie's eyes opened wide. 'Did something happen with Corey? Did the two of you…? I mean, are you two…?'

'No.' Lettie shook her head. 'Nothing happened with Corey.'

She'd wanted it to, though. When he'd come into her room and kissed her goodnight, she'd wanted more. But instead, she'd snooped through the writing desk and now he thought she was a money-grasping cheat.

'It's all right. You don't have to tell me anything you don't want to. Is there someone you could ring and talk to? Your sister, maybe?'

Lettie shook her head more vehemently. Daisy was the last person she wanted to talk to right now. She could imagine what her sister would say: *You what? You almost drowned trying to save a dog, and then you snooped through an old desk in the middle of the night? What on earth's the matter with you, Lettie?* Or even worse: *Good old Iris! Take the land and run – you know that's what she would have wanted.*

But Lettie had no idea what Iris would have wanted from this complicated situation and there was no way of ever asking her. She was gone for good and would never see Cornelius's letter.

When tears began to roll down Lettie's nose and drop onto the table, Rosie dragged her chair across the tiles and put her arm around her shoulders.

'It's OK,' she soothed, pushing the mug of chamomile tea towards her.

'I'm sorry,' sobbed Lettie. 'You're the owner of Driftwood House, not an agony aunt. You seem so together and sure of things. I bet you've never been a weird mess like me.'

'You'd be surprised,' murmured Rosie, giving Lettie's shoulders a squeeze. 'Is there anything I can do to help? You're probably still in shock after what happened yesterday.'

'No, I'm fine, honestly,' sniffed Lettie, 'but thank you. You've been very kind. Actually, I need to leave Heaven's Cove today.'

She picked up the steaming tea and took a sip because Rosie had gone to all the trouble of making it.

'Can't you stay a bit longer? You've booked until Sunday.'

'I need to go now, but I'm not asking for any money back.'

'Oh, I'm not bothered about money,' insisted Rosie, getting up from the table. 'I just hate to see you leaving when you're so upset. Does Simon know you're going? Is he the reason you're so upset?'

'No, it's nothing to do with Simon. Nothing at all. And I think you're right that I'm still upset about yesterday but I'll be fine when I get back to London.' Lettie pushed her chair back and stood up. 'Thank you for the tea but I need to go and pack my things.'

Upstairs, she threw her belongings into her case and checked on her phone for trains from Exeter to Paddington. There were a few later that day so she rang for a taxi to take her to the station.

It felt like running away. It *was* running away, but she'd go back to her little life in London, find a new job, nod at her neighbours, endure her family's matchmaking, and apologise profusely for not making the rainbow cake for Elsa's birthday. Like Iris, she would never mention Heaven's Cove again and, also like Iris, she would never forget the village. Just as she would never forget the expression on Corey's face when he'd accused her of deceit.

'I should never have come to Heaven's Cove, Iris,' said Lettie into her empty bedroom as she snapped her case closed and lifted it off the bed. 'I solved the mystery but just added to the heartache.'

She was about to carry her case downstairs when her phone beeped. It was a number she didn't recognise and she was about to ignore it when it beeped again. She opened the first message:

Hello Lettie. This is Esther. I've changed my mind and would like to see Claude. Could you pick me up and bring me to Heaven's Cove? You said you were there for a few more days.

The second message, sent just a minute later, said: *If you don't mind, of course. I don't want to be a bother but I'd feel better if you were with me.*

Lettie sat down heavily on the bed. She'd reply and explain that she was leaving Heaven's Cove. Esther could get a taxi or maybe someone else would bring her over. She'd already rescued Claude's dog and she wasn't responsible for his love life too.

She carried the case down the two flights of stairs but hesitated in the hallway. What if Esther cried off when Lettie said she couldn't collect her? She and Claude would never meet again. What would Iris want her to do? If she'd had the chance to see Cornelius one more time, she would have jumped at it.

'Oh, dear,' said Lettie, softly. She put her case down next to the grandfather clock and called into the kitchen. 'Rosie, I'll be leaving later but need to go somewhere first if that's OK.'

'Of course.' Rosie poked her head around the kitchen door. 'Are you all right now?'

'Yes, thank you. I will be.'

Two hours later, Lettie's taxi arrived back into Heaven's Cove with Esther sitting next to her in the back seat.

'I haven't been here for forty years but everything looks much the same.' Esther craned her neck to see along the lane that led to the church. 'The shops are different, but the buildings are the same.' She twisted her pale hands in her lap. 'It was very kind of you to collect me, Lettie, especially in a taxi. But I'm beginning to wish I hadn't contacted you at all.'

'Do you feel nervous about seeing Claude again?'

'I do, which is silly, really. We're both old codgers now. What if he's out?'

'We'll track him down. I don't think Claude ever goes very far,' Lettie reassured her for the third time since leaving Carro Lodge.

Lettie stole a glance at her passenger. She was wearing an A-line skirt in heavy cream cotton, a thin pink jumper with a round neck, and a cream jacket with gold buttons. There were pearls around her neck and her hair was pinned up in a bun. She'd made quite an effort before seeing her old beau.

Lettie got the taxi driver to drop them on the quay and handed over the fare, trying not to think of her dwindling savings.

Claude's cottage was ahead of them, bright in the sunshine, and Esther swallowed hard. 'Nothing's changed at all,' she murmured, before turning to Lettie. 'I'm sorry to be a nuisance but I'm not sure I can do this after all. Perhaps I'd be better off going straight home?'

'We're here now. Why don't we take it slowly and see what happens?'

Esther stared at Lettie for a moment. 'Why are you doing this for me and Claude?'

'Claude is a one-off, and you remind me of someone I used to know. She would approve of the two of you getting together after all this time. Not everyone has the chance of a reunion.'

When Lettie's eyes filled with tears, Esther patted her hand. 'Come on then. Let's get this done.'

Together they walked towards Claude's ramshackle cottage. Esther stayed by the low wall outside, leaning on her walking stick, while Lettie went to the door and raised her hand. She had no idea how this was going to go.

Chapter Thirty-Four

Claude

Claude bent down, ignoring the twinge in his lower back, and put his arms around Buster.

'You daft dog, going swimming without me there to look after you,' he said, pushing his face into the animal's soft fur.

When he raised his head, his cheeks were wet with tears that he brushed away impatiently. 'Look at me. You've turned me into a snivelling wreck. What would people think?'

The knock on the door was so quiet, he almost missed it, but Buster's ears pricked up and he abandoned the leftovers of his steak, which Claude had bought for him as a welcome home treat, and bounded into the hall.

Claude sighed. He'd had a steady stream of people to his door all morning, asking after Buster and checking out on the quiet that his owner was OK. It was kind of them but, for a quiet, private man like Claude, it had still felt like an intrusion.

For a moment, he considered pretending he was out but Buster spoiled that by beginning to bark.

'Shush, boy!' Claude pulled him away from the door and took a deep breath. One more visitor and then he'd pull the curtains, get

Buster settled in the tiny courtyard out back and pretend he'd moved to Scotland.

'Yes?' he said, somewhat impatiently, pulling open the door. His expression froze when he saw Lettie standing on his doorstep. 'Lettie!' He grabbed her hand and pumped it up and down. 'How are you? I called at Florence's this morning to ask if you were fully recovered and she said you were, but very little else. She seemed troubled so I was worried about you. Come in.'

He stepped back but Lettie stayed on the doorstep, biting her lip.

'You are all right, aren't you?'

'Yes, I'm fine today. I just…' Without another word she stepped to the side, almost into the tangle of old fishing nets propped against the side wall of his tiny front garden. Past her, Claude could see someone standing on the quayside. A short woman with white hair, dressed in cream and pink. He squinted, wishing he'd put his glasses on because her features were fuzzy. For one ridiculous moment, he wondered if she was the ghost of Lettie's great-aunt Iris, come to tell him that his time was up.

But when the woman took a few steps forward, her features came more into focus. She had an oval face, pale skin and eyes the colour of cornflowers at Cora Head. Breath caught in Claude's throat as she took another few steps towards him. It couldn't be.

They stood, four feet and forty years apart, as tourists walked by licking ice creams and gulls screeched overhead at the boats coming into harbour.

At last she spoke, her voice familiar though more tremulous than he remembered.

'Well, Claude. Here we are again.'

He couldn't speak and Lettie moved to his side and put her hand on his arm. Usually, he shrugged off any physical contact. What was the point in reminding himself of something he'd so rarely had? But he let her hand rest there, warming his skin.

'Shall we go inside?' asked Lettie gently.

Claude nodded and stood back to let the women into his home. As Esther brushed past him, he closed his eyes and the years fell away. He was thirty-five years old again. An introspective and sometimes lonely man who had finally let his guard down and allowed a woman into his heart. He was standing in this very doorway, waiting for the woman he loved. Waiting, always waiting, until he realised that she would never come again.

'Claude, please come and sit down,' said Lettie, taking his arm again and leading him into his sitting room. 'I should have told you we were coming. It's all too much of a shock.'

'No, no. It's fine,' said Claude, finding his voice at last. He sat in the dining chair with the window behind him and Esther perched on the edge of the sofa. Buster pushed his nose against Esther's hand and she patted him on the head.

'How are you, Claude, after all these years?' she asked, her eyes fixed on his face.

How could he answer such a question? So much life had happened, good and bad, since they were last together. Claude shrugged. 'Older, but much the same, as you can see.' He looked around the room, with its ramshackle furniture. This place was frozen in time, as was he. 'How are you?' he managed, noticing Lettie slipping out of the room and into his kitchen.

'Older too.' Esther smiled. 'A lot older and, I hope, a little wiser.' She continued to pat Buster, who sat at her feet. 'It's good to see you, Claude. Why did you ask Lettie to find me?'

I wanted to make sure that 'we' really did exist and our relationship wasn't a fantasy conjured up by my lonely mind.

Claude forced himself to smile. 'I think about you sometimes and wanted to see if life had treated you well.'

'That was kind of you.' Esther hesitated. 'I wasn't sure about coming. I wasn't sure what it would achieve, but I wanted to see you. I also owe you an apology and I thought it best to make that in person.'

'You don't owe me anything, Esther.'

'But I do.' When the woman he'd once loved sat forward, her face was bathed in sunlight and he could see every line, every wrinkle. She was even more beautiful now that time had etched a multitude of joys and sorrows onto her skin. 'I sent you a note to say goodbye, Claude. That was cowardly of me. You at least deserved to hear my goodbye face to face, with a proper explanation.'

'You didn't need to explain. You don't now. You still loved your husband. I knew that was always a possibility. And you were carrying his child so your ties to him were strong. It doesn't matter – it's all water under the bridge.'

A vision of deep dark water swirling around his ankles, dragging him into the depths, ran through his mind and he batted it away. He'd kept his emotions in check for so long, he couldn't let them out. They formed a solid core inside him and, without that, he feared he would collapse, like a house of cards.

'I did love Terry, in my own way, but not like I loved you, Claude.'

'Then why did you leave me?'

He hadn't meant to say that, and he shrank back in his seat. He couldn't let everything out. It would destroy him. He'd been foolish to think he could be in touch with Esther again and remain unscathed.

'I've asked myself the same question so many times over the years.' Esther sighed. 'I was afraid, Claude. The feelings I had for you were so fierce, I worried that they would burn out. You must have wondered that too?'

Claude paused and then nodded. 'You were my undoing, Esther Kenvale, and I had to remake myself after you'd gone.'

'I'm so sorry.'

'I would have taken on your child. You knew that.'

She pushed out her chin, the way she used to when trying to be brave. 'Yes, I knew. But Terry deserved to know his child and he was a good father to our son, who I love very much. He has two children of his own, now.'

'You're a grandmother?' said Claude, in awe.

'I am, and my grandchildren are the apples of my eye. My life hasn't been so bad, Claude, and I hope yours has been the same. I hope I didn't cause too much pain and you never regretted what we did have for a little while.'

Claude closed his eyes briefly. 'Although I've missed you, I wouldn't have had it any other way.'

It was true, he realised. For all the heartache and pain, their time together had been a bright flash in his grey life – like a comet whose tail spread a blaze of light until it faded away, as though it had never been.

Lettie came back into the room with the old tin tray that used to belong to his mother. On it were two china cups that she must have found at the back of the cupboard and the milk carton. Claude felt ill at ease that she'd seen his kitchen, which wasn't terribly clean, but that was the least of his concerns right now.

'I hope you didn't mind me rooting around your kitchen, Claude, but I thought you might both like a cup of tea. I couldn't find a milk jug, or any sugar.'

'Esther doesn't take sugar,' said Claude. 'Or perhaps you do now.'

She shook her head. 'No, I still don't take sugar. Just milk. Thank you.'

Lettie poured the milk into the cups and handed them out before walking to the door. 'You two must have a lot to talk about so I'll leave you in peace. You've got my phone number, Esther, so give me a call when you're ready for me to put you back in a taxi. I'll be somewhere around Heaven's Cove.'

Esther got slowly to her feet as the front door banged shut and walked to the dresser. She'd seen the faded photograph of her as a young woman that had been in this cottage for forty years. If Claude had known she was coming, that picture would have gone back in the drawer. He worried it made him seem like some sad sap who'd spent his life waiting for her.

'I've had a busy and full life since you went, Esther. I've worked at sea for years, still do sometimes when they're short-staffed, and I've been content living here with my dogs.'

'I'm glad.' Esther reached out and touched the photo, her long, elegant fingers brushing her young face.

'Tell me more about your life.'

Esther smiled and took her seat again on the sofa, with Buster at her feet. 'It's been busy too. Terry and I moved to Yorkshire and had our son, Gavin. As I said, he's grown up now with his own family. He and his wife live in London, near to my granddaughter, and my grandson lives in Cornwall.' She gazed out of the window for a moment, at the pillows of white cloud bunching over the sea. 'Terry died a while ago, of a heart attack.'

'I'm sorry.'

Esther waved away his concern. 'Oh, it was very quick. He wouldn't have wanted to linger. He had no patience for that kind of thing.'

'And now you're living in Devon.'

'I am and it's good to be back. I live in a flat in sheltered accommodation, with a warden to look after me and keep me in check because I'm so old.' She laughed. 'I'm sort of halfway between both grandchildren which seemed a good idea at the time, and I'm fairly near to Terry's side of the family. But I only have very intermittent visits from all of them. Life is so busy for younger people these days.' She paused for a moment, lost in thought, before continuing. 'You never had children yourself, then, Claude?'

He shook his head, surprised by the wave of sorrow that engulfed him. 'No kids, no wife,' he said gruffly.

'I wanted children and so did Terry,' said Esther quietly. 'That was one reason I decided to stay with him. You'd said you weren't keen on having kids.'

Had he? Claude couldn't remember ever saying so. It was true that he'd never felt particularly comfortable around children, but with Esther it would have been different. The shadowy corners of the room were suddenly filled with the ghosts of the children he and Esther might have had together.

'It's all in the past now,' he said, and the woman he'd once loved nodded.

'You're right. We should look to the future now we're reunited, thanks to Lettie.' She looked through the window at Lettie, who was sitting on a bench outside, gazing out across the ocean. 'She's a lovely young woman, and very caring. How did you come to know her?'

Claude smiled. 'I'm not quite sure. She kind of wormed her way into my life and now I'd rather like it if she stayed. But she'll be going home soon. She's not from round here.'

'An outsider?' Esther raised an eyebrow, and Claude smiled again.

'A dreaded grockle, dropping litter and ruining the village.'

Esther laughed. 'Still the same old Claude, I see.'

'Actually, Lettie's family are from Heaven's Cove so I suppose she can count herself an honorary villager. Did she tell you that she risked her life yesterday rescuing Buster from the sea?'

'She did not. What an extraordinary young woman. Tell me all about it, and about the village, which hardly seems to have changed at all.'

They talked for a while about Lettie's exploits and Heaven's Cove and politics and the state of the world – two old friends shooting the breeze, and Claude realised that a weight he'd never fully acknowledged had lifted from his shoulders.

All too soon, Esther glanced at the gold watch on her wrist and got to her feet.

'I can't keep Lettie waiting too long. It was very kind of her to bring me here in the first place.'

'Will I see you again?' asked Claude, standing up and trying to keep the panic out of his voice. He couldn't bear the thought of losing her again.

Esther walked towards him and reached up to rest the palm of her hand on his cheek. Her eyes, more piercing blue than ever against the white of her hair, gazed into his.

'It's too late for us, Claude, to be anything more than friends, but I would like to stay in touch. Perhaps we can talk on the phone and meet up every now and again?'

'I'd like that,' said Claude, briefly pressing his hand on top of Esther's. 'I'm just glad to have you back in my life.'

Esther's eyes filled with tears but she smiled. 'You're a very special man, Claude. I knew it forty years ago and I know it still.'

When she walked from the room, Claude sank back onto his chair. And he watched from the window as she met up with Lettie and the two of them got into a taxi.

This time he could watch Esther go, because he knew she would be coming back.

Chapter Thirty-Five

Lettie

After waving goodbye to Esther's taxi, Lettie walked through the village, a muddle of thoughts and emotions.

Esther had told her the reunion went well and she'd be keeping in touch with Claude. And knowing the two of them would be forging a new friendship made Lettie's heart glad. But her thoughts kept returning to Corey and the distrust on his face when he'd accused her of deceiving him and his grandmother. Lettie had tried to finish the Allford-Starcross feud by finding out the truth about Iris and Cornelius, but all she'd ended up doing was rekindling it.

'Sorry, Iris,' murmured Lettie, dodging pushchairs and children waving ice creams. 'It's all been a bit of a cock-up.'

And although time was marching on and she should be heading back to Driftwood House to collect her case, she decided to take a walk first – to clear her head and try to make sense of all that had happened over the last two weeks.

Reaching the edge of the village, where clustered cottages gave way to winding country roads with high Devon hedges, she could smell the sea and hear gulls calling to each other above her head.

Lettie climbed up the steep path until she came to the top of Cora Head. Then she walked towards the edge of the cliff. She felt a familiar tremble in her legs but kept on walking until she reached the end of the land. If she could survive Buster's rescue, she could manage to stand here, high above the sea that was crashing into the cliff face below.

The sea looked magnificent today, with a huge swell that was sending white-crested rollers towards the beach. The sky had clouded over but the sun had pushed its way through and a shaft of light was falling on Heaven's Cove, making cottage windows sparkle and brightening the bunting outside The Smugglers Haunt. In the heart of the village, not far from the ancient church, Lettie could see the dark roof that covered Cornelius's shrine of a bedroom – a family tragedy from so long ago that had reached out from the past and spread its heartbreak across the decades.

And now, according to the papers she'd found and to Florence herself, this piece of land belonged to Lettie. This magnificent headland she was standing on. She could hardly believe it. She'd never owned land or property, and that wasn't about to change. There was no way she could accept it, and yet...

She imagined building a house here, one like Driftwood House, and enjoying the peace and the amazing view all year round. She imagined herself in the doorway, in the early morning light, with Corey standing beside her. She shook her head. Where did that come from? Corey thought she was a deceptive cheat. Tears sprang into her eyes and she blinked furiously until the view became less smudged and blurry.

A chilly breeze had started winding its way around her bare arms and making her shiver. It really was time to leave this place and head back to her real life in London. She'd simply never mention the piece of land again. Florence and Corey would just have to keep it.

With one last look at the view, she made her way down the headland path and walked towards the village store for a sandwich because she'd hardly eaten all day. It would also give her a chance to say goodbye to the store owner, Bert. He'd always been cheerful when she'd called in to buy bits and pieces over the last couple of weeks. But she deliberately walked the longer way round to avoid walking past Florence's cottage.

She was in the store, choosing between coronation chicken and egg and cress, when a car screeched to a halt on the narrow pavement outside. Simon jumped out and rushed into the shop.

'Lettie! I was just on my way to Driftwood House when I saw you coming in here.'

'Hi, Simon,' said Lettie, deciding on egg. 'Now's not a good time because I'm heading back to London.'

'I don't blame you. I've done a fair bit of business around these parts over the last couple of weeks but I can't wait to get out of this hole either.' His voice was so loud! Lettie cringed as Bert looked up from the counter and glared at them. 'But I hear you have good news.'

'You know more than me then.'

Simon grinned. 'You know what I mean.'

'I really don't.' Lettie knew she sounded fractious but she wasn't in the mood for some strange kind of guessing game.

'I hear that congratulations are in order because you're now the owner of a prime piece of village real estate. Well played!' When Lettie said nothing, he grabbed hold of her hands and continued: 'You own the headland – Lovers' Link, Cora Head, whatever you want to call it. Word in the village is that Florence has given it to you, for some reason I have yet to understand.'

'How the hell did you hear about that?' asked Lettie, removing her hands from Simon's grasp.

'Is it true then? Wow, respect! How on earth did you pull that off?'

'Tell me how you heard,' repeated Lettie, not interested in Simon's congratulations.

'You know what this place is like – a total gossip mill. Usually they seem to be talking about me these days, but I overheard people in the pub discussing you owning the headland. That's amazing, Lettie.'

'How did people know in the pub?'

'You and Corey were talking about it in the street, apparently. Arguing, I hear, which I can't say I'm surprised about because that man is a total arse and I'm glad you've come to your senses.'

'Is nothing private in this place?'

Simon grinned again. 'Seems not. So how come the headland is now yours?'

Lettie sighed. If rumours were flying around, she might as well take the chance to set them straight. 'I found out that Cornelius, Florence's brother, left it to my great-aunt and her descendants. There's a deed outlining his wishes.'

'You what?' Simon looked confused in spite of the wide grin on his face. 'Oh, whatever. Nice one, Cornelius! So you're sitting pretty then.'

'Hardly.'

'Of course you are. You sell me the land and pocket the dosh and go off and do whatever it is you want to do. Go and lie on a beach for a while, a better beach than Heaven's Cove. You can go to the Seychelles or Barbados.' He gave her a wink. 'I might even come with you.'

'What would happen to the land?' asked Lettie, as an unpleasant image of Simon in swimming trunks, flexing his muscles on a white sand beach, flitted through her mind and swiftly out again.

'Like I told you, it's perfect for holiday homes.'

'Two or three?'

'Yeah,' he said slowly, drawing out the word. Then he winked again. 'Or more if I can get away with it, which I'm pretty sure I can. More of a holiday village than a couple of houses.'

'That's not what you told Florence.'

'She doesn't understand business,' he said airily, 'not like you and me. And she's far too invested in this tin-pot little village in the back of beyond.'

'It's her home. She belongs here.'

'Fair enough, but the headland no longer belongs to *her*, so you and I had better start discussing money.'

He licked his lips, leaving a slick of saliva.

'There's no point discussing anything, Simon.'

'What do you mean?'

'You could offer me ten million pounds for the headland and I wouldn't be interested.'

Simon's smile faltered. 'What are you saying?'

'I'm saying I don't want a holiday village built on Cora Head, at any price.'

'Why not? At the end of the day, we'll be back in London, so who cares what happens here?'

'I do,' said Lettie quietly.

'Why?'

'Because Heaven's Cove is where Iris grew up and met the love of her life, and it's a beautiful village that should be preserved.'

Simon laughed as though he didn't believe her, before stopping abruptly. 'You're kidding, right? It's a tiny place that smells of fish and seaweed, and I'm talking about a load of money here. Not ten mill – that's ridiculous – but enough to change your life. You're not going to turn that down, are you, babe?'

Being called 'babe' put Lettie's teeth on edge.

'I'm afraid I'm not interested,' she insisted.

'Not even if I offered you—'

'I don't want to know,' interrupted Lettie. What was the point in finding out how much she was turning down?

Simon's mouth twitched in the corner as though he was suppressing a smile. 'Are you planning on playing hardball, Miss Starcross? You're taking on an expert negotiator here. Just think of what you could do with a huge windfall.'

'Oh, I am,' said Lettie, pushing away ideas of what she could do with it. She'd have enough to fund a different kind of life – if she took his offer, if she had no morals and decency whatsoever, if Corey was right to mistrust her. She took a deep breath. 'But I'm afraid, whatever you offer, the answer is still no.'

'You're being ridiculous. Just sell me the land.'

'The land isn't mine to sell.'

'But you said—'

'I said Cornelius had left it to Iris but I doubt the deed he left is properly legal.'

'You can go through the courts.'

'I wouldn't accept the land anyway, even if a judge told me categorically that it was mine.'

Simon's mouth flapped open. 'Why on earth not? Oh God, don't tell me that you're mooning over Corey Allford. Just because he turned up in a big boat and rescued you, that doesn't mean you owe him a piece of land that could make you more money than you probably earn in ten years.'

Ten years? thought Lettie, wistfully, imagining the security and freedom that money would buy. But it wouldn't buy peace of mind.

'My decision isn't because of Corey. Not really. It's because this village and the people in it are amazing, and Cornelius and Iris don't want it to be spoiled.'

'It's just a couple of holiday homes!'

'Or a holiday village?'

Simon's cheeks reddened. 'That was just me exaggerating a bit.'

'It doesn't matter because the land isn't morally mine.'

'Morals don't come into it.'

'You've made that very clear.'

'Florence's brother wanted you to have it.'

'He wanted Iris to have it. But that was a long time ago. Iris is gone and I've only been here for two weeks. Florence has loved that land for her whole life and it's special to her because of her brother.'

'But we could make a killing on it, Lettie.'

Lettie glared at him. She hadn't felt this irritated since she'd told the adhesives customer to get lost. 'That's the difference between you and me, Simon. I don't want to make a killing. I know it's disappointing for you, but you've made some other good deals in Devon so I'm sure you'll be all right. Now, I really must go and do my packing.'

When she started walking away, Simon called after her: 'Think of the brand new car you could be driving, all the holidays you could have and all the shoes you could buy. You'd be a fool to turn this down.'

'I told you,' called Lettie, over her shoulder. 'Sorry, Simon, but I'm not selling the headland, to you or anyone else. It belongs to the Allfords.'

That was that, then, as far as any kind of continuing relationship with Simon was concerned, thought Lettie, walking towards the quay to say goodbye to Claude. Daisy would never let it drop, if she found out. *He was perfect, Lettie. What the hell were you thinking?*

But Daisy was so wrong. Simon was the type of man her family said was right for her, but he wasn't. He was good-looking and charming and he had a good job and his own flat and a big car. But he wasn't particularly kind, and he thought mostly of himself.

Lettie would tell Daisy so, but she probably wouldn't tell her about inheriting the headland… and refusing it. She really never would hear the end of that. So it would remain a secret, to be taken out every now and then before being pushed to the back of her mind.

She'd always remember these past two weeks as a time when life slowed down and seemed to make more sense. When she connected with Iris once more and learned a lot about herself in the process.

She didn't regret her stay in Heaven's Cove one bit. But there was one regret she couldn't shake. Regret that she and Corey had parted on such bad terms – and that he believed she could be so devious and deceptive. She would write to him and his grandmother when she got home and reiterate that she was renouncing her 'ownership' of the headland. If Florence said it was hers to keep, then she would have to accept it was hers to give back. Perhaps then he might believe her. But, by then, it would be too late. She and Corey would never see each other again.

Sighing, she knocked gently on Claude's door. If he wasn't in, she would leave a note to say goodbye.

The door was suddenly wrenched open and Buster ran out and leaped up at her.

'You've made a friend for life there,' said Claude, standing in the doorway. He looked different. His long grey hair was still a mess and his bushy beard was untamed, but he looked lighter somehow. Less weighed down by life.

'He's a lovely dog.'

Lettie patted Buster's head until his jumping stopped and he nuzzled his nose into her side.

'Do you want to come in? I owe you more thanks. You found Esther and brought her here to see me. I'll never forget that.' He peered at her closely. 'But you look upset. Are you all right after what happened?'

'What do you mean?' asked Lettie. Had Claude heard about Cornelius's gift of land too?

'What I mean is, it must have been frightening to be trapped on the rocks like that, with the tide coming in.'

Lettie's shoulders relaxed. 'It was scary at the time, but I'm fine now, honestly.'

'Good, because you were very brave and you brought Buster back to me.'

'I was happy to help.' Lettie hesitated. 'I wanted to let you know that I'm leaving Heaven's Cove.'

'When?'

Lettie was touched by the emotion on Claude's craggy face. At least someone would be sorry to see her go.

'I'm going today.'

'Why so soon?'

'I've been here for two weeks and it's time to go home.'

'Did you find out what you wanted about your great-aunt?'

'I did, thank you.'

'Good.' Claude shook his head. 'I can't wait to be rid of most outsiders, with their yelling and bad manners and dropping litter everywhere. But you're different, Lettie Starcross. You belong here.'

Lettie's lip wobbled at that. She certainly felt an affinity with this village, as Iris once did, that was hard to explain.

When she didn't reply, Claude leaned forward and whispered: 'You could always stay.'

'I can't stay at Driftwood House for ever,' said Lettie, in the no-nonsense tone of voice Daisy often used with the children.

'No, but you could stay here, next door.'

'What do you mean?'

'The cottage next door used to belong to my parents and now it belongs to me. It's a holiday let at the moment.' Claude grimaced. 'Holidaymakers and me, we don't mix well. I'd rather have someone I know next door, someone I like.'

When Lettie reached out and put her hand on Claude's shoulder, he didn't pull away.

'That's really kind of you, Claude. In many ways I'd love to stay, but… things just haven't worked out and I need to get back to London.'

'London? Pah.'

'My family need me.'

'Families? Pah.'

He pulled such a face, Lettie laughed, before being distracted by the sound of a text message arriving from her mum: *I hear you'll be back later. Can we sort out a trip to Lidl tomorrow? We need more loo roll x* Lettie sighed and pushed her phone back into her pocket. Maybe Claude was right. But life didn't always turn out the way you wanted.

'So…' She pulled her shoulders back. 'It's goodbye, Claude. I'll send you a postcard of the sights when I get home.'

Claude nodded, looking downcast. 'I'd like that and maybe you'll be back down here again soon?'

'Maybe,' answered Lettie, wondering if she'd be like Iris and never return. How awkward would it be to bump into Corey or Florence in the street? It would be dreadful if Corey remembered her and ignored her, and even worse if he didn't remember her at all.

She hesitated, unsure whether hugging Claude would be appropriate, but he resolved the dilemma by sticking out his hand.

'Goodbye, Miss Lettie Starcross. It's been a privilege to know you.'

'Goodbye, Claude. You too.'

Lettie took his huge paw of a hand and shook it, feeling a rush of sorrow. Leaving the place Iris had once called home hurt.

Chapter Thirty-Six

Lettie had said goodbye to Driftwood House and to Rosie. She'd had a last look at the stunning view from the clifftop and had marvelled afresh at the glittering ocean stretching to the horizon and the quaint cottages below her, huddling together on the edge of the land.

She'd also replied to Mum's text, saying she'd sort out a Lidl trip as soon as she could, while determining to set up online shopping deliveries for her parents. Her mum wouldn't like it. She enjoyed her shopping trips, but she could always have an exciting trip to Tesco with her friend, Moira, who regularly offered to take her.

Lettie glanced at her watch and frowned. The taxi was late and she'd miss yet another train if it didn't get a move on.

Usually, Lettie was happy to come home from holiday, however much fun she'd had. The urge to up sticks and escape to the sunshine for good was short-lived, and the pull of her normal life in London was enough to entice her back to reality. But not this time. Life had changed in the few short weeks since Iris had died, she realised. She'd changed. And a growing feeling of belonging in Heaven's Cove was hard to shake.

'Get a grip, Starcross,' she murmured to herself, picking up her case and deciding to walk down the cliff path. She could meet the taxi in the lane at the bottom. 'Go home, forget this place, and get back to normal.'

Going back to normal would be relatively easy in practical terms. She'd find another tedious customer care job and her family would keep her busy, as always. But forgetting this special place and the people in it wouldn't be so simple.

She pictured Corey in his yellow uniform battling through rough seas to reach her and Buster. She could almost feel his arm around her shoulders, and the brush of his cheek against hers when he'd later kissed her goodnight. And she could still picture his disappointed face when he thought she'd deceived him. The fact that he hadn't believed her would hurt for a long time.

'Well, damn you, Corey Allford,' she said out loud to the seagulls swooping over her head as she picked her way down the path. 'I hope you enjoy your lonely, distrustful life.'

There was no taxi in sight when she got down to the road and she'd just taken out her phone to ring the taxi firm again when she heard pounding feet behind her.

'I had to stop you,' puffed Corey, his face lobster-red. He bent over with his hands on his thighs, breathing loudly in and out. 'Ran… all… way,' he gasped. 'Not as fit as I thought. Terrible stitch.'

Lettie could have cried, because seeing Corey was going to make leaving all the harder. 'If you're here to have another go at me, don't bother because I'm leaving Heaven's Cove, and you don't need to worry because I have no intention of selling Cora Head to Simon.'

'I know. I heard you had an argument with him in Bert's shop.'

Lettie shook her head. 'Of course you did.'

Much as she'd grown to love Heaven's Cove, she would never get used to the village grapevine. In London you could drop dead and no one would notice.

'Look, can we talk?' asked Corey, massaging his side. His face was returning to its normal colour and his breathing had eased.

'I've got a train to catch.' A black car had just turned the corner and was heading towards them. 'And my taxi is here.'

'Can't you get the next train?'

'I could but what's the point, Corey? I'm leaving the village so I might as well go now.'

'But I need to apologise. I've been such an idiot. I shouldn't have doubted you and accused you of being so… I don't know…'

'Horribly deceitful?'

'Yeah, fair enough… horribly deceitful. I should have believed you when you said Iris knew nothing about Cornelius leaving her the land.'

'Of course you should have. Did you think I almost drowned on purpose, just so I could wheedle my way into Cornelius's room for the night?' Lettie's voice was rising in frustration and Corey took a step back.

'No, of course not. I wasn't thinking logically at all.'

'And what about Simon? Did you really think I'd be in cahoots with a complete idiot like him?'

The corner of Corey's mouth twitched. 'He really is an idiot, isn't he?'

'A complete, grade A version. So it's all the more insulting that you thought he and I were working together.'

Corey wrinkled his nose. 'Actually, I thought at times that you might be going out with him.'

'Really? Jeez, you're worse than my family when it comes to pairing me off with totally unsuitable men. Simon just kept hanging around and turning up like a bad penny.'

'He seems to have a talent for doing that.'

When the approaching car stopped behind Corey, Lettie picked up her suitcase.

'Look, thank you for apologising but I do need to catch the next train.'

Only when she stepped past Corey and looked at the car properly, she realised that it wasn't a taxi at all. The battered black car belonged to Florence, who was sliding out of the driving seat.

'For goodness' sake, why did you bring your grandmother with you?'

'What?' Corey spun around. 'What the hell are you doing here, Gran?'

'I'm trying to stop history repeating itself,' replied Florence tartly, leaving the engine running and the car parked at an odd angle across the road. 'There have been far too many misunderstandings between Starcrosses and Allfords over the years.'

'How did you know where I'd be?' demanded Corey.

'It was pretty obvious after I'd rung to tell you what Bert mentioned about the ruckus between that property development man and Lettie in his shop. By the time I'd driven home, you were gone.'

'It was still a stretch to know I'd have come here.'

'Hardly. You were happier than I'd seen you for ages planning your afternoon out with Miss Starcross, and like a bear with a sore head since your fight with her.' She turned to Lettie. 'Are you still leaving with no plans to return?'

Lettie nodded, thrown by the Allfords turning up en masse, out of the blue.

Florence frowned and addressed Corey. 'Then you need to tell Miss Starcross the truth about Grace.'

Corey winced and stared at the ground. No one said anything for what seemed like an age, the calling of birds overhead filling the silence, until he spoke. 'Will... will you take a walk with me, Lettie? Gran will look after your case.'

'Like I said, I have a train—'

'Please.'

And he looked so flustered, so pained, Lettie followed when he started walking along the lane. What was the truth about his ex-wife? she wondered. What had happened to hurt him so much?

'Where are we going?' she asked after a while.

Corey shrugged. 'It doesn't matter. I just need to talk to you, alone.'

He led the way along the narrow lane. Bees droned lazily in the high hedges that edged the empty road, and the air was heavy with heat that settled on top of Lettie like a blanket. After a while, he turned off the road and climbed over a stile. Lettie followed and they walked through a field, dotted with sheep, which rose towards the top of a hill.

'What is this all about, Corey?' asked Lettie, coming to a halt. 'I'm sure Bert told your gran that I turned down Simon's offer of buying the land. I'm not going to sell it and I'm not even going to accept it. The headland was left to Iris, not to me. I don't have a proper claim on it and I don't want to have one.'

'Even though it could help you change your life.'

'I'm not going to change my life at the expense of someone else's.'

'I know. I think I've always known.' Corey shook his head. 'You're a decent person, Lettie. I just find it so hard to trust people after Grace...'

'I'm not Grace.'

'No, you're not.'

He shoved his hands into the pockets of his jeans and scuffed his feet in the grass, as sheep nearby raised their heads and stared.

'What did your wife do to make you so distrustful? I know your marriage broke up and that's sad, but marriages end all the time.'

Corey breathed out slowly. 'If you want the whole sorry tale, we went to London for Grace's career. I told you that, but what I didn't say was that Grace fell pregnant a year after we moved there. She wasn't too pleased but I thought it was anxiety at such a big change, and I was so excited at the thought of being a dad. Far more excited than I'd ever have imagined. We were happy, or at least I thought we were, and I thought we'd be a happy family of three.'

'So what happened?'

'Grace settled into her pregnancy and I couldn't wait to meet my son or daughter for the first time.' He cleared his throat and closed his eyes. 'But when she was almost eight months pregnant, I discovered that she was cheating on me. With an entrepreneurial businessman, a dickhead very like Simon.'

'And the baby?' whispered Lettie, already knowing the answer.

Corey opened his eyes. 'The baby was his. Grace was sure, and a test after he was born confirmed it.'

'He. So the baby was a boy.'

'Yeah.' Corey gazed into the distance, his jaw set. 'My son who never was. She stayed with the other man. They're the happy family now and I'm living with my grandmother and finding it very hard to get close to anyone else. It was the lies that did it. I trusted Grace utterly and yet she'd been lying to me for months. It made me distrust myself because how could I read people properly if I'd misread my own wife so completely?'

Lettie wasn't sure what to say. She could only imagine what such a betrayal of trust would do to your self-esteem and your view of the world.

'It wasn't your fault, Corey,' she managed, knowing that her words were totally inadequate when it came to mending the hurt he'd suffered.

'It felt like my failing. But I'd started to trust you…'

'Until I came across the letter and your gran said the headland was mine.'

Corey nodded. 'With Grace, the little things finally added up – why she sometimes worked late, why the passcode on her mobile had changed, why she wasn't happier about our baby.'

When he stopped and swallowed hard, Lettie reached out and placed her hand on his arm.

'This is so painful. You don't have to tell me any of this.'

'But I do because after you found the letter and deed I put two and two together, like I finally did with Grace, but this time I came up with—'

'—a lot more than four?'

'A hell of a lot more.' The ghost of a smile flitted across his face. 'It's all a bit of a mess, isn't it?'

'You could say that.'

Corey sat down on the grass and Lettie sat beside him and nudged him with her shoulder, desperate to try and make him feel better.

'Families, huh?'

'Yours will be glad to have you back.'

'They certainly will. Mum's organised a shopping trip to Lidl for loo roll already, and Daisy will have me childminding before my feet have touched the floor. And I've got a few jobs to apply for, including one that involves farming foodstuffs.'

'What about the different kind of life you wanted?'

'Ah well, you know.' Lettie shrugged. 'Real life, and all that.'

She glanced at Corey, who was staring across the fields towards the sparkling sea. 'You *can* trust me, you know. Not everyone wants to deceive you. You were horribly hurt and let down by one woman but not everyone is like that. What are you going to do? Never trust anyone again and end up lonely and alone, like Claude, one day?'

'Much as I respect Claude, that wouldn't be my first choice.' He moved his gaze from the sea to her face. 'But what about you? If you don't branch out and make a different kind of life for yourself you might end up alone, like your great-aunt.'

'Or worse, with a perfect man who buys me a steam mop for my birthday.' When Corey wrinkled his nose quizzically, Lettie laughed. 'It's a family thing. Just ignore me.'

'I would, only you're so very hard to ignore.'

Lettie stopped breathing as Corey leaned closer. His dark eyes, full of pain and… something else, searched hers. And then he kissed her. It wasn't a brief kiss on the cheek this time. His lips were warm on hers and his hands became tangled in her hair as the kiss went on and on. The tickle of grass on her skin and the bleating of sheep nearby disappeared. All she knew was heat and desire and belonging.

'Sorry.' Corey dropped his hands and moved back, pressing his lips together. 'You're about to leave Heaven's Cove so this is lousy timing. I shouldn't have done that, or I should have done it before.'

'Yes, you should have. You absolutely, definitely should have.'

When Lettie closed the gap between them and pressed her lips against his, he put his arms around her and they fell back onto the grass, startling sheep nearby who trotted away.

Lettie had never much been one for kissing. It had often been a bit of a let-down with the men she'd dated – a brief, clumsy interlude with boyfriends who were keen to move on to more. But this felt different. Lettie felt different as Corey kissed her again and she kissed him back. It was slow and measured and right.

Lying on the grass with Heaven's Cove stretched out in front of her and Corey Allford's arms around her felt exactly right. It felt like the door into the kind of different life she needed.

They broke apart when a car horn sounded from the road.

'It's not Gran, is it?' asked Corey, groaning. 'I get my terrible timing from her.'

Lettie squinted towards the lane. 'No, I think it's my taxi at last. Your gran must have told the driver we'd walked on.'

Corey stood up slowly and pulled Lettie to her feet. 'I guess you'd better go, then and I apologise for getting you all… grassy.' He pulled a blade of grass from Lettie's hair and tried to smile but didn't quite manage it. 'You don't want to miss your train.'

He thought she was still leaving. He thought she still could leave after what had just happened. But Lettie knew what she wanted to do. As she started to walk towards the road, Corey called after her: 'Aren't you going to say goodbye?'

Lettie stopped and turned. He looked so vulnerable and hurt, it broke her heart.

'There's no need. I'm just going to tell the taxi driver that I don't need a ride to the station after all. I'm sure my family can manage without me for at least a few more days. I'll be back in a minute. Honest.'

Corey gave a long, slow smile that made his dark eyes twinkle. 'I'll trust you, Lettie Starcross.'

Chapter Thirty-Seven

Four months later

A winter storm was due any time, according to Claude, who seemed to be better at predicting the weather than the Met Office.

Fortunately, at the moment it was bright and blustery. But Cora Head was exposed and Lettie huddled against Corey, who put his arms around her and pulled her close. The wind was whipping at her legs, and gulls squawked as they were buffeted by the strong currents. Ahead of them, the grey sea was flecked with white crests.

Lettie snuggled further into Corey's coat and thought about everything she still had to do that day. Her parents would be arriving for Christmas at the weekend, and Daisy and her family too. Lettie couldn't wait to see them even though her parents staying with her in Claude's holiday let would be a squeeze. It was a good job that Daisy had rented a cottage in the village for her, Jason and the kids.

But they'd all get together for a traditional meal at Lettie's on Christmas Day, and Claude and Esther had been invited too. With them and Corey and Florence as well, Christmas Day was going to be manic and they'd probably end up eating in shifts at the small kitchen table, but it would be so good to see them all.

Lettie did miss them. Well, maybe not the shopping trips and endless babysitting. But her new life in Heaven's Cove kept her too busy to dwell on the distance between them.

It was all go these days, partly thanks to the brand new Heaven's Cove Cultural Centre she was setting up at the village hall, next to the tourist office. Claude had been so delighted to discover that Lettie was staying after all, he'd agreed to her request to put his archives on display. And he was getting quite excited about the centre's grand opening that was planned for the spring, in time for a new influx of 'outsiders'.

Added to that, Lettie was also studying Devon history part-time, and working three days per week in customer care for a local business selling stationery. Talking about box files and paperclips wasn't thrilling, but changing your life took time – and she was doing pretty well already. Her family were also getting used to her being almost two hundred miles away and were managing just fine.

'Are you OK, Letts?' whispered Corey, as Florence stepped forward to inspect the wooden bench that had just been delivered. It had been placed to overlook the sea and a brass plaque had been attached to it: *In loving memory of Iris Starcross, who never forgot Cornelius Allford or Heaven's Cove.*

'I'm absolutely fine.' Lettie stood on tiptoe and kissed the tip of Corey's nose, before calling across to the elderly woman who had become so dear to her over the last few months. 'How are you, Florence?'

Florence ran her fingers across the plaque and smiled at Lettie. 'I'm fine, too, because all is as it should be.'

She was right, but there was one more thing to do. In his letter, Cornelius had asked Iris to '*Take every chance to be happy, but throw a flower into the sea and think of me sometimes.*' Moving away from Corey,

Lettie pulled a single yellow rose from the bag slung across her body and walked close to the edge of the cliff. When she threw the flower towards the ocean, the wind took it and carried it out far beyond the land. It danced in the breeze as it swirled down, down and into the churning water.

Lettie returned to the man she loved and gazed out across the sea which reflected the pale washed blue of the sky. It felt as if the past had come full circle as she stood here, in Corey's arms, with Iris's necklace safe beneath the thick wool of her coat.

Thank you, Iris and Cornelius, she said in her head, with the sound of seagulls above her and the faint bustle of Heaven's Cove below. *The key to your heart turned out to be the key to mine.*

A Letter from Liz

Dear reader,

Thank you so much for choosing to read *A Letter to the Last House Before the Sea*. I really hope you enjoyed Lettie's story – and Iris's and Claude's, too. If you did, and you'd like to keep up to date with all my latest releases, just sign up at the following link. Your email address will never be shared and you can unsubscribe at any time.

www.bookouture.com/liz-eeles

This is my second standalone story set in Heaven's Cove – and I love writing about the village so much, I'm writing a third novel that's also set on the rugged Devon coast. That book, full of mystery and romance, will be published soon. And in the meantime, if you haven't read my first Heaven's Cove novel, *Secrets at the Last House Before the Sea*, you can find out how Rosie uncovered a huge family secret, fell in love with Liam, and came to be running Driftwood House.

If you did enjoy *A Letter to the Last House Before the Sea*, I'd be grateful if you could write a review. I'd love to hear what you think, and it makes such a difference in helping new readers to discover my books for the first time.

I also love hearing from readers directly, and you can get in touch via my website, on my Facebook page or through Twitter and Instagram.

Thanks so much,

Liz x

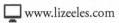 www.lizeeles.com

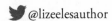 lizeelesauthor

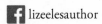 @lizeelesauthor

 lizeelesauthor

Acknowledgements

This book would never have been written without my fabulous editor, Ellen Gleeson, nudging me towards writing women's fiction. I'm so glad I listened and gave it a go. Thank you, Ellen and Bookouture, for guiding me in the right direction and providing the support I needed to make this book happen.

I'm grateful, too, to friends and family who've encouraged me along the way.

Thank you to my (he would say) long-suffering husband, Tim, who copes admirably with the highs and lows of having a slightly stressy author for a wife. I had great fun striding across Dartmoor with you in glorious weather, and finding the inspiration for this story.

And finally, I'd like to give a shout-out and thank you to the brave volunteers, men and women, who risk their lives at sea to save others.

Made in the USA
Columbia, SC
02 March 2022